THE
BLUE
DOOR

THRESHOLD SERIES

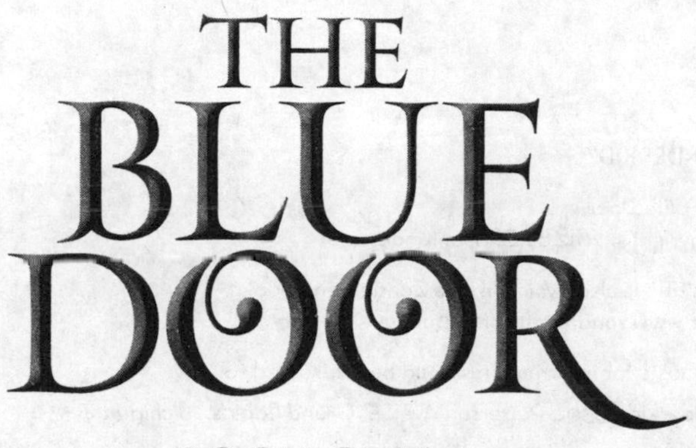

BOOK ONE

CHRISTA KINDE

ZONDERVAN.com/
AUTHORTRACKER
follow your favorite authors

We want to hear from you. Please send your comments about this book to us in care of zreview@zondervan.com. Thank you.

ZONDERKIDZ

The Blue Door

This title is also available as a Zondervan ebook.
Visit www.zondervan.com/ebooks

Requests for information should be addressed to:

Zonderkidz, 5300 *Patterson Ave SE, Grand Rapids, Michigan 49530*

ISBN 978-0-310-72419-3

Editor: Kim Childress with Leslie Peterson
Cover design: Cindy Davis
Interior design and composition: Greg Johnson/Textbook Perfect

Printed in the United States of America

12 13 14 15 16 /DCI/ 20 19 18 17 16 15 14 13 12 11 10 9 8 7 6 5 4 3 2 1

Can you believe it? Thank you for encouraging me to try, Simone.

TABLE OF CONTENTS

1

THE INVISIBLE BOY

A shining column erupted from the ring of stones set into the floor of a circular room, carrying with it the figure of a young man wreathed by shifting tendrils of blue light. "You called?" he cheerfully inquired.

"I did," rumbled a deep voice as a tall, dark man stepped forward. "We may have a problem."

Ash blond brows lifted in surprise. "I'm not the one you usually turn to in an emergency, Harken. Surely one of the others ...?"

An upraised hand halted his protest. "This situation calls for more ... delicacy."

"A direct intervention, then?"

"I'm afraid *that* has already been accomplished."

"Who?"

"Shimron's new apprentice."

"That shouldn't even be possible."

Harken offered an eloquent shrug. "Nothing is impossible."

"You have to admit, it's highly irregular."

"And well he knows it. The boy is frightened."

"I'll hurry," he promised. "Is there a message?"

"How about *Fear not*?"

Prissie stepped along a narrow rut leading through her grandpa's orchard, placing her sandaled feet with care so as not to raise any dust. The overgrown lane wasn't a proper road since it was only used during harvesttime, but it was one of her favorite places to escape from the constant noise of home. "Margery's birthday party's in two more weeks. April's email said she was actually thinking about inviting *boys* this year. Thank goodness she changed her mind. It would have ruined everything!"

At fourteen, there were many things that frustrated Prissie, but the thing she hated most was that she didn't have anyone to talk to about them. Margery and the other girls from school all lived in town, but she was stranded in the middle of nowhere with too many brothers for company.

"They're supposed to post class assignments pretty soon, and I'm crossing my fingers that we'll all have the same homeroom." She flipped a long, honey-colored braid over her shoulder, then added, "I don't know what would be worse — being separated from my friends, or having *him* in my class again. He's so annoying!"

Prissie paused and peered up and down the path. "Doesn't it feel like someone's watching?" she asked hesitantly.

Crouching down, she softly called to Tansy; the striped tabby happily butted her head against Prissie's hand and began to purr. "Zeke better not be up to his tricks. I don't want any stalker brothers ruining things; this is my first chance to talk to Milo since Sunday."

The cat meowed, and Prissie tickled her under the chin before standing and glancing around, unable to shake the feeling of being watched. She turned in a full circle, eyes alert for a telltale head of tousled blond hair. Finally, she shrugged and continued toward the main road, the matriarch of their hay loft trailing in her wake. "It's *sad* that getting the mail is the most exciting part of my day," she sighed.

Prissie wasn't exactly *bored*. Their farm was a lively place, what with school being out for the summer and the house jam-packed. There was gardening to be done, the orchard to mow, chickens to tend, and kittens to tame. But all of that stuff was the normal kind of busy ... not the *exciting* kind. "Grandpa likes to say the Pomeroys have deep roots, but all that really means is that we never go anywhere. Not like Aunt Ida," she informed the cat.

Her dad's younger sister had left West Edinton as soon as she'd married and rarely made it back for visits. Uncle Loren worked for a mission board, and they traveled the world, visiting faraway places like China, India, and Africa. Prissie keenly missed the vivacious woman who'd been her "bestest" friend until she was nine, but Aunt Ida found ways to stay connected. A steady trickle of postcards and packages made it into the twin mailboxes on Orchard Lane, which was *one* of the reasons Prissie liked to get the mail personally.

The other reason was Milo Leggett.

Put simply, Milo was their mailman. Though young, he

was an upstanding member of their community, a Sunday school teacher at Prissie's church, and an all-around nice guy. There probably wasn't a soul in West Edinton who didn't know Milo, and since he handled all their mail, he knew everyone back.

Whenever he was around, Milo acted as though the Pomeroy clan was his own family, and Prissie liked to think they *were* special ... and not only because they were the last stop on his daily route. As far as she was concerned, it was the one good thing about living so far from town, because about once a week — usually when there was a package to deliver — he'd stop in and stay a while.

He had an easy smile, a pleasant laugh, and it was Prissie's studied opinion that Milo's eyes were an uncommonly wonderful shade of blue. She fussed with the skirt of her pink sundress and said, "At least *he* doesn't treat me like one of the boys." People always seemed to think that a country girl with five brothers would turn out to be a tomboy, but Prissie did her best to set them straight by being very, *very* ladylike.

"If you don't hurry along, we'll miss him," she primly informed Tansy.

Most of the apple trees in this part of the orchard were the dwarf variety, their gnarled branches weighed down by unripe fruit. However, a long row of standard apple trees lined the lane. The full-sized trees took up too much space to be practical, but Grandpa Pete harbored a smidgen of nostalgia under his gruff exterior. They had been his mother's favorite apples, and since he couldn't bring himself to tear them out, they stayed.

Prissie gasped, stopping dead in her tracks. To her amazement, someone was sitting in one of Great-grandma's trees, and he was definitely watching her. Bright, black eyes peered at her with lively interest. She stared right back in utter confusion. Theirs was a small town, and she knew everyone who lived nearby. Outside of harvesttime, it was unusual to see a stranger out their way, and this boy was definitely strange. Cautiously, she stepped closer.

He wore odd clothing — a long tunic over loose pants. The beige fabric's unusual sheen shimmered in the sunlight, and the decorative patterns that edged the deep vee of the collar and the wide cuffs of each sleeve shone as if they'd been stitched with silver threads. His features were delicately exotic; pale golden skin and almond-shaped eyes were set off by glossy black, shoulder-length hair.

The boy looked comfortable enough as he leaned against the tree trunk, one foot braced on the rough bark of the low branch on which he sat, the other swinging casually. He was barefoot, and Prissie cast about for any sign of shoes, a pack, or even a bicycle in the vicinity. Nothing. Since it was too early in the season for apple thieves, she decided to err on the side of hospitality. "Hello!" she called.

The boy's eyes widened in surprise, and he looked around uncertainly. Finally, in a soft, lyrical voice, he asked, "Are you speaking to *me*?"

Prissie tilted her head to one side and, in a fair imitation of her grandmother's brisk tones, replied, "And who *else* would I be talking to?"

He only blinked at her, seemingly at a loss.

She smiled to lessen the sting of her retort. "Hi, I'm Prissie ... Prissie Pomeroy." Pointing at the roofline of their barn, which was easily visible over the tops of the trees, she added, "I live right over there."

The boy's eyes never left her face, and he was frowning in concentration.

"Do you live around here?" she asked, and when he didn't reply, she tried again. "I haven't seen you around. Are you new to the area?"

"I am," he admitted slowly.

"That explains why we haven't met," she announced, glad to have hit upon a reasonable explanation. "So what's your name?"

The oddly dressed boy swung a leg over the branch, lightly dropped to the ground, then straightened. He was shorter than her by a few inches. As he walked slowly toward her, he answered, "I am called Koji."

She thought his response a bit strange, but she politely extended her hand. "Nice to meet you, Koji."

The boy stepped right up to her, ignoring her hand and searching her face with keen interest. "You can see me?" he asked quietly.

"Obviously."

"I thought so," he mused aloud, his expression troubled.

It was Prissie's turn to frown. His words made little sense.

"Then may I ask you a question?" Koji asked earnestly.

"Sure."

"Why were you praying to your cat?"

"E-excuse me?"

Black eyes strayed from Prissie to Tansy, then back again. "I heard you, and I was wondering ..."

"You were *listening*?" she gasped, trying to remember exactly what he might have overheard.

Koji nodded slowly, and Prissie huffed and propped her hands on her hips. "Well, I might have been talking out loud, but I wasn't praying ... and *certainly* not to a cat. That's just *weird*!"

"I thought so, too," the boy replied seriously.

Shaking her head, Prissie said, "Come on," and resumed walking.

"Where are we going?" he inquired, taking up a position in the lane's neighboring rut.

"Just to get the mail," she replied. "It should be here any minute."

"That is good," Koji said, sounding rather relieved.

As they walked side by side, Tansy wandered off, stalking something that moved through the long grass beneath the trees. Prissie didn't mind since cats didn't make very good conversationalists. "So, you said you're new here?" she prompted.

"Yes," he acknowledged. "That is why I am not sure how this is supposed to work."

"Are you an exchange student or something?"

"No."

"You must be staying *somewhere* nearby if you're barefoot," she pointed out.

"It is not far," Koji replied carefully.

They reached the end of the lane, and Prissie deftly opened the green metal gate in the white-painted board fence that surrounded their property, holding it wide and waving the boy through. "Watch out for the ditch," she instructed as she swung the gate back into place and re-twisted the wire that kept it secure.

Orchard Lane was the northernmost street in West Edinton as well as the last turn off of Centennial Highway before leaving Milton County. A handful of other families lived on the narrow gravel road, but after a few miles, it dead-ended in a wide turn-about in front of Pomeroy Orchard.

Matching white mailboxes surrounded by a profusion of purple coneflowers stood at the end of a long driveway, and Prissie made a beeline for them. An oval-shaped wooden sign hanging beneath them bore their farm's logo — an overflowing bushel basket of apples. The neat block letters on the side of the first mailbox said, *Peter & Nellie Pomeroy,* and the second one read, *Jayce & Naomi Pomeroy.* Prissie perched on the top rail of the fence behind them, then patted the space next to her. "This is where I wait," she announced.

Koji obediently climbed up beside her, murmuring, "Thank you."

Prissie wasn't sure *what* to think of the peculiar newcomer. Although he was a boy, he spoke quietly and politely, a refreshing change from her boisterous family. She wanted to make sure Koji was okay before turning him over to her brothers, who were always glad for a new playmate, but something about the shy way Koji watched her made her want to take him under her wing. Her brothers knew better than to pick on someone just because they were different, but she had a feeling that this guy would end up being teased at school.

"I've never seen clothes like those before," she commented.

Koji glanced down at himself and touched the softly draping cloth. "Are they uncommon?"

"People around here definitely don't dress like that," Prissie replied. After a moment's thought, she diplomatically added, "They look comfortable, though."

"I did not expect to be seen," he admitted. "Are they inappropriate?"

"Oh, no . . . just different. Don't worry about it," she replied reassuringly. "So, how old are you?"

Koji opened his mouth, then closed it again. Finally, he answered, "I am . . . uncertain."

Prissie shook her head in disbelief. "How can you not know how old you are?"

"How old do I look?"

"Let's see . . . you're definitely older than Zeke, who's eight, but I doubt you're as old as Beau. He's thirteen. What grade are you in?"

"Grade?" he asked blankly.

"Yes, what grade are you going into this fall?" she repeated. When he didn't answer, she prompted, "You *do* go to school, don't you?"

"I am an apprentice."

Just then, the sound of an engine carried down the road, and they both looked toward the car that rattled toward them, kicking up a small cloud of dust. The faded green four-door rolled to a stop in front of the mailboxes, and Milo leaned out the window. "Hey there, Miss Priscilla!"

Milo was the only person besides her mother who called her by her full name, and Prissie loved it. Pink blossomed on her cheeks as she replied, "Hello, Milo."

To her surprise, he didn't acknowledge her companion but said, "Zeke was down here yesterday, and he said you were helping your grandma."

"We were packing pickle jars," Prissie explained, but her lips turned down. It wasn't like Milo to ignore someone. She cleared her throat and arched her brows at him. "This is Koji, a new friend." The boy beside her squirmed, and Prissie elbowed him gently. "Don't worry; Milo's okay. We've known him for ages."

"I apologize," the mailman smoothly interjected. "I didn't intend to be rude. I simply wasn't sure … well, never mind that, now. Hey, Koji … I see you've met Miss Pomeroy."

"Yes."

"How is it that the two of you became acquainted?" Milo gently asked.

Black eyes pleaded for understanding. "I don't really understand, Milo. Did I do something wrong … maybe?" The fidgeting boy nervously pushed his hair back, tucking it behind one ear, and Prissie's eyes immediately bugged out. The tip of Koji's revealed ear came to a pronounced point.

"Well, *that's* done it," Milo sighed. Propping his chin on his fist he chided, "My, what big ears you have."

Koji started and guiltily pulled the hair back forward. "Sorry," he mumbled before peeking at Prissie out of the corner of his eye. "Do not be afraid?" he asked, sounding more than a little uncertain.

"Are you supposed to be some kind of elf or something?" she demanded.

He quickly shook his head, then looked helplessly at Milo. "What should I do?" he asked in a small voice.

"That's a very good question." The mailman ran a hand over close-cropped blond curls. "Well, these things don't happen without a reason," he said with determined cheerfulness.

"That is so," Koji agreed.

Prissie looked between them. "Do you *know* each other?"

"We do," Milo said with a small smile.

"This doesn't make any sense," she muttered, hopping down from the fence and approaching the mailman. "What's going on?" she demanded, a spark of temper hiding her underlying nervousness.

Milo turned off the engine and unfolded his lean frame from the parked car. Gesturing reassuringly, he said, "I can explain, but I think it's best if we have a little chat with Harken. He'll know what to say."

"Who's Harken?"

"The gentleman who owns the used bookstore on Main Street," Milo calmly replied.

"I know Mr. Mercer," she acknowledged hesitantly. "He's nice."

For several moments, lines of concentration creased Milo's forehead, and then he asked, "Miss Priscilla, is your mother home?"

"She's in the garden," Prissie said, nodding in the direction of the house.

"If I can arrange things, will you come with us into town?" Milo asked.

Prissie's heart did a little flip. Yes, it would be nice to find out why Koji looked like he'd wandered away from a film crew, but what *really* mattered was the chance to go somewhere with Milo. "Sure!" she replied, smiling brightly.

Milo looked somewhat taken aback, but he nodded and said, "As it happens, I have a package to deliver. If you'll lead the way, I'll do so personally!"

"Perfect!" Prissie exclaimed.

"Providential," the mailman corrected, leaning over to collect his final delivery of the day from inside the car. Pocketing his keys, he gestured for her to precede him, and once they were on their way up the long drive, he asked, "Will you do me a favor, Miss Priscilla?"

"Of course!"

"Stay with Koji, and let me do all the talking."

"That's fine," she agreed, fairly bursting with excitement. Momma just *had* to say yes!

Naomi Pomeroy was on her knees in the vegetable garden that she and Grandma Nell fussed over every summer. At Milo's friendly hail, she stood and dusted off her pants, but before she could return the greeting, two boys exploded from around the side of the house. *"Milo!"* hollered the eight-year-old, who veered in order to barrel into the mailman.

Milo taught the third and fourth grade boys at the same church the Pomeroys attended, and Prissie's younger brother was one of the mischief-makers who kept him on his toes come Sundays. "Hey there, Zeke!" laughed Milo, roughing up the boy's unruly blond mop. In a twinkling, Zeke clambered up onto the mailman's back, while the youngest member of the Pomeroy family wrapped himself around his leg. "And it's young master Jude!" A third boy ambled over much more slowly, but no less eagerly. A few years had passed since Beau had been in Milo's class, but the brown-haired teen grinned self-consciously when the mailman mussed up his hair as well. "How've you been?"

"Good," Beau replied with a shrug. "You?"

"Never a dull moment!"

"Boys," Naomi chided. "Give Mr. Leggett some room to breathe."

"It's no problem, ma'am," the mailman assured. "Though you may want to rescue this package." He extended the day's batch of mail, which he'd cradled protectively against his chest. "It'd be a shame for it to travel all the way from Portugal only to be thwarted on your very doorstep."

Prissie's mother accepted the small box and its accompanying stack of envelopes and flyers. "Oh! It's from Ida!" she exclaimed, smiling with pleasure.

"Is it for all of us or just Prissie again?" asked six-year-old Jude.

"This one is for your grandpa and grandma," Naomi announced. Her energetic young son was still draped over Milo's shoulders, and she waved the box temptingly in front of Zeke's nose. "Would you like to take it to Grandma Nell?"

"I dunno," he replied reluctantly, tightening his grip on his teacher, half-throttling the man.

"I'll do it!" volunteered Jude eagerly.

"No! Me!" Zeke exclaimed.

Prissie looked on with a mixture of envy and embarrassment as her brothers vied for Milo's attention. She was a little surprised that no one had commented on Koji's presence yet. Normally, Zeke would have asked a dozen barely polite questions by now, and Jude wasn't shy when it came to strangers. Glancing down at their ignored guest, she smiled apologetically.

"Your family sure is noisy," Koji quietly remarked.

"Yeah, they are," she murmured back.

"It gives your home a pleasant atmosphere."

Prissie sniffed. "You don't have to live here."

After a short dispute, the two youngsters were off like a shot toward the smaller of the two houses that shared Pomeroy Orchard's front lawn, Zeke with package in hand, and Jude carrying the rest of Pete and Nell's mail.

Once they disappeared inside with the sharp slap of a screen door, Milo spoke up. "Mrs. Pomeroy, I was wondering if I could borrow some able assistants for the rest of the afternoon?"

"What did you have in mind?"

"Nothing *too* dangerous," the mailman replied lightly. "I'm going into town to help Harken Mercer for a couple hours. He received a shipment of used books from upstate, and he has a lot of boxes to unpack."

"Many hands make light the work," Naomi quipped. Glancing between her remaining children, she asked, "Any volunteers?"

Prissie glanced at Milo, who nodded. "I'm going," she declared.

"Yeah, I'll go," Beau agreed.

Again, Koji was overlooked, and Prissie cringed over her mother's baffling rudeness. Meanwhile, Naomi instructed, "Have them back by six and then stay for supper. Grandma Nell always makes enough for an army."

"It would be a pleasure! Thank you, ma'am."

"You can stay for dinner, too," Prissie whispered to Koji.

His black eyes sparkled, but he hesitated before answering, "I do not think it will be permitted, but thank you."

"What was that, Prissie?" her mother asked, giving her daughter a strange look.

"Huh?"

"I was asking if you wanted to change. It sounds like dusty work."

"No, I'm fine," she insisted with a toss of braids. There was no way she was going into town with Milo wearing grungy work clothes.

They trooped back down to the car parked in front of the mailboxes, and Beau offered to take the backseat. While he and Milo stacked plastic mail bins to make room, Koji scooted into the front seat, taking the spot in the middle.

Prissie slid in next to him, puzzling over her family's behavior. It didn't make any sense ... *unless* ... Slouching a little so that the seat provided cover, she whispered, "Can I see them again?" Koji nodded and pushed back his hair, revealing the pointed tip of one ear. "If you aren't an elf ... are you some kind of a fairy?"

He blinked and said, "No."

"Alien?"

Koji looked vaguely insulted. "No."

"Well, you're not a normal boy," she accused in a hushed voice. "My family acted as if you weren't even there, and I think it's because they couldn't *see* you."

"People should not be able to see me," Koji replied with a small frown.

"Milo can see you," Prissie countered as the mailman slid into the driver's seat and started the engine.

"Yes, I can," the mailman amiably confirmed, keeping his voice low.

"Why?"

"Because we're the same ... well, mostly," Milo smiled, then spoke louder for the benefit of her younger brother in the back. "Everyone buckled?"

"Yeah," Beau replied.

Prissie was losing patience with answers that weren't answers. Milo was a fixture in their town and in her life. He was a normal guy who liked to joke and tease. He'd never been mysterious, and she didn't like the sudden change one bit. As they took off toward the highway, engine noise and the clatter of gravel helped cover Prissie's question. "The same ... *how*?" she demanded in a hoarse whisper.

"I am not sure if I should say," Koji answered, his shoulders hunching miserably.

Milo gave the boy's knee a reassuring pat, then checked on Beau in the rear-view mirror. "The truth is best," he said, offering Prissie a lopsided smile before turning his attention back on the road. "Go ahead, Koji."

The boy straightened and bravely met Prissie's gaze. "The *truth* is ... we are angels."

2

THE CURIOSITY SHOP

Did you hear, sir?"

"You don't have to call me *sir.* We're off duty."

"Yes, sir," his young partner replied, hurrying on. "Did you receive Harken's message?"

"Message?" the balding man answered distractedly. "Was there one?"

"A moment ago, sir."

"Then, no. I'm afraid it escaped my notice." A throat cleared, and the older man finally straightened from his task. Icy gray eyes peered over wire-rimmed glasses, and he quietly asked, "Has something happened?"

"Yes, sir. Apparently, there's this girl…"

Milo ushered Prissie and Beau through the front door of The Curiosity Shop, setting off a cheerful twinkle of notes from the tiny wind chime suspended just inside the door. He walked briskly down the center aisle, poking his head around the corners into the alcoves along one side of the shop, making sure there were no other customers. "Harken!" he sang out. "I've brought guests!"

The Curiosity Shop was mainly a secondhand bookstore, though Harken Mercer had accumulated an odd assortment of paraphernalia over the years — outdated maps, sea shells, star charts, historical time lines, geographical samples, and sheet music cluttered flat surfaces or were tacked up wherever the walls weren't lined with bookshelves.

Naomi had brought the Pomeroy children to this shop almost as often as the local library, and all of Prissie's memories of it were good ones. Whenever she poked around through the shelves, she always discovered something she hadn't known she was looking for. That's probably why Momma liked to call Harken's store "The Miracle Shop."

"Prissie Pomeroy," greeted the proprietor, his deep voice rolling from the direction of the back room. He strolled through the door, a stack of books in his arms. Harken was a tall man with skin as black as his smile was white. "And Beau as well? Excellent!"

"Good afternoon, Mr. Mercer," the siblings chorused. Momma insisted on manners, and all her children could use them in a pinch — even the boys.

Once again, Koji was ignored, but Prissie doubted it was because Harken couldn't see him. The old man's kind brown eyes briefly strayed to their invisible companion, and they held a smile of welcome.

Prissie didn't really know much about the shop owner other than that her father looked up to him a great deal. According to Dad, The Curiosity Shop had been on Main Street ever since *he* was a kid, and Harken was well-known and well-liked by the other West Edinton business owners.

"Has Milo told you why you've been recruited?" Harken inquired.

"Work," Beau promptly answered, though his attention was wandering. He'd inherited Momma's nose-in-a-book tendencies and was scanning the nearest shelves.

"Right you are, my boy," the shop owner chuckled. "I've already divided the shipment in half. These boxes will need to go into the storage shed behind the building," he explained, pointing to a good-sized stack in front of the register. Choosing a set of keys from a hook, he tossed them to Milo. "If you would be so good as to unlock the shed."

"Happy to," the mailman replied with a wink, and he ducked through the door into the back room.

"The rest of these," Harken continued, gesturing to a smaller pile, "will need to be unpacked and shelved."

"What kinds of books are in here?" Beau asked as he tilted his head to read the box's label. "Any stories? You don't have many."

It was true. Probably the strangest thing about The Curiosity Shop was that Harken didn't stock much fiction. Prissie had noticed it as well, but she'd never asked because it seemed a little rude. Though she narrowed her eyes accusingly at her brother, she was just as eager to hear the old man's answer.

"This shop's contents reveal the avenues taken by my own curiosity. These books are a reflection of my personal interests." Harken gazed around the store, then spread his arms wide. "You can learn a lot about a person from what they choose to read."

Prissie's eyes darted to the nearest shelf, which held an entire row of books on the Middle East — archaeological histories, travel guides, volumes of photography, and even a few cookbooks. Since Harken seemed to be inviting it, she joined Beau in wandering around, taking note of the different kinds of books in his collection: old sets of encyclopedias, stacks of travel magazines, academic journals, nature photography, space exploration, and oddly enough, books of crossword puzzles.

"So you're mostly into information?" Beau asked. "Do you have a computer? Because you can find even more on the Internet."

The old man nodded. "I use the computers at the library when the need arises, but I've found that I prefer books. It may take me longer to find what I need, but I learn unexpected things along the way. Many times, the journey is just as important as reaching the goal."

"*These* are stories," Beau called from one of the alcoves. "Well, sorta."

Harken joined him and pulled one of the books from the shelf. "Yes, these are stories — life stories." One entire bookcase was dedicated to biographies and autobiographies, and from what Prissie could see, most of them were of noted Christian thinkers, missionaries, evangelists, and pastors. "I'm also fond of parables," the old man admitted.

Milo reappeared and placed Harken's keys onto the counter beside the register, then grabbed a couple of boxes. "Is anywhere in the shed fine?" he asked as Beau hauled a box into his arms as well. The shopkeeper agreed, and Milo and Beau carried them out.

"Now that we have a moment ..." Harken gave Prissie a considering look, but he turned to the boy standing just inside the door. "Hello, Koji. You've had an eventful day."

"Yes," he agreed, glancing shyly at Prissie.

"Why can *you* see him, Mr. Mercer?"

"Because I'm an angel as well," he gently revealed.

Prissie shook her head. "But you've always been here, and everyone knows you! My dad's bakery is half a block away, and I remember coming here when I was little!"

"You were fond of books with castles in them," he said with a smile. "Your father always called you his princess, and I think you believed him."

"That's right! You remembered," she replied, somewhat awed.

"It's part of my job to pay attention, although Jayce and I have been good friends since he was your age," Harken said. "It's been a pleasure to watch his hopes for the future flourish."

Prissie tried to fathom this new information, but angels simply didn't fit into her notion of normal. "But this is impossible! How can *you* be an ... an ...?"

"An angel," he finished for her, nodding seriously. "It's true, Prissie."

"Why would an angel live in a little place like West Edinton?" she asked skeptically.

"A small town isn't of greater or lesser importance," Harken explained. "Milo, Koji, and I all have a part to play in a grander scheme — one that is beyond our ability to understand. In this way, we're not much different from you."

"Are you saying that there are lots of people around here who are actually angels?" she demanded nervously.

Harken made a soothing motion with his hand. "No, child. We're few and far between, and it's very rare for anyone to see us for what we truly are."

"Did I do something wrong?" Koji inquired, shifting from foot to foot.

"No, young one," Harken assured. "This wasn't your doing."

Prissie's discomfort grew, and she searched her mind for what little she knew of angels. "Does that mean that one of you is supposed to be my guardian angel?" she demanded.

"No, neither of us is a Guardian," the old man answered patiently.

"But ... I *have* a guardian angel?" she persisted.

"Of course you do."

Glancing around the otherwise empty shop, Prissie asked, "Where?"

Harken smiled softly. "Close."

"Don't I get to meet my angel?"

The old man's smile widened, and he said, "One day, I'm sure you will, but today is not that day."

"Oh," she mumbled in disappointment.

Harken placed his hand on his chest and said, "Milo and I are Messengers. We're go-betweens, directed by God. Koji here is an Observer; he watches, listens, and learns, tracing the hand of God in the lives of mankind."

She looked between the two of them, wanting to tell them they were crazy, then desperately said, "You don't *look* like angels."

"And what is an angel *supposed* to look like?"

The sound of footsteps came from the back room, and Prissie's mouth snapped shut as her brother and the mailman returned. "Sorry it took us so long; I managed to drop a box, and it took a while to pick up everything," Milo said sheepishly. "Did we take too long?"

He and Harken exchanged a long look, and Prissie saw her chance to escape. She needed a little room to think. "I'll take one," she offered.

"Me and Milo can handle these, Priss," Beau said.

"Milo *and I*," she corrected. "I'm here to help, so I'll help, too."

Prissie lifted the box, which was really quite heavy for its size, and headed into the back room, which was another warren of shelves. Cartons and stacks of boxes were everywhere, and against the far wall were two doors, one green and one blue. As she stood contemplating her options, Beau nearly bumped into her, his arms manfully weighed down by two boxes. "Which door do we use?" she asked.

Her brother gave her a strange look. "Is that supposed to be some kind of trick question?"

Prissie huffed. "There's no reason to be rude. I was only asking!"

"There's only *one* door, Priss," he said sarcastically. "Use it." She gawked after him as he trudged across the room and turned to push open the green door with his hip. Cocking a brow at her, he disappeared into the late summer sunlight.

For a long moment, she stood still, but then she set her box on the corner of a desk and tiptoed to the blue door. It looked old — partly because the color had faded to a milkier hue in spots, and partly because people just didn't make doors like this one anymore. The entire surface had been intricately carved. Leaves, fruit, and flowers nestled among crisscrossing vines in an ornate border. Two trees stood in the center, their uppermost branches twined together.

The doorknob shone like a luminous crystal; flashes of different colors lurked beneath its smooth surface. When she took hold it hummed beneath her palm, sending an almost musical note through her body, right down to the soles of her feet. "First an invisible boy, now an invisible door?" she murmured.

"So you can see this as well," Harken remarked. Milo strode past with another couple of boxes in his arms, but not without giving her an encouraging grin. Koji padded into the room on bare feet and brightened.

"Where does it lead?" Prissie asked.

"That's an interesting question," the shopkeeper replied. "In one sense, it leads nowhere; in another sense, it leads us toward heaven. Since you're capable of *seeing* the door, let's see if you can step through it."

Koji's dark eyes sparkled. "I hope so!"

His excitement lessened Prissie's nervousness enough for her to try. The knob turned easily, its latch clicked softly, and a warm glow seeped through the narrow opening she'd created. She hesitated on the threshold, looking back at Harken for permission to proceed. "By all means," he urged. "There's nothing to fear beyond this door."

Taking a deep breath, Prissie gave the door a push; it swung outward, and she stepped through ... and into a garden. There were trees all around, so it felt as if they were within a forest glade, but that was impossible. "This isn't what's behind the shop," she said, turning around to take in the scenery. There was supposed to be a parking lot, a storage shed, her brother, and a bright, sunny summer afternoon. "What's wrong with the sky?"

"That is how *this* sky appears," Harken answered. "Tell me what you see."

"Grass, trees, and the sky looks like water," she replied.

"It does, doesn't it," the old man calmly agreed.

"Is it water?"

"No. That's merely a trick of the light."

"Nothing else?" asked Koji, his gaze directed at a spot just past her shoulder.

She slowly turned once more, but finally answered, "That's all. Where are we?"

"We've stepped outside of time. Some would call this *beyond the veil,*" Harken supplied. "For us, it is a home away from home, a gathering place that offers privacy, fellowship, refreshment."

"Umm ... right. This is your break room," Prissie said in a tight voice.

Hearing something in her tone, Harken frowned. "In its fashion, yes."

Prissie turned on her heel, rushing toward a much more familiar world of cardboard cartons and overstuffed bookshelves. The two angels followed more slowly, and when they caught up to her, she faced them. "I don't believe you."

Koji's head tipped to one side, confusion plain on his face. "Which part?"

"This is crazy ... completely ridiculous," she muttered. Fixing Harken with a stern look, she repeated, "I *won't* believe you."

Just then, Milo strolled through the door, laughing as he talked with Beau. He trailed off the moment he caught the mood in the room and looked uncertainly between Harken and Prissie.

His sparkling blue eyes grew sadder … and older … and Prissie's lip trembled. "No," she whispered stubbornly. "No, there must be some mistake."

"Miss Priscilla?"

Milo raised a hand, but she turned her back on him and addressed Harken with extreme politeness. "My dad's bakery is right over there, and I think I'll go see him. Like Beau said, he and Milo can handle the rest."

"What's going on, Sis?" asked her brother, perplexed by her sudden change in attitude.

"It's nothing," she lied. "I'll be with Dad and catch a ride home with him."

"You better call Mom and let her know," he cautioned.

"I'll call from the bakery."

"Miss Priscilla?" Milo tried again, but she darted from the room, through the shop, and out the front door without a backward glance.

3
THE HASTY RETREAT

"Why has this child been put in danger?" demanded a pacing angel with a drawn sword. "She is confused, *frightened*!"

"Gently, my friend," soothed a serene old-timer with snowy white hair. "We do not yet know how far into our midst Miss Pomeroy will be drawn. Her acquaintance with Koji may be the limit of her involvement."

"That is enough to draw the *wrong* sort of attention!"

"Alas, that is so."

The gentle admission cooled the warrior's temper. With a pleading look, he asked, "Why has it been given to *her* to see such things?"

The old one merely shook his head. "Who can know the mind of God?"

Once the large stack of boxes was transferred into the shed, Harken set Beau to work opening the ones that needed to be shelved. As soon as the teen was caught up in his task, the shopkeeper took an armload of leather-bound tomes and moved to the far alcove, beckoning for Milo and Koji to follow. The mailman scooped up a few more books and joined the older angel.

Koji's face was a portrait of confusion. "She does not *believe* in us?"

"That's what she said," Harken replied with a patient smile.

"But that will not change anything," the boy pointed out.

"I know that," the old man said, pointing to himself. "And you know that," he stated, gently tapping Koji's chest. "However, many humans believe that they can influence reality with what amounts to willful blindness. If they are confronted with something that doesn't appeal to them, they often refuse to acknowledge it."

"So she is going to ignore us until we go away?" Koji asked.

"That's the sum of it," Milo agreed, scrubbing wearily at his face.

Koji looked between the two adults and asked, "*Are* we going away?"

"No, young one. Things cannot go back to the way they were before."

"Will she tell?" Koji asked worriedly.

"I don't think so," replied Milo.

"She isn't going to go around telling people about something she doesn't want to believe herself," Harken explained.

"Have you ever had to reveal yourself to a human before, Harken?" Milo asked curiously.

"Not for many years, and then only in dreams," his mentor replied. "I wonder at the purposes of bringing this girl into our midst."

"She did not seem very pleased," Koji unhappily pointed out.

"She might be a little scared," Milo suggested.

"Of *us*?" the boy asked.

"Perhaps a little, yes," Harken agreed. "But I daresay she's struggling with disappointment as well."

Milo drooped visibly. "Some of this is my fault. Could I have handled it better?"

Harken clapped his shoulder. "No, my boy. We'll give her time to get over the surprise; in the meantime, I will ask for direction."

"Yes, that's good," Milo said resignedly, then looked to his comrade. "I've always treated her the same as everyone else."

"I know," soothed Harken. "But now you don't have to."

"I don't believe it. I *won't* believe it," Prissie muttered over and over as she hurried past the local paper, the post office, and the town hall, which housed a tiny branch library. Story time was underway in the big gazebo that stood out front, so she checked for cars and dashed across Main Street, heading for the comforting familiarity of Loafing Around, her father's bakery.

Though Prissie didn't know all the details, she'd overheard enough snippets of adult conversation to know that Grandpa had a hard time accepting his son's career choice. Pete Pomeroy had wanted his only boy to take over the farm and orchard, carrying on the family business, but Dad had gone to cooking school instead. The tension between them had eased considerably with the birth of Pete's first grandson. Grandpa poured all his love for the orchard into Tad, and by the time the little guy was four, he'd tell anyone who asked that he was going to be a farmer. Momma said it was hard to tell if Tad loved the farm because he loved *it* ... or because he loved Grandpa. In the end, it hardly mattered; Pomeroy Orchard's future was secure.

The bakery offered a bit of everything, but Jayce Pomeroy's specialty was bread, and they were famous for their dinner rolls. Soft, light, golden-brown potato rolls had been the Saturday Special since day one, and people actually lined up for them. It was the closest thing Main Street ever had to a traffic jam. Two years ago in shop class, Prissie's next older brother Neil had made Dad a sign with routered lettering; it was proudly displayed on the bakery's front door and invited patrons to *Get Your Buns in Here.*

Prissie frowned at the sidewalk until she neared her destination, then glanced up to see a guy standing in front of the bakery, his nose practically pressed to the window. "What are *you* doing here, Ransom?"

Ransom Pavlos was a classmate, and for the last couple years, he'd been the bane of her existence. The gangly teen casually sat back on the seat of his bike and shifted the wide strap that crossed his chest. "None of your business, Miss Priss," he smirked.

"This is *too* my business!" she declared. "It's my dad's bakery."

He glanced through the display window and muttered, "Your dad's, huh? Well, that changes things."

"What's *that* supposed to mean?" Prissie demanded.

Reaching into the pouch angled across his back, he fished out a newspaper and tossed it at her feet. "It means I'm not interested," he replied before pedaling away.

"Hey! she called after him. "You're not supposed to ride on the sidewalks!"

Ransom lifted a hand in farewell, but otherwise ignored her words.

Prissie scowled after him, then bent to pick up the tightly rolled copy of *The Herald*, letting her old, familiar disgust with Ransom push Milo far from her mind. "Whatever," she grumbled as she shoved through the bakery's front door, setting its bell to jangling. Inside, she sniffed and smiled. It was impossible not to, because the bakery smelled just as it should — spicy, yeasty, sweet, and safe. Her father might wear the apron in the family, but he was her daddy, and this place was a little piece of home.

The woman sitting on a stool behind the counter set aside her knitting and smiled bashfully. "You haven't been by in a while, Prissie," she greeted. "That sure is a pretty dress! Is it new?"

"Hello, Pearl," she replied, beaming under the compliment. Pearl Matthews was a statuesque young woman with warm brown skin and wiry black hair who always noticed the right kinds of things.

"Are you out doing errands with your momma?"

"Not today," said Prissie, her smile faltering. "It's just me and Beau." For several moments, she stared at the other woman, wondering if she was really *real* ... or if she might be an angel, too. *No.* She shook off the notion as impossible. Pearl had a husband and a little girl, while Milo and Harken were both single, with no families that she'd ever heard of. "Is Dad here?"

"Where *else* would he be?" Pearl teased. "He's up to his elbows in peaches."

"We brought in two crates, and Louise put him to work," drawled a voice from the corner.

"Oh, hello, Uncle Lou!" Prissie exclaimed, embarrassed to have overlooked him.

The quiet old man rarely made eye contact with anyone and spent many a morning camped out in the corner of the small seating area, sipping coffee, reading the paper, and waiting for handouts. His wife was the bakery's only other employee.

Louise Cook, a tiny, spunky woman in her late sixties, just couldn't get the hang of retirement, so Prissie's father had offered her a place in his kitchen. For the last three years, she'd been turning out dozens of delicious pies on a daily basis. Jayce was fond of saying that he was hard-pressed to keep up with her, and he was only half-kidding. Auntie Lou wore big, floral aprons, handed out cookies to growing boys, and didn't take *no* for an answer. It didn't surprise Prissie at all that her father had been roped into peeling fruit.

Louise's husband wasn't really named Lou. Zeke had been the first to mix up their names, and even though Mr. Cook's given name was Paul, "Uncle Lou" stuck.

"Is that the afternoon edition?" he inquired.

Prissie glanced down at the paper still clutched in her hand. "Oh, yes! Would you like it?"

"If you please," he smiled, and she hurried to present it to him. "How's your summer been, young lady?"

"The usual," Prissie sighed. "Lots of gardening and canning."

The old man shook out the paper, adjusted his glasses,

then tapped the lead article on the front page. "County fair's just around the corner. You planning on entering anything this year?"

"I am!" she replied confidently. "I can't compete with Auntie Lou or Grandma Nell, but I'm going to enter a pie in the junior division."

"Oh, that'll be wonderful!" chimed in Pearl. "What kind?"

"I'm still testing recipes," Prissie hedged.

"If you're looking for inspiration, there are a few beauties left in the case," prompted Uncle Lou. He shooed the girl toward the display, and she crossed to check out Louise's pies.

Pearl joined her in *ooh*-ing and *aah*-ing over a lattice-topped cherry and an old-fashioned buttermilk pie decorated with whipped cream and raspberries. "I want a piece of *that* one," the tall woman confided, pointing to a nut pie that definitely had chocolate in it. "It's a new recipe, and it looks heavenly!"

Prissie cringed at her choice of words, but nodded in agreement.

Uncle Lou kept his eyes on his newspaper as he nonchalantly said, "Your pa might let us test a few, being as it's the end of the day."

"Are you trying to get Prissie to sweet-talk a piece of pie for you?" Pearl scolded.

The old man peeked from under bushy white brows. "I wouldn't object to a wee wedge — or a warm-up?" He lifted his coffee cup hopefully, and Pearl shook her head in mock dismay.

Prissie smiled as the two entered into their usual routine of polite wheedling and gentle bossing that always ended in Uncle Lou's favor. She was feeling better by the minute, and then, the kitchen door swung wide, and her father strode through, dressed in chef's whites and wiping his hands on a well-spattered apron. The minute he spotted her, he broke into a wide, boyish grin.

Jayce Pomeroy was tall and broad, with brown hair and blue eyes that sparkled with good humor. While Prissie didn't necessarily want her friends to find out that her dad spent most of his day wearing a hair net, that didn't stop her from hurrying forward when he opened his arms. "There's my girl! What are you doing here, princess?"

She explained the bare minimum, and her father nodded his understanding. "Then call your mother and tell her we're bringing home peach cobbler tonight!"

A couple hours later, soft chimes sounded when Mr. Pomeroy opened The Curiosity Shop's front door and stepped inside. He lifted a hand to greet his old friend. "Good afternoon, sir! I hear you're in possession of one of my lot."

"I am at that!" Harken gestured broadly at Beau, who was hunkered down in the corner, poring over an illustrated history of nearby Sunderland State Park. "As you can see, he's enjoying the fruits of his labors."

The teen stirred enough to blink blue eyes at his father over the top of the oversized book before breaking into an enthusiastic grin. "Hi, Dad! Mr. Mercer's letting me keep this! It's pretty cool ... it even has maps of the caves!"

Jayce raised his eyebrows at Harken, who waved his hand. "The boy *earned* it."

Milo strolled out of the back room, a hammer in hand. "Hey there, Mr. Pomeroy! Did Miss Priscilla make it over to the bakery all right?"

"Sure, sure ... that's partly why I'm here," her father replied, causing the two angels to exchange a quick glance. Jayce shoved his hands into his pockets and addressed the shop owner. "My wife tells me that Milo's coming to dinner, and she asked me to invite you as well ... unless you have other plans?"

"Well, now," Harken replied thoughtfully. "That's very generous, but I don't wish to impose."

"Don't even think it," scoffed Jayce. "You know Naomi, it's always the more, the merrier. She said my mother's pulled out the stops, and Prissie and I made dessert."

The old man's low chuckle filled the shop. "I would be honored to accept your hospitality, Jayce. Thank you for thinking of an old bachelor like me."

"You and Milo are most welcome," Jayce assured.

"Yo, Prissie, anybody home?" demanded Neil, her next brother up the family order.

Snapping fingers in front of her eyes startled Prissie out of her thoughts, and she looked in confusion at her oldest brother Tad, whose lips quirked in amusement. "Where've you been?"

Pointed ears, shining clothes, blue doors, and forest glades filled her mind, but she wasn't about to admit it. "Sorry, what?"

Neil rolled his eyes and half-stood to reach across the table and snag the butter dish sitting in front of her plate. "Here ya go, Milo," the sixteen-year-old declared. His blue eyes twinkled with mischief as he added, "Please excuse our sister; she's not usually this neglectful of our guests. You must be a special case."

"Thank you, Neil," the mailman politely replied, though his gaze rested uncertainly on Prissie.

If she hadn't prided herself so highly on good posture, Prissie would have slouched ... or slid right under the table. Having Milo over for dinner was a rare treat. On any other day, she would have fought tooth and nail to claim a place of honor at his side, but tonight, Grandma Nell had needed a firm hand to haul onto her usual seat between her mother and Tad.

The Pomeroy's table was a long, wide, solid piece of craftsmanship that had dominated the farmhouse kitchen for the better part of a century. Its wooden surface showed years of wear, scarred and smoothed by turns, and it could accommodate the entire family with room to spare. With a dozen people crowded around it, dinner was even more lively than usual, which made it easier for Prissie to hang back. Normally, she was in the thick of every discussion, but tonight, she joined Tad on the sidelines.

"You feeling okay, Priss?" he murmured. Tad was eighteen and heading into his senior year at high school. Her big-big brother's serious gray eyes considered her, then turned back to his plate, but after taking a bite of mashed potatoes, he glanced her way, still waiting for an answer.

"It's been a strange day," she whispered back, offering a strained smile for reassurance.

He nodded once, then gave his attention to the main thread of conversation, which was happening at Dad's end of the table, where Grandpa was seated across from Harken. "Saw the notice last week. Can't hardly believe it's almost time for *Messiah* rehearsals to pick back up again," Pete Pomeroy remarked.

"They *are* starting earlier this year," Harken replied. "The director wants to give everyone time to learn the new arrangements."

Harken attended Holy Trinity Presbyterian, a picturesque stone church noted for its stained glass windows and pipe organ, and every December, they hosted a full-scale performance of Handel's *Messiah*. They pulled choir members from the whole community, and the annual production was the highlight of the holidays for many locals, especially Grandpa Pete.

"Not sure I approve of them trying to snazz up the classics," the old farmer grumbled. "Adding the symphony was classy, but electric guitars and whatnot? I just don't know."

"Oh, don't be such a fuddy-duddy, Peter," scolded Nell. "I think it sounds fun!"

Pete had been growling out the low notes with the bass section for upwards of forty years, with his wife lending her strength to the alto section. Prissie could understand his lack of enthusiasm over the plans to mix things up and modernize the score. Harken smiled and offered, "Times change, but the message remains the same."

Grandpa harrumphed, but Milo spoke up before the old man could voice another complaint. "I'll be taking part for the first time this year. A friend from Deo Volente roped me into it."

"Oh, yeah?" Neil asked, perking up. "Tad, Beau and I have been going to Deo Volente at Harper's Elementary School, though you should know kids call it DeeVee. They have an amazing band. It'd be great if you joined."

The meal continued, and conversation rambled from one topic to the next. Eventually, plates were pushed back and Dad made a comment about Beau's new book. The teen grinned at Harken. "I'll gladly work for books."

"Oho!" cheered Neil. "Someone's finally figured out how to get Beau's nose out of a book!"

"Lure him with the promise of more," Tad teased.

Beau made a face at his older siblings, but joined in on the laughter that rippled through the room. Harken's deep chuckle lasted longest, and then he said, "I'll send word when the next shipment comes in, and you can have your pick. If you and Prissie can make time for me with what's left of the summer, I'd appreciate it."

As everyone's attention swung in her direction, Prissie hastily excused herself from the table to refill the water pitchers. Her back was very straight as she pulled ice cube trays from the freezer and busied herself in front of the sink. When she stole a peek over her shoulder, Momma was starting to stand, but Harken raised a hand, saying, "Let me. I need to settle up with your daughter for the help she offered earlier."

Naomi smiled and nodded, and Milo dove into the fray, turning the conversation in a completely new direction. "Say, Neil, has the football team started meeting yet?"

"Next week," the teen answered. "We had sports camp last month, so Coach gave us a couple weeks to rest up before practice starts up again. I've seen you at some of the games. You a football fan?"

"I go to *all* the home games," the mailman enthusiastically replied.

"No kidding?"

Milo nodded. "I have a special place in my heart for the team. Any chance you'll you be a starter this year?"

Neil shrugged and said, "Dunno yet. Hope so."

Prissie tried to mentally brace herself to face Harken, but at the same time, she couldn't help darting glances into the corners of the room, at the doorways, and even out the windows, half expecting Koji to appear. It wasn't the same as earlier, when she felt as if she was being watched. No, this time, it was the uncanny knowledge that she probably *was* being watched, even though she couldn't see or hear the watchers. The sudden self-consciousness was making her jittery.

Prissie was so caught up in her inner turmoil that she started violently when a dark hand reached past her to turn off the tap and rescue the overflowing pitcher. "He stayed behind," Harken offered in a low voice.

"Wh-what?"

"Koji," the old gentleman explained. "He stayed behind this evening because we thought you might be uncomfortable—seeing the unseen."

"Oh," she breathed, glancing at the table, where Milo was deeply immersed in a discussion of the West Edinton Warriors' chances in their division this coming year. The mailman had shed his official postal service uniform in favor of a casual shirt in a shade of blue that really did wonderful things for his eyes. He gestured broadly while he talked, comfortable in their midst.

Prissie had always felt as if he belonged to them, but she was no longer sure that was true. For some reason, Milo's smile *hurt*, so Prissie went back to not looking at the man ... angel. "Why did everything have to change?" she asked in a tight voice.

"Nothing's changed, Prissie," Harken corrected. "You're now seeing certain things the way they truly are."

"Is there a difference?"

"Yes, there is," the angel assured. Very gently, he laid a hand on her shoulder, and she tensed, but grudgingly met his eyes. "I have a message for you, child."

"From who?"

Prissie darted a quick glance at Milo, but the old man shook his head and said, "First of all, don't be afraid."

She swallowed hard and gave a little half-shake of her head. "If you say so."

He pulled his hand away with a sigh. "I told you, Prissie, I'm only the messenger." She tentatively met his gaze, and Harken nodded approvingly. With calm solemnity, he intoned, "Priscilla Pomeroy, the time has come for you to give away some of your trust."

4

THE STUBBORN STREAK

A bent form scrabbled along a dank passage and slipped into a small chamber whose entrance was hidden in the cleft of a rock. "There's a development, my lord," he announced in a hoarse voice.

"What now, Dinge?" inquired a figure seated upon a heap of boulders in the center of the cave.

"I overheard some saying that a *message* has been delivered."

His leader leaned forward, and a faint dissonance, like the sour note in a musical chord, echoed off of the walls. "To whom?"

"A fourteen-year-old girl."

A misshapen shadow lurking in the pitch sneered, "Probably just a two-bit molly-coddler soothing away nightmares."

"No," snapped the news-bringer, drawing himself up importantly. "I would not waste our lord's time on something so trivial."

"What then?" prompted the leader on his tumbledown throne.

"A firsthand encounter," Dinge revealed excitedly. "A message delivered in person."

"Means nothing," jeered the naysayer. "What's a girl of that age going to do, huh?"

Dinge hissed his outrage. "Murque, you *fool*! Don't you remember what happened the *last time* a message like this was dismissed?"

"Uhh ... what?" he replied dimly.

"A virgin conceived," smoothly replied their leader.

"What're the chances *that'll* happen again," grumbled Murque, earning a scathing look from Dinge.

The central figure rubbed small circles against his temple with the tips of graceful fingers. "Which Messenger?"

"Harken."

Their lord stilled. "Oh?"

"Yes, lord."

"That definitely changes things," he mused aloud.

The first Sunday of every month, First Baptist Church hosted a potluck dinner following the morning service. Prissie's mother and grandmother were firm believers in bringing enough to feed your own family with some to spare, and since there were *ten* Pomeroys to account for, the procession from the parking lot to the church's basement kitchen was always a long one.

Mr. Pomeroy and his three teenage boys were weighed down with piping hot pans wrapped in towels, and Zeke and Jude brought up the rear, swinging bags of Loafing Around's famous dinner rolls. Grandma Nell took possession of the pie carrier, and Mrs. Pomeroy precariously balanced a platter of brownies on top of her Bible and notebook, though it was rescued by an usher and passed along to one of the efficient kitchen ladies as she walked through the door.

Milo was one of the greeters this Sunday, and he stepped forward with open hands and a warm smile. "Good morning, Miss Priscilla. Can I help?"

Prissie sailed right past him holding her nose and her rice pudding high. "I've got it, thanks," she replied crisply.

The mailman let his hands fall to his sides as he bleakly watched her march toward the stairs leading down to the fellowship hall. Jayce, who'd been relieved of his burden by another kitchen lady, shook his head at his daughter's stiff back, then strode over and casually addressed Milo. "Care to tell me what happened?"

"Sir?"

"I thought maybe the dinner at our place was a fluke, but my Prissie seems to have had a change of heart where you're concerned."

Milo winced and rubbed the back of his neck. "I suppose I've disappointed your daughter," he offered.

"In what way?" her father inquired. His tone was reasonable, but he looked every inch a man prepared to defend and protect his daughter.

"I believe she's finally seen, well, sir, the age difference alone," Milo offered uncomfortably.

"Sure, sure ... I get it." With a heavy sigh, Jayce dropped a hand on the young man's shoulder. "It was kinda cute when she was little, the way she took a shine to you. Puppy love or whatever."

The mailman shoved his hands deep into his pockets. "I'm sorry, sir."

"Have you done anything you *should* be sorry for?" Jayce inquired, an edge back in his tone.

Milo quickly straightened and earnestly met the man's gaze. "No, sir! Absolutely not."

"Then stop looking so guilty," Jayce urged. "Girls are just ... girls. Naomi says it's part of growing up."

"I asked Harken for advice, and he believes everything will work for the good."

"He's a wise man," Mr. Pomeroy mused. "The two of you kind of look out for each other, don't you?"

"I rent a room over his shop, so we're neighbors."

"Love thy neighbor, and all that?" Jayce asked with a chuckle.

"And all that," Milo agreed. "Sir, should I stay away from your family for a while?"

Prissie's father absently tugged at his tie, his expression serious. "You've been a good friend ever since you moved to town, and I hate to see this kind of rift develop."

"Yes, sir."

"No, I don't want you to suddenly disappear from our lives," Jayce said decidedly. He glanced in the direction his daughter had disappeared. "Prissie's a lot like my father; she's not one to let go of a grudge quickly. If there's any way to make up with her *before* her mind is set, I'd do it quickly."

The strains of organ and piano drifted from the sanctuary,

signaling the nearing of service time, and Milo smiled as he took a step back. "I will, sir. And thank you."

"For what?"

"Your trust," he replied, excusing himself with a polite nod.

In the kitchen, Prissie and Beau prowled the perimeter, assessing the other offerings with a practiced eye. The countertops were crowded with an assortment of glass casserole dishes and foil-topped pans, and crock pots vied for outlets. "Two kinds of meatballs," she whispered.

"But *three* people brought baked beans," her brother replied in a low voice. Giving her a small smile of triumph, he added, "And I only saw two lasagnas."

"So far." With a significant nod at the fridge, she reminded, "There've been more Jell-O salads lately, so Jude might win again."

It was a game of sorts, with pot luck predictions made in the car on the way to church. The tally wouldn't be official until they actually walked through the line at lunchtime, because there were always latecomers whose contributions threw everyone off.

Beau peeked under the foil covering a pan and wrinkled his nose at a broccoli casserole before casually lifting the corner on the next pan, which contained cheesy potatoes. "Say, Priss, how come you blew off Milo?"

"I didn't blow him off; I just didn't need his help."

"I've heard about girls playing hard to get and stuff, but did you see the look on his face?"

Prissie sniffed. "I can't say that I did."

"Hmm," Beau hummed distractedly, gazing critically at a pot of meatballs. "You know that look Jude gets if a hen pecks him when he's gathering eggs?"

Immediately, Prissie's littlest brother appeared in her mind's eye. Jude loved the whole farm, but the hens were his special favorites. When he felt he'd offended one, he'd follow it around the yard, wide eyes brimming with unshed tears, apologizing. It was sweet and silly, because he wouldn't hurt a fly, let alone one of their flock.

Beau watched her face, then nodded. "Whatever he did, even if it was nothing, he's sorry, and he wants to make up."

"Do you mean Jude or Milo?" Prissie asked suspiciously.

Her brother just shrugged and edged closer to the fridge.

Grandma Nell bustled around the church kitchen, quite at home in the midst of the potluck chaos. She gave her grandchildren a knowing look, then pointed toward the door. "Out you get," she ordered. "Service is starting!"

Prissie had never been more grateful for an excuse to retreat. "Yes, Grandma," the siblings chorused and took off.

Milo didn't sit near the Pomeroys that morning, but Prissie could see him on the other side of the sanctuary, standing behind Pearl's husband, Derrick, and making faces at their eighteen-month-old daughter, Amberly. The mailman wasn't the kind of person to stake out a favorite spot and sit there every week; he was always there, but never in the same place twice. All throughout the first two hymns, the little girl waved shyly at Milo, and Prissie thought it was cute, but sort of unsettling. Did the toddler know that the smiling man she was reaching for wasn't what he seemed? More important, was it okay for him to trick her by pretending to be normal?

While she made a halfhearted stab at the second verse of a chorus, Prissie watched Milo like a hawk, unsure if her resentment was directed toward him or the child who had claimed his attention. Amberly giggled, and Pearl smiled on indulgently when the mailman held up a hand so the little girl could pat it; but then Milo seemed to sense Prissie's gaze and turned his head. His happy smile faded, becoming something uncertain, and the expression looked so *wrong* on her usually carefree friend that Prissie had to look away.

Muffled *thumps* of closing hymnals and the shuffle of feet signaled that the congregation was taking their seats. Prissie carefully arranged her skirt and crossed her ankles before idly scanning the bulletin as one of the elders went through the announcements. It didn't take long for her attention to drift.

First Baptist Church wasn't as grand as the Presbyterian church on Main Street, but to Prissie's way of thinking, it was everything a church was *supposed* to be. Traditional white clapboard, double doors, polished wood pews, and a cross on the wall behind the pulpit. They didn't have stained glass windows, but the lady's guild made beautiful banners that hung between the windows along each wall. They were changed out every month to fit the seasons, and for August, everything was in summery shades of green with snippets from the Psalms on them: "He shall be like a tree," and "His leaf shall not wither."

The soft rustle of pages alerted her that Pastor Albert Ruggles, or Pastor Bert as he liked to be called, had already taken the pulpit and given the morning's text, so she stole a peek at Tad's Bible to see where to turn.

In spite of the heat of the day, their pastor wore a navy blue suit and greeted them with a smile as sunny as the yellow of his tie. "If you'll recall, we've spent the last few weeks in a study of the life of Abraham. This morning, we pick up his story in Genesis 18.

"Whenever people tell this story, they like to skip to the end ... cut to the chase ... deliver the punch line, as it were. They'll tell you that this is the story of Sarah, the woman who laughed at God, and how the Lord got the last laugh. Sarah gives birth to a miracle baby, and they name him Isaac, which means *laughter!*" Pastor Bert chuckled, and a few titters came from the audience.

"It's a wonderful story, and one I'm sure Isaac heard many times when he was growing up. But today, I'd like to back up and slow down, because if you look at this section of Genesis in a different way, it's the story of two men, each visited by angels."

Prissie's wandering thoughts jolted to attention.

As her pastor recounted Abraham's generosity toward the strangers who appeared on his lands, comparing it to Lot's treatment of his angelic visitors, Prissie glanced Milo's way, only to remember that he was downstairs, teaching Zeke's class. She wondered if they were having the same lesson and decided to drill her younger brother about it later. Who better to teach about angels than an angel?

Prissie flipped through Genesis, skimming for more details about the angels and not having much luck. She was frustrated that the text didn't go into more detail about the most interesting part of the account. When she finally tuned back into Pastor Bert's sermon, he was wrapping things up. The pastor looked out over the audience and smiled. "To close, I'd like to remind you of the admonition in Hebrews 13:2 — 'Do not forget to entertain strangers, for by so doing some have unwittingly entertained angels.'

"That's exactly what happened to Abraham and Lot, and it ties in nicely for us today. I believe this is a call to God's people to be genuine in their generosity. Reach out to those around you, be they friend or stranger, and give them a smile, a helping hand, a listening ear, a kind word, a shared meal. You never know when you might be entertaining angels unaware."

Afterward, Prissie followed Jude through the line, carrying his plate as he pointed to the foods he wanted to sample. Once he was perched on a chair next to Grandpa, she watched carefully, waiting for Pastor Ruggles to get into line and slipping into place behind him. He chatted amiably with one of the deacons, but when he finally picked up his silverware, she saw her opportunity. As he spooned chicken and rice onto his plate, she spoke up. "Excuse me, Pastor Bert?"

He glanced up and smiled. "Hello, Prissie. What can I do for you?"

"I was hoping you could answer a few questions, since you're an expert on God and things."

The pastor's brown eyes warmed, but he didn't laugh, for which she was grateful. "Well, let's see, I don't know about the 'expert' part, but I'll do my best, young lady. What's on your mind?"

"Angels, mostly," she admitted, cutting a glance in Milo's direction. "I guess I'm a little confused. I thought they mostly lived in heaven."

"I'm sure they call heaven home," he agreed. "But I suspect they leave from time to time, carrying out the Lord's work."

"They have jobs?" Prissie asked. "Like working in a store or as a teacher or something?"

He laughed softly. "Wouldn't that be something? No, I meant that God has given them responsibilities. *Some* may spend their lives in heaven, singing the Lord's praises, but others serve as messengers or guardians."

"And observers?"

"Well, let's see," he mused aloud. "It does say in First Peter that they're eagerly watching God's plans play out in our lives — 'things which angels desire to look into.' I wonder what they find so fascinating, don't you?"

"So they're really *real*?" she whispered, half to herself. It was harder than she expected to mesh the Bible stories she'd grown up hearing with real life.

"Why, yes," Pastor Bert said as he took a scoop of spaghetti hot dish, not noticing the way Prissie paled. "As real as you and me. They're referred to throughout the Scriptures in a very matter-of-fact way, and those who encountered angels *knew* they were dealing with supernatural beings."

Her questions felt stupid, but she needed to check. This was too important, too close to home to leave to chance. "Do you think they're here in West Edinton?"

"Of course! They're probably all around us — the unseen armies of heaven!" he replied enthusiastically.

"Oh," she murmured, hugging her empty plate to her chest. "But wasn't that mostly in Bible times? Nobody sees angels anymore, right? That would be strange."

"Messengers from God may be rarer now because all we need to know can be found in the Scriptures," speculated

Pastor Bert. "Or maybe we're like Elijah's servant, and we don't have eyes to see what's all around us."

The man reached the end of the serving table and picked up a glass of iced tea. "Anything else, Prissie?"

"One more question," she begged. "What would you do if you saw an angel?"

"That's a puzzler," he said, gazing upward. "If I was face-to-face with an angel — or face to *floor* come to think of it," he interjected with a wide smile. "There must be a *reason* they always introduce themselves with the words, 'Fear not!' "

"Yes they do that," Prissie mumbled, trying not to fidget as she waited for his answer.

"From what I've read, angels don't turn up without a reason," said Pastor Bert. "If I had the incredible privilege of meeting an angel face-to-face, I believe I'd want to know if they had a message for me."

She blinked. "Is that all?"

"All?" her pastor echoed incredulously. "Think for a moment! The messenger may be a dazzling angel, but the message is *God's*! Whether it might be encouragement, direction, correction, or a call to action, I would definitely want to hear a personal word from the Lord!"

"I hadn't thought of it that way," Prissie managed.

"One thing's certain," Pastor Bert concluded. "In the Bible, whenever someone met an angel, their life was never the same again!"

She wondered why he seemed to think this was a *good* thing.

"Well, little lady, if that's all, I think you'd better give it another try."

"Wh-what?" He chuckled and nodded at her empty plate. "Those are mighty slim pickin's!"

"Yes, sir," Prissie murmured, tacking on a belated, "Thank you."

She returned to the end of the line, but only lingered for a moment. Confusion robbed her of her appetite, so she ducked into the kitchen to see if she could lend a hand. If what Pastor Bert said was true, she had nothing to fear from angels. On top of that, she'd already received a rare and precious message. The only problem was it didn't make any sense.

5

THE RUDE AWAKENING

A tall warrior slapped his knees and took a seat beside an angel who wore his age gracefully, like a crown of silver. Lifting one callused hand, he said, "Shimron, I can still count the number of weeks your apprentice has been under my watch-care on these fingers. I cannot remember the last time so much trouble was stirred by a single misstep."

"*Was* it a misstep?" the Observer inquired.

"I have good reason for misgivings," countered the big angel ruefully.

"The stirrings had already begun before Koji arrived," Shimron pointed out. "He would not *be* here if that were not so."

"I know it," he replied grimly. "But he is so very *new*. What compelled you to choose an apprentice so young?"

Shimron smiled benignly. "For the most part, Koji was no different than any of the other potentials in his class. Inquisitive. Eager. Hopeful."

"But?"

"I was asked countless questions that day," he reminisced. "But he was the only one who wanted to know why I was sad."

The warrior's gaze softened. "The boy saw through your brave front."

"Koji sees the world with uncommon clarity," Shimron concurred with a nod.

Prissie was only three when it happened, so she couldn't really remember much, but in her dreams, she was always falling.

For a little girl brimming with determination, the barn was a wonderful place to explore — a warm, sweet-smelling paradise where sunlight streamed through dusty motes. Pigeons cooed in the rafters, and chickens scritched and scratched their way across the floor. Young Prissie had a vague sense of wanting to be Grandma's helper and find the eggs their hens would sometimes hide in the loft, but five-year-old Neil lured her with the promise of kittens. Their mother cat had a new litter, and he wanted to be the first to find it. Her chubby legs barely managed the stretch between rungs on the ladder leading to the loft, but he pushed her up from behind.

The kittens were nowhere to be found, and Neil took off to continue his quest in the machine shed, leaving his baby sister alone amidst the golden bales. Soft clucks from one corner of the loft betrayed the presence of a lone chicken, and Prissie squealed in delight over her discovery. Abandoning her egg, the hen bolted out of the little girl's reach, and Prissie followed, giggling as she chased it in ever-widening circles across the plank floor. When the hen leapt off the edge, awkwardly flapping to a safe landing below, her pursuer stumbled, teetered, and fell.

A shrill scream, a tilting world, and helpless whimpers. She clearly remembered her fear in that moment, for it remained with her.

According to Momma, Prissie was too scared to make sense, so no one believed the next part. But in her dreams, she still felt strong arms and heard a gentle voice. "You frightened me, little one," soothed a strange man who cradled her close to his chest. "I was almost too late."

Her eyes were blurred with tears, so Prissie couldn't recall his face, but she had a lingering impression of long, brown hair ... tanned skin ... and warm hands.

"Don't let your big brother lead you astray," he urged. "And if your mother says not to play in the loft, you must listen."

The little girl's lip trembled, but she nodded before squirming to be let down. He released her, and she ran to the house to find Momma.

Prissie woke with a start, the dream fading from memory, leaving her with an unsettled feeling that was difficult to face alone. For a moment, she thought of going to her mother for comfort, but she quickly dismissed the idea. She wasn't a baby any longer. "Just a dream," she mumbled into her pillow, trying to reassure herself.

As the only daughter in a houseful of sons, Prissie had been granted an enormous privilege; she was the only member of the family with a room of her own. It was a tiny niche at the very end of the hallway, and the ceiling slanted so sharply that one corner of her door was angled. There was just enough space inside for a narrow bed, a bedside table, and a creaky old wardrobe, but there was one feature that transformed her sanctuary into something sublime. Halfway up the wall, a window seat spanned the width of the gable, and if there was one thing Prissie loved, it was the window set above it.

According to Grandpa, all four of the house's peaks had boasted stained glass windows when he was a boy, but damage or renovations had claimed the other three over the years. This one remained, a relic from another era, and it was her treasure. A simple geometric pattern of diamonds in soft shades of green, blue, peach, and gold filtered sunlight or shone in moonlight. Grandma Nell had quilted Prissie's bedspread in the same colors, and the hues were echoed in the braided rug, which had graced the smooth floorboards since Grandpa's mother's day. The overall effect may have been a little old-fashioned, but it suited Prissie.

No one else was allowed in her room, so when she turned onto her back, she was startled to see Koji perched on her window seat, gazing at the stars through the multicolored panes. His hair was tucked behind pointed ears, and the stained glass made patterns of color on his upturned face. She had to admit that at that moment, he looked the part of an angel. "Koji, what are you doing in my room?" she whispered.

The boy turned to meet her gaze. "This is a very pretty window; it reminds me of home."

"You have stained glass windows where you come from?"

"Something very much like them," he replied, reaching up to trace the edging of a blue diamond.

"Are you homesick?" Prissie asked curiously.

He frowned thoughtfully, then said, "I do not think so."

"What are you doing in my room?" she repeated.

"I wanted someone to talk to."

Prissie glanced at her clock, which told her it was shortly after two in the morning. "But it's the middle of the night!"

"I do not sleep," Koji answered with a small shrug.

"Well, I *do*," she grumbled, pulling her sheet up over her face. "Find someone else to talk to."

"You are the only one who can answer my questions, though."

She folded down the blankets and studied him suspiciously, curious in spite of herself. "What kinds of questions?"

Meeting her gaze solemnly, he bluntly asked, "Why are you avoiding Milo?"

Prissie opened and closed her mouth, then said, "I'm *not* avoiding him."

Koji tipped his head to one side. "You used to follow him around."

Blushing hotly, she answered, "That was before I knew he wasn't *real*."

"Milo *is* real."

"But he's not who he said he was! I *thought* he was a normal guy."

"So are you avoiding him because he is an angel?" Koji persisted.

"No, it's because he *lied*," Prissie corrected.

Koji's black eyes sparkled in the moonlight. "Did you *ask* him if he was an angel?"

"Of course not? Who would ask something like that?"

"Then, he did *not* lie," the young angel earnestly declared.

"He has been doing his job faithfully for many years; your accusations are unjust."

"His *job*?"

"He is very good at it," Koji explained. "Milo has many friends, and I envy him."

"You're jealous?" Prissie sat up in bed and frowned at him. "Can angels *be* jealous?"

"Yes," he candidly replied. "He has been able to interact with humans every single day, but I am only allowed to observe. There are so many questions I want to ask!"

Thinking back to Pastor Bert's words, Prissie asked, "Why are you so fascinated by people?"

"It is my nature," Koji replied. "I am an Observer, so I wish to know, to understand, to discover, to explore . . ."

"Right," she interrupted. "But *why*? There has to be a *reason* you're watching us."

"It is my purpose."

"You do it because you have to?"

Koji shook his head. "I want to."

"But what if you *didn't* want to?" Prissie challenged.

"I *do* want to," he replied patiently.

"But only because you *have* to want to?" she persisted. "What if you wanted to do something else, like be a Messenger so you could talk to people."

"An Observer is what I am." A slow smile spread across the boy's face, and he turned to face her fully. "You truly do not understand."

His delight only added to Prissie's frustration. "Of course I don't!"

"I will try to answer your question if you will explain some things to me?" he bargained.

"Only if I don't have to answer your questions in the middle of the night."

"Agreed!"

"Thank goodness," Prissie muttered.

"I will answer your question about why you are interesting," Koji offered.

"Well?" she prompted.

Koji pointed to himself, then at her as he said, "I act according to my nature, but you often act contrary to yours."

Prissie frowned in confusion. "What do you mean, my *nature*?"

"It is human nature to sin," he said bluntly. "Yet you frequently manage not to."

"Oh."

"Do you have any other questions?" Koji asked hopefully.

With a flop, Prissie lay back down and turned her face into her pillow. "No," came her muffled reply. "Why don't you go talk to Harken or Milo, since they probably don't need sleep either?"

"Harken is away, and Milo does not wish to talk."

"Why not?"

"He is too sad."

Prissie turned her head just enough to peek at Koji out of the corner of her eye. "Can angels *be* sad?"

"Yes," Koji agreed, turning his eyes back toward the stars twinkling beyond multicolored panes. "Very sad."

6

THE SECOND OPINION

"It's not the first time a girl's had a crush on you, Goldilocks."

"I know," sighed Milo.

"I take it you're kinda fond of this one?"

"Prissie's *special,*" Koji interjected.

"She *must* be if she can see you, squirt!"

"*Every* individual has value," Milo flatly stated.

"That's a given, but this is different. You're getting the chance to be totally *genuine* with a person!"

The angel gave a short, bitter laugh as he raked his fingers through long blond hair. "Only to discover that she was much happier with the lie."

"We *don't* lie," his friend corrected. "They assume."

"Then why do her eyes accuse me?"

"You did not do anything wrong!" protested Koji.

"Milo's just a softie," teased the other angel, earning a halfhearted glare. "It's okay to care about them, you know."

"I care about all of them."

"You and me, both," agreed his friend, then snapped his fingers. "Here's what you do. Smooth things over, then bring her around."

"You want to meet Prissie?" Koji asked, eyes aglow.

"Absolutely! She's already met a few of us; what's one more?"

"I *could* talk to Harken about it," Milo said slowly.

"Then it's settled!"

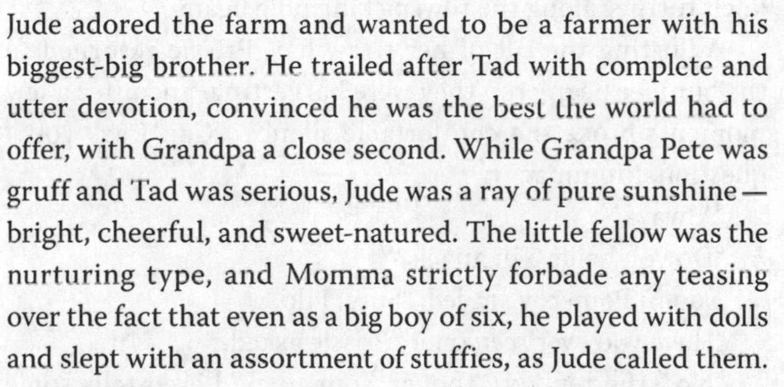

Jude adored the farm and wanted to be a farmer with his biggest-big brother. He trailed after Tad with complete and utter devotion, convinced he was the best the world had to offer, with Grandpa a close second. While Grandpa Pete was gruff and Tad was serious, Jude was a ray of pure sunshine—bright, cheerful, and sweet-natured. The little fellow was the nurturing type, and Momma strictly forbade any teasing over the fact that even as a big boy of six, he played with dolls and slept with an assortment of stuffies, as Jude called them.

One of Jude's greatest loves was the chickens that had free range of their farmyard. He gave them all names and chatted to them as if they were people. No one could coax an egg out from under a crotchety old hen like he could, so Neil called Jude "the chicken whisperer." This year would be the first time the boy showed one of his hens at the county fair. A stack of wire cages stood ready in the barn, waiting to house their entries in the fair's upcoming poultry competition.

Maddie, which was short for Madder, as in "than a wet

hen," was a beautiful Ameraucana with black and white feathers. The name had been Tad's idea, so of course, Jude thought it was wonderful, even if it hardly suited her. Maddie was a good-tempered chicken, tame and smart; she was one of five hens who never strayed far from the boy whenever he was out in the yard. Her eggs were always a soft shade of pale green that rivaled Grandpa's duck eggs for beauty.

Prissie stroked Maddie's comb with the fuzzy end of a "tickle weed" and smiled when the hen closed her eyes and endured the attention. "You're going to win a ribbon for Judicious, aren't you, girl?" she murmured, using Tad's nickname for their youngest brother.

"There's a fair chance," Momma agreed from where she knelt further along the row, picking pole beans.

Adjusting the tilt of her straw hat, Prissie returned to the bumper bean crop they were harvesting, and after a few moments broke the comfortable silence. "Can I ask you a question, Momma?"

"Always."

"Do you believe in angels?"

Naomi Pomeroy smiled. "Sure, I do."

"Have you ever *seen* one?" Prissie asked.

"No," she replied, "though your uncle Loren tells some pretty amazing stories from his travels. You should ask him about it."

"Did Aunt Ida's last letter say when they'll be back?"

"A few things are still up in the air, but possibly for Christmas," Momma replied.

Prissie nodded, but steered the conversation back where it belonged. "What else do you know about angels?"

"Well, let's see," she mused. "Off the top of my head, I

can say for sure that angels were used to announce things. There were a lot of them in the Christmas story, and not just Gabriel. An angel spoke to Zacharias to tell him that Elizabeth would give birth to John the Baptist, and an angel spoke to Mary's husband Joseph in dreams ... twice, I think."

"*Everybody* knows that!" Prissie sighed.

"Only if they've heard it before, sweetheart," her mother gently chided. She gathered her thoughts, then said, "One verse in the gospels implies that every child has an angel—a guardian angel."

There it was again, as if it was common knowledge. Messengers. Guardians. "Are there other kinds of angels?"

Momma picked up her pail and moved to the next bean tower. "Umm ... Isaiah describes some fantastical creatures, and in Revelation the angels sound pretty fierce. Paul talks about 'powers and principalities' in conflict, so I've always thought some angels must be well-armed, battle-ready types."

Prissie's mind was spinning. "The Bible talks about angels that much?"

"Didn't you sign up to read through the Bible in a year?" her mother asked lightly. "We started Isaiah two weeks ago."

"I'm a little behind, I guess," she hedged, quickly changing the subject. "Do angels have wings and halos?"

Mrs. Pomeroy threw a handful of beans into her pail and answered, "That's how artists usually portray them, but I don't know if they're literal or just a convention that was adopted somewhere along the way. There's usually some truth behind a legend." She paused in her work, propping her hands against her lower back for a stretch. "Wings *would* be nice. Can you imagine what it would be like to fly?"

Prissie cast a sidelong look in her mother's direction and noted the familiar, far-away look in the woman's gray eyes. Naomi was a little on the flighty side, and it was obvious that her mind was off in another world. "So angels are real," Prissie stated, bringing Momma back to earth. "Do you think there are people who can see them?"

"There are stories, but it's hard to know if they're true. It's certainly possible, but the instances seem to be rare," she replied, giving her daughter a teasing glance. "Why have *you* been visited by winged messengers?"

Squirming uncomfortably, Prissie gave her full attention to picking beans. "Not *exactly*," she said, comforting herself that it wasn't a lie since Koji, Milo, and Harken lacked feathers. "I was just curious."

Momma was summoned back to the house by Jude, who brought news of Zeke's discovery that he could make taller towers out of building blocks if he used peanut butter between the layers. Prissie stayed behind to finish up in the garden. The beans were done, which only left a long line of green onions, their spiky tops poking out from the midst of thick weeds. With a sigh, she knelt at one end of the row and began the slow task of removing the weeds without uprooting the bulbs.

Maddie clucked softly from the shallow depression she'd created under the broad leaves of a nearby zucchini plant, and when Prissie looked up, Koji was crouched down beside the hen, watching the bird intently.

Sitting back on her heels, Prissie asked, "Can she see you?"

"She knows I am here," he replied. Maddie cocked her

head to one side, as if listening to something, and Koji smiled as he mirrored the action. "And that I bear her no ill will."

"Obviously."

The young angel stood and wriggled his bare toes in the dirt for a moment before dropping to his knees across from Prissie. "May I help?" he inquired, tentatively touching the tips of an onion.

"You'll get your pretty clothing dirty!" Prissie protested.

"Our raiment cannot become stained," Koji explained, and he stood back up to show her how the dirt simply fell away from the shimmering fabric. "Without spot or wrinkle."

"That's from the Bible," Prissie remarked.

"Indeed."

She turned her attention back to weeding, keeping a close eye on Koji to make sure he was doing it right. "So, why are you back today?" she asked.

"I wanted to see you."

"Why?"

"Because you can see me," he replied simply.

Prissie squinted at him from under the brim of her straw hat. "Is being invisible lonely?"

"No ... and yes."

"What's *that* supposed to mean?" she challenged, scooting a little farther down the row. The job was going much faster with two of them working together.

"It is part of what I did not explain very well last night," he replied. "May I try again?"

"If you must."

"Sin taints everything, like this garden." He held up a weed as proof. "And you as well."

Prissie lowered her head to hide her blush. "I do the best I can," she grumbled. "It's not fair to criticize."

"I speak the truth, nothing more." She shrugged defensively, and Koji continued, "When a human has been forgiven, they undergo the most beautiful change I have ever seen." Prissie looked up in surprise, and met the young angel's steady gaze. His dark eyes glowed with warmth, gladness, even joy. "It is truly lovely."

"What is?" she whispered, her heartbeat quickening.

"The presence of God," Koji replied in a low, reverent voice. "Those who have been forgiven are touched by His Spirit. I can tell because I have met Him."

"You've *met* the Holy Spirit?"

"Yes."

"You mean, you talked to him just like you're talking to me?" Prissie pressed, disbelief coloring her tone.

"Yes," Koji confidently repeated. "When I am close to those who belong to God, I am not lonely, for He is with them. I also like being with the others in my Flight," he confided. "When Abner sings, it feels like home."

"Is Abner an angel, too?" she asked.

Koji nodded. "We gather in the garden behind the blue door each day."

Intrigued in spite of herself, Prissie asked, "What do you do?"

"Talk ... listen ... sing."

"I've heard Milo before, and Harken, too. Do you sing as well?"

In answer, Koji straightened, threw back his head and, without a trace of embarrassment, sang a simple song of praise to the Creator. As he thanked God for His presence with His people and for the onions they were tending, his sweet treble voice made Prissie's skin prickle into goose bumps.

After the last note faded, Maddie's approving cluck broke the silence that stretched between them. "Did you make that up?" Prissie asked in awe.

"Yes."

"I wish I could do that," she sighed.

"Do you want to sing together?" Koji invited.

Prissie shook her head self-consciously and returned to weeding. "I want to sound like you."

When she moved farther down the row, her companion didn't move with her, and she glanced up to find him studying her closely. The expression on his face was one Prissie was beginning to equate with being *observed*. "What? Did I say something strange?"

"No." He scooted along the line of onions so he was across from her again and set back to work. "Do you covet my voice?"

"I wouldn't put it like that," she muttered unhappily. "You should just take it as a compliment." Again, Prissie could feel his gaze, but she refused to meet it.

"I have thanked Abner for his songs," the boy shared. "At that time, he asked me which was more important: the singer or the song?"

Prissie thought about it. A poor performance could ruin an otherwise decent song, but the best singer in the world would never be heard if they didn't perform. "I guess you need both?" she ventured.

Koji tipped his head to one side and explained, "The singer gives voice to the song in his heart, but its beginning and end belong to God. *He* is most important."

"So it was a trick question?"

"Among angels, it would be considered a joke."

7

THE BAKER'S DAUGHTER

"Can't we *do* something about that Messenger?" grumbled Murque. "He's *up* to something, going from house to house."

"He's a mailman, idiot," snapped Dinge. From their hiding place within the shadow of a lilac hedge, the two demons watched Milo's car roll to a stop. "If we *could* get to him, he would be gone."

"We pick off Messengers all the time."

"Yeah, well this one has a Guardian," the crouching demon whispered hoarsely. "There! See?"

Murque swore under his breath, then muttered, "I thought only *people* had Guardians. He's just a poser."

"Their Flight's been more cautious since midsummer."

An unholy gleam lit his cohort's eyes. "Lost track of one of their own, didn't they?"

"That they did," Dinge replied with a rusty laugh.

Prissie didn't *do* rough and tumble. She wore dresses, had excellent posture, and strove to attain what she considered the best of feminine beauty. Jayce and Naomi couldn't really explain where their daughter got all her notions, but they saw no harm in letting her have her way.

"Where are you off to in such a hurry?" Jayce called as his daughter passed by.

"Grandma's," Prissie replied. "I need to practice."

"Sure, sure," her father replied. "It's a good thing there are two kitchens on this farm, or Zeke and I would be out of luck." Her younger brother grinned from his perch on a step stool, proudly wearing one of his father's aprons. Wednesdays were always their dad's half days, so he came home early to hang out with them around the house, often making a mess of their kitchen in the process.

She regularly experimented with new recipes herself, usually with less-than-stellar results, but she was determined to conquer the culinary arts. The only problem was ... she wasn't very good at it. To be perfectly honest, she was terrible at it.

Jayce had offered to teach his daughter everything he knew, but she was privately frustrated with him for being so comfortable in an area where she struggled. It was much easier to go to Grandma Nell for lessons, so Prissie conveniently ignored the fact that her father and brother were bonding by making candied rose petals.

A half hour later, she was liberally sprinkled with flour

and grimly gripping the handles of a rolling pin. "Gently, sweetie," urged Grandma Nell. "You need a delicate touch when it comes to pastry."

"I know," she tersely replied.

"You should accept the advice of those who are wiser than you," remarked Koji, who'd stationed himself on top of her grandparents' refrigerator. Prissie shot him a dark look, which he met with an uncertain smile.

"Lighter, *lighter*, dear," urged Grandma Nell, demonstrating again with a deft turn of her round of dough. With sure hands, she rolled out the pastry, transferred it into a waiting pie tin and then crimped the edges.

Prissie banged at her lump of dough and sighed in dissatisfaction when the crust tore. With a scowl, she folded it over to try again.

Grandma peered over her shoulder. "You should have just patched it."

"But it wasn't *right*!" argued Prissie.

"It's okay to have a little imperfection," the older woman tutted.

"I can't have any mistakes if I'm going to win a ribbon at the fair!" she protested.

"People expect a homemade pie to have a few irregularities. Trying to hide them only makes matters worse because overworking the crust toughens it," Grandma Nell explained. "Don't worry so much about how it looks; taste is the important thing."

"Yours always look perfect," Prissie pointed out dejectedly.

"I've had a few more years of experience," her grandmother chuckled. "Speaking of taste, have you decided what kind of pie you're making for the competition?"

"Will the apples from Great-grandma's trees be ready in time?"

"Oh, I dunno. It'll be close, but you might find enough ripe apples to work with."

"I will ask Abner to help if you want," offered Koji from overhead.

Prissie knew she'd heard that name before. "Who?"

"What, dear?" asked her grandmother, who was mixing up a crumb topping.

She made a shushing motion at the boy and replied, "Grandpa always brags about those apples and the pies his mother made from them."

Nell's blue eyes sparkled. "That's the truth, and for good reason. Pete's mother loved those trees! Their apples were the secret behind her pink applesauce, which was the prettiest color, and without a drop of food coloring to help things along."

"I maybe remember it ... a little."

"You were only five when she passed on, but you loved the color pink even then," Nell smiled. "I'll see if I can hunt up her recipe. She was real particular about the blend of apples, and that may translate into a winning pie."

"Shouldn't I make up my own recipe?" Prissie asked.

Grandma Nell shook a floury finger in her direction. "Those who are smart learn from those who are wise. And it *will* be your own recipe if you're adapting Mother Pomeroy's pink applesauce into a pie."

Prissie's eyes took on the shine of anticipation. "I want to! Can I?"

"I don't see why not," her grandmother said with an indulgent smile. "But first things first, roll out your crust."

"Yes, ma'am!" Prissie exclaimed, using her rolling pin to give the dough a zealous thump that made Nell—and Koji—wince.

"My pie looks pitiful," Prissie mourned as she slid it into the oven next to her grandmother's. "Neil is going to make fun of it; I just know it."

"I would like to taste your pie," Koji declared.

"I could probably sneak you a piece," Prissie offered. "Momma wouldn't mind."

"Perhaps ... perhaps if I ..." the boy began, suddenly looking nervous. "Prissie, if Harken and Shimron obtain permission for a change in my status, would you accept it?"

Prissie couldn't understand why Koji would need *her* approval for such a thing, but there was no mistaking the hopefulness shining in his dark eyes. Planting her hands on her hips, she asked, "Is it something *you* want?"

"Very much," he replied seriously.

"Then, why don't you?"

Koji's smile was truly beautiful.

Just then, someone rapped smartly on the screen door. No one in the family ever knocked, and most folks who dropped by simply gave a holler, announcing themselves. "Who could that be?" she murmured.

As if in answer, a cheerful voice hailed, "Special delivery!"

Koji hopped lightly from the top of the fridge and darted toward the front porch, calling, "Milo, she agreed!"

Prissie followed much more slowly, wringing a dish-towel between her hands. The mailman waited just beyond the welcome mat in his uniform—a long-sleeved shirt with the postal service's logo stitched onto the arm. "Hello, Miss Priscilla," he greeted, nodding pleasantly at Koji. "I had a feeling you would be here. There's a package for your grandmother."

He lifted a parcel about the size of a shoebox, and Koji looked expectantly at Prissie. "Can Milo come in?"

"I guess," she allowed. "Grandma's in the garden."

He nodded. "I'll wait."

Koji ignored the uncomfortable silence that snuck into the room and helped things along by interrupting it. "Where is the box from?"

"Spain," Milo replied.

"Do you know someone in Spain?" the young angel inquired of Prissie.

"My Aunt Ida," she replied curtly. "It's where she and Uncle Lo were going next after Portugal."

The conversation stalled again, but thankfully, Grandma Nell bustled up the path from the garden, a basket under one arm, and a bunch of hydrangeas in her other hand. Milo quickly moved to open the door for her. "Good afternoon, ma'am!"

"Oh, Milo! What a nice surprise!" she exclaimed. "Come on through, and I'll find you a little something. Prissie, fetch me a vase for these. You know where they are."

She gladly escaped and took her time choosing from the empty vases lining the shelf over her grandmother's laundry tub. "Unbelievable," she grumbled, unhappily patting her flour-streaked apron.

"What do you not believe?" inquired Koji curiously.

Prissie whirled, startled that the young angel had followed her. "Milo's timing," she groused.

"His delivery was punctual."

"That's not what I meant," she snapped. "I wasn't expecting to see him today."

Koji's face took on a look of concentration. "I thought you said you were not avoiding him."

"I'm *not*!" Prissie protested.

"Are you unhappy to see him?"

"N-no, but I'm a mess, and I don't know what to *say* to him!"

He considered this for a moment before asking, "What would you speak to Milo about if nothing had changed?"

She shrugged moodily. "Things."

Koji accepted her answer without hesitation. "He would still like to hear about things. I know it."

When Prissie returned to the kitchen with a cobalt blue vase, Milo was already seated at the table, a tall glass of iced tea and a plate of lemon bars set before him. Grandma turned from the sink where she was rinsing tomatoes and said, "Lovely, sweetie. Now, go sit with Milo, and we'll have a look into Ida's box together."

Trying to hide her nervousness, Prissie slid into the chair next to Milo's. A glance in Koji's direction showed that the younger angel had returned to his perch on the refrigerator, which offered a decent view of the proceedings while keeping him out from underfoot.

Grandma Nell bustled over and thumped a red enamel colander and a bowl of freshly picked beans between the two. Without batting an eye, Milo reached for a handful and began snapping the ends off. At Prissie's startled expression, he smiled. "I've been doing this for quite some time. Your grandmother trained me when I first started my route."

She couldn't decide whether she should be annoyed that her grandmother had been quietly hogging so much of Milo's time over the years ... or amused at how much the mailman looked like one of her big brothers. They always looked so awkward when Grandma bossed them into helping snap beans or shell peas. "Does she ask you to hunt duck eggs, too?" she asked before she remembered to hold back.

Milo's eyes took on a sparkle, and he shook his head. "I haven't been asked to do that yet, but two winters back, I received lessons in knitting."

"How did that go?" Prissie asked in amazement.

"Not very well," he admitted.

"Oh, I dunno," Grandma remarked as she placed the vase of flowers on the counter. "You and Pete had some good visits while you were learning to cast stitches."

"No argument there," Milo replied. "Though Harken wasn't terribly impressed with that lumpy scarf I produced. He thought it looked more like a fishing net!"

Prissie giggled and reached for a handful of beans. "That wasn't very nice!"

"Maybe not, but sadly, he was right."

Grandma Nell brought a pair of scissors with her to the table and carefully sliced through the packing tape. She peeled back the heavy brown paper, taking care to save the postmark, then opened the box. Setting aside the letter that had been placed on top of the other items, she murmured, "What have you been up to, my girl?"

Ida's boxes arrived at regular intervals from cities all over the world, depending on where she and her husband might be visiting. Uncle Loren worked for a missions organization and traveled from church to church, offering encouragement to the many men and women who served the Lord in faraway places. "Did she send the usual?" Prissie asked.

"Of course," chuckled Grandma Nell, fishing out a small sheaf of papers and a clear plastic freezer bag from under something folded into tissue paper.

While Pete and Nell Pomeroy loved hearing from their daughter, they didn't like for her to fritter her money on useless things. Early on, Grandpa had jokingly announced that as a farmer, he was mostly interested in dirt. The first time Ida sent him a small bottle of sand from the shore of Honduras, a tradition was begun. Now Ida always included a soil sample for her father, one for every place she visited.

Grandma's standing request was for church bulletins. Not all churches used printed announcements, but Ida always found something — a missionary's photo postcard, conference fliers, or cuttings from local papers. Over the years, Grandma Nell's collection had grown to include news from many foreign lands in many foreign languages.

Of course, there were always other things as well — small gifts that reminded Prissie of her aunt Ida's enthusiasm for life, no matter where it took her.

"Oh, look at *this*!" Grandma exclaimed, shaking out a black shawl with a deep fringe. "Spanish lace! Gracious! Ida knows better than to send something this fancy to me!"

In spite of her grumbling, her grandmother looked pleased over the present and swung it around her shoulders with a swirl of the silky tassels.

"It's pretty, Grandma! You should wear it to church!"

Milo was spared from making any fashion comments by taking a large bite of lemon bar and chasing it down with a swallow of his tea. However, he reached over and tapped the corner of the bulletin. "May I see?"

"Help yourself," Grandma Nell replied as she opened her daughter's letter and unfolded a sheet covered in Ida's distinctively loopy penmanship. Some smaller cards fell out, and she looked even more excited than she had been about the shawl. "There are recipes this time! Now where are my glasses?"

As her grandmother bustled into the bedroom for her reading glasses, Prissie stole a look at Milo. The mailman had gone back to snapping beans, but his eyes followed the text of the announcements in the church bulletin Ida had sent. "Can you read Spanish?" she asked in surprise.

"Yep," he replied calmly, then cautiously added, "Language is no barrier for someone like me."

Prissie knotted her fingers together. The lull was getting awkward again, and she didn't like it. Taking a deep breath, she asked, "Does it say anything interesting?"

Milo brightened somewhat and pulled the folded paper closer. "This is talking about some services they've been having, and how they've pulled in some new attendees — folks who've never been to church before."

"That's good," Prissie murmured.

"It is glorious!" interjected Koji from his perch.

Milo returned the boy's triumphant look with a bright smile. "Sure is!"

Grandma Nell returned, her glasses balanced on the end of her nose as she scanned Ida's letter. "Ida's excited about how well their meetings have been going. Isn't that just wonderful?"

"Glorious," Prissie mumbled with a sidelong glance at Koji, who swung one leg over the edge of the fridge.

"Sure is!" Milo agreed with sparkling eyes, completing the loop.

Grandma Nell read further and shared, "They're going to be in Greece next. Loren is excited about the chance to visit all of the historical sites."

"I didn't know Uncle Lo liked ruins," Prissie said vaguely.

Milo casually commented, "I'm sure you remember that Paul's missionary journeys took him through Greece. That's probably what he has in mind."

"Oh ... well, *obviously,*" Prissie replied with weak bravado.

"Sure enough," Grandma Nell agreed. "Ida says he can't wait to visit Ephesus."

Draining the last of his tea with a rattle of ice cubes, Milo stood. "Thank you so much for your hospitality, ma'am, but I should be on my way." Carrying his dishes to the sink, he paused in the act of turning and remarked, "Something smells good!"

"That would be Prissie's pie," Nell slyly remarked.

"No kidding?" the mailman inquired, looking impressed.

"Grandma's, too," Prissie protested, blushing under the attention.

"Yes, but one is Prissie's," Grandma declared in her no-nonsense way. "Sweetie, go on and walk Milo to his car. You've plenty of time before your baking's ready to come out of the oven."

"Yes, Grandma." Prissie pushed her chair back and sent Koji a pleading look. Much to her relief, the boy hopped down, quickly joining her and Milo as they filed out the door and down the walk.

Once they were out of earshot of her grandparent's house, Milo spoke up. "Miss Priscilla, I want to apologize."

She stared resolutely at her feet. "What would you be apologizing *for*?"

Milo ran his fingers over the top of his curling hair and replied, "For contributing to your unbelief at a time when faith is needed most."

She wrinkled her nose. "I'm not even sure what that *means*. Apologies should make *sense*."

"Can you suggest a better one?" he gently prodded.

Prissie's steps lagged at the thought, but no matter which way she turned their situation around, she couldn't think of anything with which to accuse Milo.

Koji broke in. "Are you growing accustomed to the idea of angels, Prissie?"

"What choice do I have?" she sighed. "Every time I turn around, there you are."

Unfazed by the edge to her tone, Koji persisted. "You do not fear us."

"Obviously," she huffed.

"There are more of us," Milo quietly announced. "Others you could meet, if you're interested." They reached his car, and he opened the door. "I would be honored to introduce you."

"I'll think about it."

Milo nodded patiently and slid into the vehicle, then leaned out the open window. "I'm glad there was a package today," he said earnestly.

"It was providential?" she asked breezily.

"Positively," he agreed. "I'll be waiting for your answer."

8

THE HELPFUL NUDGE

"Are they in danger?" Milo asked worriedly.

"Undoubtedly," Harken answered. "There are many who would thwart God's purposes."

"At least they're not alone."

The senior Messenger shook his head. "A mixed blessing, since it draws the interest of our enemies."

Milo confessed, "It's kind of frustrating. Miss Priscilla has been given the *barest* glimpse of heavenly things. I want to show her *more*, but in many ways, she's still blind."

"Things have a way of unfolding," Harken reminded. "I feel this is just the beginning."

The eastern horizon was just beginning to blush when a knock on the front door of Loafing Around caught Jayce

Pomeroy's attention. He waved at the figure darkening his doorstep, but finished sliding trays of warm muffins into the bakery case before crossing to undo the lock. "Good morning!" he greeted. "It's a little earlier than I usually open, but I've been known to make exceptions for paperboys."

"No, sir, but thank you, sir," the teen replied, nervously adjusting the strap on his newspaper bag. He cleared his throat, then launched into what had to be a very brief but carefully prepared speech. "Excuse me, sir. My name's Ransom Pavlos, and I was wondering if you're looking for part-time help?"

"Sweeping up and taking out the trash don't take much time in a shop this size, and I already have someone to run the register," Jayce answered. Noting the flicker of disappointment on Ransom's face, he made a quick decision and added, "There are always dishes to do, I suppose."

"I don't mind doing that kind of work," the young man quickly assured. "But I want to learn the trade. I want to bake."

"You're interested in breads?" Jayce asked curiously.

"And pastries, yeah," Ransom replied, holding the older man's gaze.

"Why don't you come in," Mr. Pomeroy invited, holding the door wide. He waved the teen to one of the tables and took a seat across from him. "*Patisserie*—it's not the aspiration of every young man."

"Was it yours?"

"It was," Jayce replied evenly.

"I want to decorate cakes, too," Ransom confessed, color rising in his cheeks.

"No kidding!" the bakery owner replied, nodding approvingly. "Yeah, that'd be cool."

Jayce grinned broadly. "I think we can work something out. When can you start?"

Ransom straightened. "Seriously?"

"Sure," Mr. Pomeroy replied, chuckling at the young man's obvious relief.

"Early mornings or after school," the teen replied. "If you can match what I get for my morning paper route, my dad won't put up as much of a stink when I give it up. He's not exactly pleased about my plans."

Jayce nodded and confided, "Mine wasn't either. He was *very* disappointed that I didn't want to drive a tractor."

"Mine's set on some kinda office job. I dunno exactly," Ransom shrugged.

"Do you want to come back now and explore the kitchen?" Mr. Pomeroy offered.

For a moment, the teen looked tempted, but he shook his head. "I gotta finish my route."

"Fair enough," Jayce replied. "Come back whenever you can, and we'll work out the details."

"Tomorrow?"

"Not unless you're willing to meet me at First Baptist," Mr. Pomeroy casually invited. "You're welcome to."

"Uhh ... not my thing," Ransom mumbled. "Is Monday good?"

"Sure. The bakery's closed, but I'm here all afternoon doing prep. You can lend a hand, and we'll take it from there."

"Yeah," the teen agreed, smiling crookedly. "Thanks, sir."

Prissie twirled, admiring the way her skirt flared out, before taking a seat on one of the benches inside the gazebo in front of town hall. She'd bought the snowy white sundress with its pattern of red poppies to wear to her best friend Margery's birthday party next week, but couldn't resist giving it a test run on the off-chance that she would run into Milo. Of course, she didn't really *want* to see him, but it might be nice to be seen.

Being angry with someone she cared about made Prissie unhappy, so she'd been relieved when the mailman had acted more like himself when delivering Aunt Ida's package to Grandma's. Maybe it *was* possible to pretend nothing had happened, and then everything could go back to normal.

She'd seen neither hide nor hair of Koji all day, which seemed strange after all his tagging along. It was easy to convince herself that she didn't miss having him around, but harder to explain why her world suddenly felt off-kilter.

Even Margery and April hadn't responded to her offer to meet up while she was in town. The only messages in her inbox for the last few days had been an update notification from Uncle Loren's missionary blog and a forwarded email full of silly cat pictures from Grammie Esme.

Giving one of her braids a firm pat, she opened the book she'd just checked out from their library and flipped through the pages. The travel guide detailed the natural splendor and cultural highlights of Greece with big, glossy photographs and easy-to-digest blurbs. "This is where Aunt Ida will be going next," she murmured to nobody in particular. Momma was still in the little one-room library, helping Zeke and Jude make their picks.

At first, when she heard steps, she assumed Beau had decided to join her, but the footfalls came too fast to belong to her brother, who walked very slowly while poring over a new book. When the newcomer stepped lightly into the gazebo, she looked up ... and blinked.

A young man with glossy auburn hair that fell smoothly to his shoulders strolled to the opposite side of the wooden structure to peer up and down Main Street, giving her the chance to look him over. He was handsomely dressed in a neat summer suit with a white linen jacket. Prissie darted a glance toward the library doors, hoping the rest of her family wouldn't take long. They didn't get many strangers in West Edinton, and something about this one made her uneasy.

When she peeped back at him, he was leaning against the far railing, his hands in his pockets as he watched her. "How do you do?" he politely inquired.

"Very well, thank you," she automatically replied, giving him a cautious smile. "Are you visiting in town?"

"Oh, I'm from around here," he replied, gesturing vaguely to the east.

"Really?" she replied doubtfully.

He smirked. "Do you know *all* the locals?"

The challenge in his tone irked her. "No, but you don't really fit in."

"You don't think so?" he inquired. With a smile, he touched the red handkerchief tucked into his breast pocket, then waved at her. "I think I fit in perfectly ... with *you*."

It was true. Dressed as he was in red and white, he couldn't have coordinated better if he'd tried. "I guess we *do* match," she said with a weak laugh.

"They say imitation is a form of flattery," he suavely replied. "So, tell me, have you spoken to Mr. Leggett recently, or are you still giving him the cold shoulder?"

"You know Milo?" she asked, sitting up a little straighter.

"Doesn't everyone?" the stranger laughed.

"I suppose so," Prissie cautiously admitted. "Since he's the mailman."

"Oh, Mr. Leggett is *more* than an acquaintance," the young man announced. "I've known him for years ... centuries even." Prissie's eyes widened, and he held up a finger in a shushing motion. "That's right, Miss Pomeroy; I'm an angel, too. My name is Adin."

Prissie slowly closed her library book and hugged it against her chest. "Do you have a message for me?" she asked wonderingly.

"I'm not a Messenger, though I know the routine," he replied with a benign smile. Cutting a small bow, he announced, "You've been *chosen,* highly favored one."

"I'm not sure what you mean," she said uncomfortably.

"Oh, I think you do," Adin countered. "What are you afraid of, Miss Pomeroy? Do you think the servants of God would harm you in any way?"

She straightened. "Don't be ridiculous! They would *never* ..."

"I understand you have some qualms about dealing with us," he calmly interjected. "I don't blame you, not *one bit,* but I happen to think that you're overlooking a golden opportunity! Don't you want to have an adventure?"

"No, I don't," she replied crisply. "I like my life just fine."

Adin's brows arched in surprise. "Most people wish for more, but you show wisdom beyond your years. Such contentment is admirable!"

A pleased smile flickered across Prissie's face, and she relaxed slightly. "Really?"

"Still, I think you should give us a chance," he mused aloud. "You must be needed for something important if the unseen realms have been revealed to a young lady such as yourself."

She nodded thoughtfully. "It makes sense that there would be a *reason*."

"Few are called upon to take a prominent place in the grand scheme of things," Adin declared. "God must have something *amazing* in store for you! He probably *needs* you."

"Why *me*?"

"And isn't that the same thing they *all* asked? Ruth, Esther, Mary—I could go on." Adin smiled winsomely and stepped closer.

"I really don't think I'm anything like them," Prissie murmured, a blush spreading across her cheeks.

"So modest," Adin sighed. "It's no wonder you were chosen."

"What should I do?" she asked.

His expression grew solemn, and he took another step. "Trust your heart. You're a good girl with a good head on your shoulders; do what seems right."

Just then, a high, clear voice called out, "Prissie! Prissie! Look at my stories!" She spotted Jude trundling along the path, a precarious pile of books in his arms. When she turned back to apologize to Adin, the angel was gone. Her youngest brother thumped up the steps and exclaimed, "I found all kinds of ones about *chickens*!"

Prissie inspected his stack and assured him that she was properly impressed by his haul, but the back of her mind was busy mulling over Adin's advice ... and his appearance. Milo was good-looking, but in a dusty, down-home way. No one would *ever* mistake the mailman for an angel, but Adin was more what she expected an angel to be — confident, well-spoken, and a little bit mysterious. Both Koji and Milo had mentioned *other* members of their group that she could meet. Maybe if there were more like Adin, it wouldn't be so bad.

While they were in town, the family dropped by the bakery before heading back to the farm. The boys cheerfully accepted the cookies Auntie Lou doled out, but Prissie begged for a private word with her father. Jayce offered her a table-for-two or a turn around the block, and Prissie opted for the walk. In a big family, one-on-one time with parents was usually brief, so once they were back outdoors, she plunged right in. "You know Mr. Mercer really well, right? You trust him?"

"Sure, sure," Jayce replied easily, hooking his thumbs into the apron ties at his waist and gazing up at the sky. "The Curiosity Shop's been there since I was your age, and I used to go in there and read cookbooks. We'd talk … more like I'd talk, and he'd listen. He helped me find the courage to do what I'd always wanted to do. Harken's a good man."

"So when you decided to become a baker, it was because of him?"

"Not entirely, no," her father replied. "I prayed about it, of course, and I asked my mother's advice. Circumstances dictated as well, because the bakery's previous owner was nearing retirement and agreed to sell the place to me once I finished my schooling."

Prissie kicked at a rock. "Everything just came together?"

"Looking back, it seems that way, but at the time, it felt like I was taking a huge risk."

"If you have to make a decision, how do you know you're making the right one?" she asked.

Jayce chuckled. "It's not an exact science. Life is full of opportunities and crossroads that give us a chance to apply our gifts and abilities in new ways. Sometimes there's no right or wrong answer." Prissie looked at her father as if he was crazy, and he laughed aloud. "Choices are rarely that simple."

"That doesn't help much," she grumbled.

"You have a decision to make?" he inquired.

"Yes, although it doesn't seem like I have much of a choice."

"Have you talked to your mother about it?"

"Sort of," she admitted.

"That's good," he said. "Do you want to go into specifics?"

Prissie shook her head. "Sorry, it's too weird to explain."

"Fair enough," Mr. Pomeroy replied. "Well, then as long as you've gotten wise counsel, all I can say is to watch the circumstances. They have a way of nudging us in the right direction if we're paying attention."

"Okay, Daddy," she said in a small voice.

Back inside Loafing Around, Prissie discovered that her brothers had been commandeered by Auntie Lou to peel carrots, and her mother was sharing a cup of coffee with Uncle Lou. Once Jayce excused himself to wash up and get back to work, she hesitated on the edge of her choice, then made it.

"Momma, do I have time to run over to The Curiosity Shop?" Prissie begged.

Naomi Pomeroy glanced at her watch. "Is half an hour enough?" she asked.

"More than enough."

A soft chime accompanied her entrance into Harken's bookstore. The old man looked up and smiled. "Hello, Prissie." Holding up a finger, he raised his voice and called, "We have company, Milo!"

For a few seconds, she caught distant notes of music — achingly sweet and strangely uplifting — and then there was a soft click, like a door closing. Milo appeared in the next moment, and his eyes took on a shine. "Hey, there, Miss Priscilla," he said warmly. "Welcome back ... ?"

His greeting held a question that was echoed in Harken's expectant expression. Neither pressed; they simply waited. Looking from one to the other, Prissie drew a deep, shaky breath, then blurted, "Okay."

Harken and Milo exchanged a glance, and the bookstore owner inquired, "Okay?"

"Yes. Okay. I'm willing to listen ... or whatever," Prissie said in a rush. "I don't understand what's going on, but if you guys need me, I don't feel right about refusing."

"Well, now, that's fine," Harken pronounced with a wide smile. "I don't know what's in store any more than you do, but your decision brings me great joy."

"Miss Priscilla, I, too ..." Milo managed before his voice cracked. With his hand over his heart, he closed his eyes and smiled. The simple rapture of his expression made it difficult for Prissie to breathe, and tears prickled behind her eyelids. Meeting her gaze once more, he earnestly said, "I have been waiting."

As Prissie fought to control her emotions, Harken stepped forward and asked, "What do you want to do, child?"

She sniffed and swallowed, then glanced Milo's way. "You offered to introduce me to another angel. Let's do that."

"That's easily arranged. I'd be pleased to do so."

9

THE EXCHANGE STUDENT

Murque wrapped a hank of fair hair around his gnarled fist and yanked, forcing his kneeling captive's head backward at a painful angle. "Let's play a little game," he said in ominously sweet tones. "We ask questions, and if you give us the right answers, you go free!"

A shudder ran through the pale-faced angel.

"Likes the sound of that," Murque mocked, his gaze sliding towards his partner. "Ask him again."

Dinge bared rotting teeth in the parody of a smile. "We know it's close."

Twisting cruelly so their prisoner hissed involuntarily, Murque licked his lips. "Close enough to taste."

With a disgusted look at his partner for the interruption,

Dinge continued, “The way in is hidden, but you’ve been there. Where is it?”

The slender prisoner offered no response other than to close his eyes and endure the rough treatment.

Snarling in frustration, his captor flung him against the cave wall, and for a moment, green eyes flew wide, then rolled back as their helpless victim crumpled onto the stony ground. “Whoops,” Murque grunted, prodding the unconscious figure with his foot. “I wanted him awake for the next part. We found him such a nice, new home.”

“Just do it,” Dinge ordered.

Curling his lip disdainfully, Murque grabbed a fistful of raiment and dragged the limp angel to the edge of a gaping hole in the floor, then cast him into even deeper darkness.

Prissie felt drained, and her feet dragged all the way up the front walk and across the porch. Kicking off her sandals, she lined them up neatly under the bench, then deposited her library books on the shelf just inside the door before heading toward the kitchen. She knew she should probably change first, but right now, it was more important to nab a couple of gingersnaps from the cookie jar before her younger brothers devoured them.

Two steps past the kitchen threshold, she jerked to a stop and gaped at the boy sitting at the big table, shoveling pie into his mouth like there was no tomorrow.

“Slow down, young man,” Prissie’s grandmother chided.

“S’good,” he mumbled around his bite.

Grandma Nell placed a glass of milk next to his plate and moved back to the stove where dinner preparations were underway. "Oh, my! You're back, Prissie," she greeted, nodding to their guest. "I have some exciting news! This is Koji."

She could see that. The young angel was dressed in jeans and a T-shirt, and he wore a pair of high-top sneakers with the laces tucked in. His glossy black hair was tied back in a low ponytail, revealing ears that looked perfectly normal. Koji was bursting with excitement, and the smile he sent her was overflowing with happiness. "It is nice to meet you," he declared before taking another bite of pie.

Prissie shook her head in confusion, but Grandma Nell was still talking. "I had a call from someone on the school board, and there was a last minute mix-up. They were arranging housing for a group of exchange students and something fell through, so they needed a spot to place young Koji here. Since there's that extra bunk in with the little boys, I checked with your mother, and you know her — always room for one more!"

"I see...."

Grandma nodded happily. "He'll be in your grade at school, so you can help him find his way around, meet people, fit in."

"Oh..."

At the first opportunity, Prissie beckoned to Koji, and he followed her out back, where she sat down heavily on the porch swing. "I don't understand," she stated flatly.

The boy sat next to her and explained, "Even though I am very new, it has been decided that I should integrate. This will be so much better than watching from the outside!"

"So you're going to be living here with me?"

"Yes."

She hardly knew what to think of the intrusion, but amazement didn't even begin to cover it. "Don't you think you should have asked me first?" Prissie demanded, a touch of accusation sharpening her tone.

"I did," he replied with a smile.

Prissie thought back and groaned softly. "*This* is the change in status you were talking about?"

"Yes!" Koji confirmed, practically beaming. "It is all thanks to you!"

She stood abruptly enough to give the swing a hefty shove, but Koji rode out the crooked rocking with poise. His dark eyes followed her retreat for several moments before he allowed his feet to do the same. As Prissie walked briskly down the path toward the apple barn, where harvesttime visitors could buy fruit, he trailed after.

Just beyond the a line of parking spots, a pair of crabapple trees with deep red leaves flanked a green gate. Prissie lifted the latch and started along the path beyond, which led to one of the loveliest places on their farm.

Originally, this spot was just a duck pond, but its beautification had been a father-daughter collaboration back when Ida was a girl. According to Jayce, his little sister had started it all by asking her daddy to build her a castle in the middle of their pond so that it could be the moat. Somehow, Grandpa Pete had convinced her to downscale her grand scheme to something more doable.

Together, they'd planned and planted — weeping willows, flowering shrubs, water lilies. Each year, they added something special, and its crowning glory was a footbridge that stretched over the pond at its narrowest point. The gracefully arching half-moon bridge was a popular spot for taking pictures, both for their family and for orchard visitors. A few local couples had even had their wedding photos taken there.

Aunt Ida had dubbed it their folly—Pomeroy's Folly—after the architectural extravagances that English aristocrats added to their country estates in centuries past. The name didn't mean it was foolish for Grandpa to have built such a thing; it simply meant that the bridge served no purpose but to be pretty.

Prissie didn't stop walking until she reached the bridge's highest point. Resting her elbows on the railing, she stared down at the hopeful ducks who paddled closer, looking for handouts. She showed them her empty hands, then stole a glance at her faithful shadow. Koji remained on the pond's grassy bank, looking commonplace in his new clothes. She'd been slowly adjusting to the idea that he was an otherworldly being, but now that everyone in her family could see him too, she wasn't sure how to act.

"Grandpa likes ducks," she said, needing something to say.

Koji accepted this as an invitation to join her on the bridge and climbed toward her with shuffling steps. His movements were oddly clumsy, and Prissie realized that this was probably the first time he'd ever worn shoes. Although he was dressed like an ordinary boy, he *wasn't* one.

"You're *actually* moving in here?" she asked again.

"Yes," Koji patiently replied. "For a whole year, or at least through the upcoming school year, since I am an exchange student."

"But you're *not* a student!" Prissie protested. "You're not even human."

The angel's brows knit together. "I *did* go to school before I was assigned here; even angels have to learn. I am simply transferring into your school. Shimron said I am the first Observer granted this privilege."

"So for the next year, you're giving up shiny clothes, pointy ears, invisibility, halos, flying, and whatever *else* angels do so you can take geometry and gym class?"

Koji tipped his head to one side. "I never *could* fly."

"That's hardly the point!" she snapped. Almost immediately, she regretted her words, for the boy wilted. With a longsuffering sigh, she said, "I'm trying to understand. You *really* plan to become a part of my family and go to school like a normal kid?"

"Yes," he replied cautiously, dark eyes pleading.

Was it possible for him to keep his secret? His ears had first tipped her off, but now she thought that Koji's eyes would give him away. They were extraordinary. "And you're excited about this?"

"Very."

Prissie stared out over the water. "Can you see through walls or anything?"

"No."

"Super hearing with those ears of yours?"

He frowned slightly. "No."

"So I can still have my privacy?"

"Indeed."

"And you won't come into my room without permission?"

"Agreed." Koji smiled. "Now, we can talk without anyone thinking it is strange. They will see both of us, and they will know we are friends."

Prissie relented. "Yes, I suppose they will. But what happened to your ears?"

"They are hidden. Do they look right?" Koji asked gravely, turning so she could inspect his altered features. "I thought Abner did a good job."

"They look normal to me." Reaching out, she touched the spot where the elfin point had been; it felt just as curved as it looked.

"Milo helped me with my clothing," he added.

"You look fine," she assured him.

"I cannot wait to learn more about being human!" Koji enthused. "There are *so* many questions I want to ask!"

"Be careful with that," Prissie cautioned.

"Why?"

"If you ask weird questions, people will think you're strange."

Koji considered this carefully, then nodded. "I want to fit in like Harken and the others, so will you let me know if I do something odd? I have watched carefully, but there are many things I find difficult to understand."

"I can do that," Prissie agreed. "Are you nervous?"

"I *am* nervous, but mostly excited."

They turned back toward the house, walking slowly as they talked in hushed tones. "Grandma said you'll be staying in the boys' room, but you said before that angels don't sleep," Prissie pointed out. "What will you do all night?"

"Approximate," he replied smugly. "I can lie down and close my eyes."

"Won't that be boring, though?"

"I can visit with Harken or one of the others at night."

"How?"

"We will share dreams."

Prissie gave him a blank look. "How do you do *that*?"

Koji shrugged. "I just do. I will ask Shimron; perhaps he can explain it more clearly."

"You keep mentioning Shimron. Who is he exactly?"

"See? *You* have a lot of questions, too!" the angel laughed, earning an eye roll. "Shimron is an Observer like me. He is my mentor just like Harken is Milo's mentor."

"Do you guys always come in pairs?"

"That is right!" Koji nodded approvingly. "You are being observant, too."

"Two by two," Prissie mused aloud. "Are there lots of other kinds of angels?"

"Lots," Koji agreed, then listed, "Messengers, Guardians, Protectors. Of course, there are proper names for the orders. Malakim, haderim, cherubim — each has their function, and rank is based on aptitude and experience. We work together."

"That's pretty interesting," she admitted.

As they reached the steps to the back porch, Koji touched her arm. "I do have something very important to ask you."

"Well?"

"Will you teach me how to tie my shoes?" he whispered urgently.

At dinner that night, Jayce Pomeroy unintentionally dropped a bombshell when he announced, "I'm bringing on another part-timer at the bakery; he'll start next week."

"Has business picked up that much?" asked Grandpa Pete.

Jayce fiddled with his butter knife. "It's not so much that I *need* the help. The boy wants to give the bakery business a try, and I'm in a position to give him a chance."

"How old is he?" Momma asked.

"Fifteen," he replied. "We'll take the rest of the summer to get acquainted, and he'll switch to after school and weekends once September hits."

"Who's the guy?" Neil asked around a mouthful of mashed potatoes.

"He's a local boy, though he lives across town; his name's Ransom."

Prissie's head snapped up. "Ransom Pavlos?"

"That's right," Jayce smiled.

"Not *him*!" his daughter exclaimed.

His brows lifted in surprise. "Why not?"

"Because ..." she spluttered, searching for words. "Because he's *awful*!"

Glances were exchanged around the table before Jayce calmly replied, "Could you be more specific?"

"I *know* Ransom," Prissie explained. "He's been in my homeroom class for two years in a row, and he's got long, moppy hair and sideburns, and he wears those baggy pants."

"You can hardly expect me to turn the boy away because you don't approve of his hairstyle," her father replied. "It took courage for him to approach me like he did."

"He's the head of a gang!"

"A gang!" Grandma Nell exclaimed. "In our town?"

"Well, he and his friends look like trouble," Prissie amended sourly. "I wouldn't trust any of them."

"You sure hiring that boy is worth the risk?" Grandpa Pete asked, and Prissie shot him a smile, grateful for his support.

"Aw, Prissie, Ransom ain't so bad," Neil drawled.

"Isn't," Momma quietly corrected.

"He *isn't* running with the wrong crowds," Neil defended. "His 'gang' is on the football team. Nice enough guys. Never woulda taken Ransom for the cupcake type, though."

"Cupcake type?" Jayce echoed with a chuckle. "Should I be offended?"

Neil just grinned and took a long swig of milk, giving Prissie the chance to interject, "But he's terrible! He's always mouthing off!"

"To the teachers?" Momma asked worriedly.

"To *me*!" Prissie wailed.

Neil snorted into his glass, and Jayce laughed outright. Grandpa had to hide a smile behind his napkin, and Grandma chuckled quietly. Prissie looked to Momma for support, but Naomi only smiled and gently shook her head.

Jayce held up his hands to restore order. "I appreciate your concerns. However, I'll make my *own* judgments of the boy's character once we've spent more time together. That's that."

10

THE ANGEL'S HARP

What is it you wanted to show me?" the warrior murmured uncomfortably as he followed his companion along a path that twisted deep under the earth.

"Two things," replied Abner quietly, continuing downward until they reached an enormous cavern. The cave floor fell away on one side of the path, which hugged a sheer cliff face until it dead-ended before a huge slab — a square door, hewn from gray stone and polished smooth. Its blank face was made ominous by heavy chains that anchored it to the surrounding rock.

He glanced at his companion. "May I?"

"By all means, Captain."

Striding forward, the warrior laid a hand upon the cold

metal of the bonds. "The Deep holds," he pronounced, glancing at Abner for confirmation.

"Yes," the silvery angel confirmed. "Now for the other ... in silence, if you please."

They made no sound as they backtracked, then plunged deeper into the inky labyrinth. Finally, Abner drew to a halt and turned to his companion, raising a finger to his lips, then tapping his pointed ear. At first, there was nothing, but then a faint noise like the scrape of broken glass against stone. The captain's eyes widened in recognition, and Abner nodded gravely.

Retreating to the surface, the warrior finally broke his silence. "How long have you suspected?"

"Since midsummer."

"I will arrange for additional guards."

"Thank you, Jedrick."

On the following Wednesday, Tad pulled into the parking lot of the elementary school in Harper, the next big town down the highway from West Edinton. A large banner hanging over the gymnasium door declared it the home of Deo Volente. Tad and Neil had been coming for a couple of years now, and Beau had been attending since the beginning of summer; however, this was Prissie's first time, and she had a bad case of the jitters.

Koji nudged her with his elbow and smiled reassuringly. "Milo is already here," he whispered.

"How can you tell?"

The boy considered the question, then answered, "I just can."

Sure enough, as soon as they stepped through the school doors, he hailed them. "Hey, there, Pomeroys!"

"Yo, Milo!" loudly greeted Neil, while Tad confined himself to a friendly nod. "Are *you* the reason my sister finally decided to show up? Figures."

The mailman held up his hands and chuckled. "I only invited Miss Priscilla ... something *you* might have tried?" he challenged lightly.

The sixteen-year-old rubbed the back of his neck. "Uh, point taken. I'm going to catch up with the rest of the guys," he declared hastily and hurried into the gymnasium.

"I'll be in the sound booth," Beau announced before sloping off after his older brother.

Tad hesitated. "You okay, Priss?"

"I'll stay with Koji," she offered.

"We'll find you when things start up," he promised, then ambled away.

"Ready?" Milo invited, gesturing toward the wide double doors, beyond which all manner of noise was coming.

Glancing over her shoulder to make sure no one was paying attention, she whispered, "There's an angel *here*?"

"Come on in, and I'll introduce you," Milo replied with a smile.

Prissie's first impression of Deo Volente was the racket. Bleachers and folding chairs provided seating in front of a temporary stage against the far wall, but in the part of the gym that wasn't being used for the event, twenty-odd basketballs were in constant motion. Prissie spotted Neil in the mix, shooting hoops with some of the guys from his class.

The chatter, laughter, and constant *thud* of balls only provided a backdrop for the main noise, which was coming from the stage. "Test, test, test ..." rang out over the speaker system. A lean, balding man in a yellow polo shirt scooped up a cord and plugged in his acoustic-style guitar, then began tuning. At the same time, an electric guitar ran through a scale, ending on a wailing note. Random chords came from a set of two keyboards arranged side by side, and a rhythm was tapped out on a big drum set's cymbal.

"We're early enough to say hello," Milo explained in a raised voice as they walked slowly down the center aisle. "This is their sound check."

"Okay," Prissie replied, her voice lost in the din.

At center stage stood a man with red hair that fell to his shoulders. His clothes had that lived-in look — faded jeans and a tank top, with another shirt carelessly tied around his waist. As Prissie and Milo made their way down the aisle, he turned to speak to the other band members, giving her a clear view of the vibrant red tattoos twisting over his shoulder blades and along the backs of his arms. He tapped a sandaled foot as he counted in the others, and the drummer picked up the beat. The keyboardist struck an opening chord, and after the first few bars, the throb of a bass guitar filled the room, sending deep notes vibrating through Prissie's whole body.

This was definitely different than what Prissie was used to, but as the leader's fingers plucked a melody from his guitar strings, she was pleasantly surprised, and when he turned to face the microphone and began to sing, she slowed to a stop.

His rumpled clothing and wild looks ceased to matter when he raised a light, sweet tenor. The song wasn't one she'd ever heard before, and the lyrics painted pictures in her mind of a place she couldn't reach and stirred a longing in her heart for someone she'd never seen. Before she knew it, tears were prickling under her eyelids, and when he finished, she quickly swiped at her cheeks with the back of her hand.

Milo's blue eyes held an approving shine. "Don't be embarrassed, Miss Priscilla. That's just the kind of response Baird gets when he sings one of his songs. Come on, I'll introduce you."

"To him?" she asked in disbelief. Her eyes swung back to the red-haired worship leader who was fiddling with the strings of his guitar, idly tuning. "Are you saying that *he's* the angel."

Milo grinned and whispered, "He's not the *only* one. Tonight's admission comes with two for the price of one!"

Prissie blinked in surprise and looked more carefully at the other members of the band. Beside the balding man stood the much shorter bass guitarist, whose lank brown hair poked out from under a knotted bandana. His head bobbed in time with the tapping of one diamond-patterned, high-top sneaker. The keyboardist was tall, with olive skin and black curls; his long fingers flowed easily through a rippling series of scales. Behind the drum set sat a woman with warm skin, wide-set eyes, dozens of coiling braids, and a pierced nose. She twirled one drumstick in her gauntleted hand.

"Which one is the other angel?" she asked curiously.

"Can't you guess?" Milo asked.

"None of you look like each other, so how am I supposed to tell?"

"You *shouldn't* be able to tell," he assured her. "I was just curious to see if Kester is blending in. He's new to our Flight — as new as Koji."

"Which one is Kester?" Prissie asked in an undertone.

Milo shook his head. "First things first. Mentor and *then* apprentice, hmm?"

"What?"

"Haven't you realized yet? We come in pairs—one who has more experience, and one who's still learning the ropes," he explained.

"I figured that out already," she said loftily. When her conscience twinged, she admitted, "Koji told me about some of it."

"Harken and I have been together for quite some time. Koji here is brand new, and this is his very first assignment. Kester has been around *much* longer, but he's newly assigned to Baird." Milo grinned and added, "Between you and me, I don't think he's quite adjusted to the partnership."

"Why not?" she asked.

"Let's just say that Baird's style isn't what Kester's used to." A small smile tugged at the corner of his mouth, and with a sidelong glance, he remarked, "I don't really think this is what *you're* used to either, right, Miss Priscilla?"

That was an understatement; her church tended toward the old hymns, and the only accompaniments to their singing were an organ and a piano. She wasn't really sure *she* approved of how things were done here, which was confusing, since the worship leader was apparently an angel ... and angels should know better.

Rather than answer, though, Prissie asked, "Won't it be kind of weird for you guys to have a conference right out here in front of everyone?"

Milo chuckled. "Why? Is it so strange that I have friends outside of our home church? I'm here almost every week." Stepping up to the edge of the stage, he propped an elbow on the carpeted platform and called out to the worship leader in a sing-song voice. "Oh, Baird! I have a message for you!"

The redhead turned, and his hazel eyes lit up. Unplugging his guitar, he strolled over, calling, "What's up, Milo!" He crouched down so they wouldn't have to crane their necks to talk, and suddenly, Prissie found herself on the receiving end of an easy smile. Offering a hand, Baird said, "I haven't seen you here before."

Milo jumped in to handle the introductions. "This is Miss Priscilla Pomeroy, the one who knows about us."

Baird turned wondering eyes on the girl whose hand was still in his possession. "No kidding?" the redhead drawled thoughtfully, then broke into a huge grin. "That is *so* cool! Are you freaking out? I mean, you're not scared of me or anything, right?"

Prissie's eyes drifted to the tattoos that peeked over the curve of Baird's shoulder and the cuff that decorated his left ear. "Not really."

"I'm not what you expected though?" he inquired, giving her hand a light squeeze before releasing it.

"*Nobody* has been," she replied honestly.

Baird sat down on the edge of the stage, letting his legs dangle. "Well, some of the other guys are *much* scarier looking than I am. Me? I'm just a harmless musician, an angel with a harp!" He tipped his head to one side as he smiled, then plucked a few notes on his sky-blue guitar.

Just then, the young woman on the stage launched into an energetic drum solo. At the sound, Prissie jumped. Noting her discomfort, Baird smiled sympathetically. "You're way out of your comfort zone, aren't you, Priscilla Pomeroy?" She shrugged noncommittally, and he nodded wisely. "Well, you're not the only one. Hey, Kester!" he hollered, waving to the man who'd been at the keyboards. He stood near the back of the stage, a violin in his hands. "C'mere!"

Carefully placing the instrument in its case, Kester slowly strolled over. Baird thumped the floor at his side, and Kester hesitated only a moment before unbuttoning his suit coat and stiffly lowering himself to the floor. Prissie gazed curiously at the serious-faced man, who had a large nose and dark brown eyes. "Good evening," he greeted politely.

"This is Priscilla Pomeroy, and she's a friend of Koji's!" Baird exclaimed, elbowing the neatly pressed gentleman. "Pretty amazing, right?"

The violinist pursed his lips thoughtfully, then offered his hand. "It is a pleasure to meet you Miss Pomeroy; my name is Kester Peverell."

He spoke with a foreign accent, but it wasn't one she recognized. "It's nice to meet you, Mr. Peverell. Please, you guys can call me Prissie."

"You may call me Kester," he returned, smiling faintly. "I am most curious ... how is it that you know our true nature?"

Baird nodded eagerly. "Yeah, I mean ... I've never been outed before! Have you?"

"Yes, actually," Kester promptly replied. "At least in part. There was an old woman who claimed she could see wings whenever I sang during worship services. She was very close to the end of her time and took great comfort in songs of heaven."

"No kidding?" the redhead asked, eyes wide.

"No kidding," Kester echoed solemnly.

Baird sighed. "Man, you *really* need to loosen up a little."

"I will take that under consideration," his apprentice calmly agreed.

Milo chuckled. "Looks like Kester's a quick learner; he already knows how to handle Myron!"

"Hey, hey, hey . . . !" the redhead protested. "You're *not* supposed to spread that around. The name's *Baird*. Everybody calls me Baird."

Milo nudged Prissie and explained, "He prefers to go by his last name."

Koji, whose attention had been fixed on the basketball game underway across the gym, belatedly turned back toward the stage. "Hello, Baird! Hello, Kester!"

"*See*!" exclaimed the worship leader, waving a hand at the youngest member of the angelic contingent. "Koji! *Nice* togs . . . very youthful humanity!"

"You think so?" the boy asked hopefully.

"You're *totally* blending!" Baird assured with a wink, then bounded to his feet. "It's nearly time to start, so why don't you guys come hang out afterwards?"

"Count on it," replied Milo.

As Kester picked himself up and brushed off his pants, he discreetly prompted Baird. "Your attire?"

When the redhead snapped his fingers and handed off his guitar to the other angel, Prissie realized just how much taller Kester was than his mentor. Baird pulled on the rumpled shirt that had been tied at his waist and did up a few buttons.

Kester cleared his throat. "You are off by one."

The redhead blinked at the uneven tails of his shirt and snorted. "Good catch."

While he fixed the problem, Prissie leaned over and

whispered, "Are you sure Baird's the mentor and Kester's the apprentice?"

"Quite sure," Milo replied with a definite twinkle in his eye. Waving casually to the pair, Milo led Prissie and Koji away in a search for open seats.

"Grandma always says, 'It takes all kinds,'" Prissie remarked when Koji fell into step beside her.

"Baird is very good at what he does," Koji solemnly reported.

"Chairs or bleachers?" Milo inquired.

"Chairs," Prissie replied quickly.

As they worked their way down one of the side aisles, she waved at Beau, who wore a headset. For the last few weeks, he'd been assisting the man in charge of the DeeVee's webcast and was therefore in technological glory.

Milo found an open row, and Prissie waved Koji in first so she wouldn't have to sit right next to the mailman. She might have forgiven him for being an angel, but that didn't mean she was ready for that much closeness.

"He excels at song," Koji continued.

"And Kester doesn't?" asked Prissie.

The boy solemnly answered, "Kester is *also* very good at what he does."

"But they're partners? Doesn't that mean they do the same thing?"

"Are *any* two people exactly the same?" Milo challenged.

"I think it sounds crazy — putting together two people who don't match."

Koji shook his head. "It is a *good* match; they will learn from each other."

"Sharp eyes, Observer," Milo agreed with a wink.

Prissie straightened. "That's right! If you're a Messenger, and Koji is an Observer, what are they?"

"Worshipers," Milo answered, gesturing to the two angels on the stage. "That's about as close to harps and halos as you're going to get."

Prissie couldn't help feeling disappointed that heaven was so lax where dress code was concerned. "All that's missing is the wings," she replied with a touch of sarcasm.

Milo simply smiled and shrugged.

Tad and Neil turned up moments before the singing began and slid into the seats next to their sister. One of Momma's cardinal rules was that the family sit together, but Prissie had assumed her older brothers would wriggle out of the obligation since their parents weren't there.

"Okay there, Priss?" Tad inquired.

Before she could answer, Baird stepped up to the microphone and invited everyone to stand as he struck the first chords of a chorus she'd never heard before. Not wanting to stand out, she mouthed the words, but was quickly distracted by Koji and Milo, who were harmonizing.

Her older brother nudged her with an elbow, and she glanced up into Tad's expectant face and realized he was still waiting for her answer. Brows lifted over serious gray eyes, and Prissie responded with a small but honest smile. Even in the midst of unfamiliar territory, her family gave her a sense of belonging. "I'm fine."

Afterward, Tad and Neil pitched in stacking chairs, so Prissie lingered near the stage. Koji wanted to spend some time with his new roommate, so he was looking on as Beau finished up his responsibilities at the sound booth. However, both Milo and Baird were surrounded by enthusiastic people, and she didn't want to meet anyone new. Hanging back and trying not to make eye contact, she nearly bumped into Kester, who stood just behind her with hands in his pockets. "They are always very busy," he commented.

"No one realizes they're angels," Prissie pointed out.

Kester considered that for a moment, then inclined his head. "True."

Perhaps because he was mostly a stranger, she found it easier to ask, "Why are you pretending to be people?"

Again, Kester took his time, dark eyes searching her upturned face. "Deception is not our goal," he replied. "In the end, we are servants, here because this is where we have been told to be."

"That's the only reason?"

"No one can fathom God's purposes, but like you, we can trust and obey."

"I guess," Prissie mumbled uncomfortably, then changed the subject. "You played a violin; it was really nice."

Kester glanced at the stand where the instrument still rested, then beckoned for her to follow as he strolled up the steps onto the stage. She followed, sneaking a peek at the people still milling in the gymnasium to see if anyone was watching. "Sit here, Prissie," urged the angel, courteously pulling a chair around.

With the rest of the room at her back, she was able to give Kester her full attention. "Are all of these yours?" she asked, staring at the neat row of black cases.

"They are," he replied as he took up his violin. "Baird

frequently 'mixes things up' at the last minute. It is difficult to anticipate his requirements, so I bring a selection."

Prissie could only guess the contents of three of the cases by their shapes. "How many instruments do you play?" she inquired curiously.

"Most of them," he replied as he slipped the violin into its case.

She frowned in confusion. "You brought instruments you can't play?"

Kester shook his head. "My apologies. I was unclear. It is characteristic for Worshipers to rely on their voices; we are creatures of song. However, instruments fascinate me, so I have learned how to play each one."

"*All* of them?"

"Most," he corrected. Choosing a small recorder, he sat across from her; deft fingers caressed the polished wood of the pipe before taking position over the holes. He raised it to his lips and a mellow tune, sweet in its simplicity, brought a smile to Prissie's face, and when he finished, she commented, "It's like a lullaby." Kester dipped his head and folded his hands around the instrument, waiting. His relaxed posture and calm gaze set her at ease, and Prissie gave in to an impulse to trust. "May I ask questions?"

"You may. I will answer if I can."

Little things had been bothering her, and she blurted out the first that came to mind. "How come you're different ages?"

"Because we are," he replied simply. "Some members of our group recall time's beginnings, but most of us were brought into existence since then. Those of us who spend time here are subject to its passage."

"You and Baird look about the same age," she observed. "Shouldn't mentors be older than their apprentices?"

"They should, and he is," Kester replied. "In truth, Baird is older than Harken."

Prissie's eyes widened. "But Mr. Mercer is *old*!"

"To fit in, Harken ages at the same rate as those around him. It is the same for Milo, Koji, Baird, and myself."

"But he's not really old?"

"Not in the sense you mean."

"Don't angels get old?"

"We grow and mature, but differently than you. Koji has not progressed far beyond newly formed, so he is a fair representative of where we begin."

"Does that mean Harken looks different when he's not pretending to be human?"

"Yes."

"How different?"

"Not so much; you would know him immediately," Kester assured.

"Then you look different, too?" she badgered.

"Somewhat," he patiently answered. "Do not rely too heavily on appearances. They are not the most important consideration."

Prissie wasn't sure how to respond, but Kester smoothly filled the awkward silence with activity. Holding up a finger to request patience, he laid aside the recorder and chose one of his other cases. As he flipped open the latches, he met her gaze and announced, "You will probably like this, Prissie." A new instrument was brought to light, and the angel returned to his seat, settling it across his lap.

"Is that a *real* harp?" she gasped.

"A small one, but yes," he replied, amusement lurking in his dark eyes.

"Can you play?"

"I can," Kester assured as his fingers wandered aimlessly across the strings, plucking out a soft cascade.

"I mean, *would* you play something?" she rephrased. "Please?" With enviable ease, he returned to the tune he'd played earlier, weaving the gentle melody through an accompaniment of open chords. Awed, Prissie whispered, "It's like you're a *real* angel."

"Just like," calmly agreed Kester.

11

THE UNSEEN REALM

"Shouldn't we be *grateful* for some quiet?"

"The sudden change is suspicious. Why would the enemy retreat?"

"Could they have found it?"

"Ephron knew, didn't he?"

More questions than answers were brought before the group gathered in the sanctuary behind the blue door. Finally, a voice filled with gentle authority cut across the rest. "What do you think, Myron?"

As every eye swung in his direction, the red haired Worshiper sighed. "How many times do I have to tell you that you can call me *Baird*?"

"At least once more," his captain replied, as his fingers slid over each facet of the stone set into the pommel of his sword.

"Let me ask you this, then," Baird inquired. "Why would you want *my* thoughts? I'm no tactician."

"You do not fight, but your eyes have seen many battles. I would like your perspective."

"Are you calling me *old*?" the redhead asked with a mischievous smile.

"Are you avoiding my question, Myron?"

The Worshiper's hazel eyes grew unusually solemn, and he turned his gaze toward the shifting lights that formed their sky. "In my humble opinion, this is the lull before the storm. All of hell is about to break loose."

The following afternoon, Prissie begged a ride into town with Grandma Nell, who had errands to run. "Do you have your purse?" her grandmother quizzed.

"Yes," Prissie sighed.

"Make sure to show Koji the landmarks around town," Grandma continued.

"I will."

"Thank you for the ride, ma'am," Koji offered once he'd exited the mini-van.

"So polite," Grandma beamed. "Stay together, and when you're done, wait for me over at the bakery."

"Yes, Grandma," Prissie dutifully answered. "We'll be fine."

With a wave, Nell pulled away from the curb, and Koji turned expectantly to her. "Where are we going?"

"Here and there," she replied vaguely, striking off along the sidewalk.

He hurried to catch up. "What do you intend to do?"

"My best friend's birthday party is this Saturday, and I need a gift to take."

"You have not mentioned a best friend before."

"I've known Margery since preschool," Prissie explained. "She and I have always been friends."

"Then the search for her gift must be a matter of great importance. May I help?"

"It's not *that* big a deal," she protested. "And I don't need any help, but I'll show you around West Edinton when I'm done."

"I know all about your town," Koji declared matter-of-factly. "However, you could show me the parts you like best."

She looked at him blankly. "What for?"

"I know many things about you from observing," the young angel remarked. "I would like to hear firsthand what matters to you."

Prissie looked around uncertainly, then pointed at the town hall. "Other than Dad's bakery, my favorite place in town is the gazebo outside the library."

Koji's eyes sparkled with interest. "Why?" he inquired.

"It just *is*," she replied with a huff. "Come on, we'll start over here."

She led the way to a card store that doubled as a gift shop. The place smelled like soap and candles, and there were decorative flags and windsocks hanging in the front windows. Prissie breezed past the spinners of stationary and racks of cards without a second glance, preferring to wander up and down the aisles of knickknacks. After a few minutes, she arrived in front of a glass case filled with figurines and pursed her lips in concentration. "One of these would probably be good."

"What are those?"

"Angels, obviously," she replied. "Margery has collected them since she was a baby because her middle name is Angel."

"How strange," Koji murmured, gazing intently into the case.

"I like these," Prissie remarked, pointing to a set of four small statues depicting the seasons. Winter's angel wore fur-trimmed robes and a crown of snowflakes; summer's was dressed in a sleeveless dress and garlanded in daisies. "It's too bad Margery wasn't born in spring because I like that one best. Pink is the prettiest by far! Don't you think so?" She turned to Koji, patiently waiting for his agreement.

"I have noticed your preference for the color," he replied carefully. *Too* carefully.

"What?" she demanded. "Do you have a problem with these?"

"There are several ... *inaccuracies*."

"Really?" Prissie eyed the figurines critically. "I think they're very flattering."

Koji studied the lineup of slender, serene-faced angels. "These are all *females*."

"So?"

"There *are* no female angels," he stated emphatically.

"None?" she asked, stunned.

"And feathers," he noted, sounding mystified.

"Obviously," she retorted. "They're *wings*!"

He gazed at her, dark eyes solemn. "Angels are not birds."

"Are you saying angels don't have wings?"

"No," he replied patiently. "Many angels *do*, but they are not like these."

Prissie stooped to peer at the next shelf down in the case,

which held a large selection of fairies. "What about these?" she asked. The brightly colored figurines had butterfly wings, dragonfly wings, and a few in the back had bat-like dragon wings. "At least they have pointed ears, right?"

Koji shook his head in consternation. "I will have to ask Shimron about this. It makes sense since no one ever remembers clearly ... except in dreams."

"Do you have a halo?"

He tilted his head to one side, considering one statue's tiny angelic accessory. "I do not wear a ring of light over my head, but I can become too bright for you to bear. Perhaps that is what the sculptor wished to signify?"

"I can bear you just fine," Prissie countered, upset that her traditional gift for Margery was being criticized.

"Also, they are unarmed."

"Why would they need weapons?" she scoffed. "*You* aren't armed!"

He glanced over his shoulder and scanned the store, pausing at various points as if he was seeing something she couldn't. "Observers are not, but any angel is in danger when they are in this world."

"Danger? Why?" Prissie exclaimed, looking around the quaint little shop nervously.

"Do you not know?" Koji inquired softly. "We are at war."

A creeping sense of dread latched onto her heart. "With whom?"

"The Fallen."

"Fallen angels, as in *demons*?" she asked, her blue eyes widening.

"Protectors and Guardians do most of the fighting," he replied matter-of-factly. "Messengers are at the greatest risk, for the Fallen often target them. Observers must take great care, for the enemy is merciless to any who are caught unawares. That is part of the reason we are in teams. Those who fight protect those who do not."

"Just as a precaution, though, right?" Prissie asserted. "There can't be many bad angels in West Edinton."

Koji's brows knit. "Why would you believe such a thing?"

"This is just a quiet little town. I'll bet your 'Fallen' are much more interested in big cities."

"Prissie," he said in a low voice. "The Observer who was assigned to this team before me, Shimron's previous apprentice—the Fallen *took* him."

Prissie's mouth felt suddenly dry and she swallowed hard. "What happens to angels when they're captured?" she whispered.

"I do not know; I have never been taken before," Koji replied. "But those who have been returned bear terrible scars."

She glanced uncomfortably at the case filled with lovely winged women and backed away. "I guess I'll look for something else."

Koji carelessly swung his feet as he gazed up and down Main Street, but Prissie crossed her ankles. "When I was really little, Momma told me that if we ever got separated while we were in town, I should run to this gazebo and wait for her. She would come and find me." Prissie peered up at the neat octagonal pattern of the rafters overhead. "Good things have always happened to me here."

"Like what?" prompted Koji.

"One day when Momma was standing in line for a prescription at the pharmacy, she let me come here to wait for her. I hadn't been here very long when Milo showed up. He was new in town, and since he was a stranger, I wasn't sure if I should talk to him. But he was wearing his postman's uniform, so I guessed he was safe."

"What happened?"

"He asked if I was lost, and I told him that was impossible since this is my town." She shrugged a little, then continued, "Momma found us talking and invited him over for dinner. That night, Daddy invited him to our church, and he's been there ever since."

A pleased smile brightened Koji's face. "This is where you first met Milo!"

She nodded and focused on a squirrel dashing across the lawn, wishing she could stop the color rising in her cheeks. Already, she regretted sharing such a precious memory. Preferring to let Koji do the talking, she asked, "Are angels attracted to this spot?"

Pulling up his legs so he could rest his chin on his knees, Koji said, "It *is* very pleasant, but unless an angel is a Caretaker, places do not matter so much. We are drawn to lasting things rather than passing things."

She looked at the town hall. Its gray stone came from a nearby quarry, and its bell tower was a local landmark. Up until the Presbyterian church was built on the opposite end of Main Street, it had been the tallest structure in the area. "This is the oldest building in town; it's lasted more than a hundred and fifty years."

"No," he replied dismissively. "The things of this world

will not last. We are more interested in that which endures—promises, relationships, but mostly souls. If an angel met you in this place, it was because they wanted to talk to *you*."

That was a very nice thought, and Prissie was pleased. Wanting to extend a favor, she offered, "Is there anything you want to look at in town."

"I would like to taste things," Koji replied, sounding embarrassed about the admission. "I have seen many kinds of food, but until now, I was unable to eat them."

Prissie thought back over the last few evenings. She'd noticed the would-be exchange student eating with careful concentration, but at the time, she thought he'd been worried about his table manners. It had never occurred to her that Koji was tasting foods for the first time. Then an idea struck her. "Does that mean that the first food you ever ate ...?"

"Your pie," he proudly filled in. "I shall never forget how it tasted."

She gave him a hard look, but Koji wasn't teasing. For better or for worse, her clumsy pie had been immortalized because it held a place in the memory of a boy who would live forever. Prissie wasn't sure if she should feel humbled or humiliated. "Come on, let's go," she sighed. "The corner store has groceries."

Prissie knew their market forward and backward because it wasn't very big, and she'd been shopping there since she was small enough to ride on the bottom rack of their tiny carts. However, shopping there with Koji proved to be a fascinating experience. Seeing things through his eyes made her look at them a little differently.

Koji might have known all about the history of her hometown, but apparently, grocery stores had never been a priority in the lessons he received from his mentor. Once inside, the young angel craned his neck like a tourist, trying to take in everything at once.

With a glance around to make sure no one was staring at his odd behavior, Prissie herded Koji toward the produce section. "What looks good?"

"I am not sure."

Together, they walked up and down the aisles, and to Prissie's amazement, he was familiar with all the fruits and vegetables — at least by name. He could also name all the fish laid out on ice in the meat department's glass-fronted case. "Have you seen these before?" she asked, pointing to a row of speckled trout.

"No," he admitted.

"Then, how do you *know* this stuff?" she demanded.

"I am not sure; I just know," he replied with a shrug.

Prissie turned down one of the central aisles, and Koji slowed to a stop in front of neat rows of soup cans. Dark eyes flickered from label to label, engrossed in the different varieties. "Oh, those," she remarked scornfully. "Grandma would probably make any kind you want if we ask her, and it'll taste *much* better."

"You do not approve of ... chicken and stars?" he asked wistfully.

With a long-suffering sigh, Prissie took on the role of resident expert and tour guide. "We live on a farm, and Momma and Grandma put stuff up, so we hardly *ever* buy canned food."

"Harken keeps canned food in his kitchen, though it

is mostly for show," Koji mused aloud. "What would you suggest?"

Prissie wandered up and down, dismissing nearly everything she saw. It didn't seem right to feed an angel stuff like canned ravioli or cellophane-wrapped sponge cakes. She'd been raised on *real* food, and prepackaged foodstuffs made her cringe. Finally, she grumbled, "I *suggest* we wait until we get to Dad's bakery. But until then, let's grab something to drink and one snack each — my treat."

"Thank you!" he murmured appreciatively.

They circled the store again while Koji carefully considered all of his options, even the ones she had advised against. Finally, they ended up back in the produce department, where he waffled between a starfruit and a kiwi. "Which do you like better?" he asked.

"I'm not sure," she confessed. "I've never tasted starfruit."

That sealed the deal for him. "We can share!" he declared, looking very pleased.

Next, Prissie led him to the back corner of the store, a landmark of sorts for every kid in West Edinton. Small baskets were arranged along a series of narrow shelves under an old-fashioned looking sign that declared, Penny Candy. There were jawbreakers, taffy, bubble gum, caramels, and a vast assortment of hard candies. "Dad says that when he was a little boy, all the candy really was a penny. It's a nickel now, but we still call it 'penny candy.'" Wondering if angels were allowed to eat junk food, she ventured, "Do you like sweets?"

Koji dragged his gaze away from the brightly wrapped goodies and confessed, "Very much."

"Pick something," she urged, pulling out a small, white paper bag and counting out half a dozen root beer barrels, which were Jude's favorite. "Momma likes to keep the candy jar on the kitchen mantle stocked."

"Which do you like?" Koji asked as she counted out six cinnamon candies.

"I don't really eat candy very much," she replied aloofly.

"Oh," he replied, obviously disappointed.

She gave him an exasperated look, then rummaged through a basket filled with small suckers. "*Fine*... this is my favorite," she admitted, showing him the one she liked best.

Koji peered intently at the wrapper, on which small text was printed. "Cream soda?" he asked. "That is not a kind of fruit."

"Obviously," she retorted.

The young angel fished around in the bin, systematically inspecting the labels and extracting five more. He offered them to her like a small bouquet, then asked, "Does it taste like milk?"

"It's not cream, it's cream soda."

His head tipped to one side. "What is that?"

She led him to the long row of beverages and located bottles of the stuff. "I guess it tastes like vanilla? Maybe?" she hazarded. "It tastes *good*, okay?"

Koji nodded and smiled. "I will trust you in this matter."

As they walked toward the front registers, something caught Prissie's eye. On impulse, she reached out and plucked the item off the shelf, watching to see when the observant young angel noticed the small box of star-shaped pasta riding along the belt toward the checker. When he did, his expression of surprise was quickly followed by one of delight, and Prissie felt as though she'd been rewarded. Somehow, an angel's smile managed to capture the purest essence of joy.

Back outside, Koji walked quietly at Prissie's side, hugging their one shopping bag to his chest. She was glad he was so happy over such a simple thing, but her mind was already racing ahead. There had to be something that would be good for Margery's birthday present, but *what*?

Suddenly, Koji snatched her hand, pulling her to a stop. Prissie tried to extract herself from his grasp, but Koji's attention was fixed on a point farther down the road. When she looked in the same direction, nothing seemed to be out of the ordinary. "Koji?" she whispered. "Let go of me!"

He nodded sharply, but not at her, then got in front of her. His voice was calm enough, but his eyes were wide, *urgent*. "You have shared your food with me. Maybe I can share some of ours?" he offered.

Without waiting for an answer, he tugged her back the way they'd come. "Where do angels shop?" Prissie asked, trying to joke but falling flat.

"We do not," he replied seriously. "Abner's flock keeps us supplied. I think perhaps *now* you will notice them."

The way Koji was acting, you would have thought they were being chased down the street. Prissie glanced over her shoulder and stifled a groan. Not half a block away, a familiar group trooped out of the local delicatessen. The *last* thing she wanted was for Ransom and his gang to see her holding hands with a boy on Main Street. Once more, she tried to pull free of Koji's grasp, but he wasn't having it.

"Almost there," he assured.

"Fine," she hissed. Keeping her head down, she picked up her pace until they were jogging together. He didn't release his hold until they clattered through the door to Harken's shop.

"What's all this?" the shopkeeper called.

Koji indicated the street and said, "Things are stirring, so Tamaes sent us ahead."

"Who?" Prissie asked.

Harken's expression grew solemn, and he moved to look out the front window. "Well, now, that was probably wise."

"He suggested showing Abner's flock to Prissie. May I?"

The old man's brilliant smile flashed. "An excellent suggestion! Shall we go into the garden?" He gestured toward the back room.

Prissie preceded them through the maze of boxes toward the mysterious blue door that seemed to beckon to her. Glancing first at Harken for permission, she reached out to touch the irridescent gleaming knob, which hummed softly against her fingertips.

She paused on the threshold, gazing at the lovely glade that wasn't really a part of her world, but Koji gently pushed her forward. "It is safe *inside.* Come on, Prissie. We need to close the door."

Everything was as she remembered it — soft grass carpeted the small clearing, and the surrounding trees reaching toward the rippling lights in the sky. Maybe because she was expecting it this time, she didn't feel quite as unsettled by the otherworldly aspects of the angels' sanctuary.

Harken stepped past her, humming under his breath as he strolled into the center of the glade, scanning the forest. Koji eagerly shed his shoes and socks, then wriggled his toes in the grass with a blissful expression. Setting his foot gear next to their grocery bag, he trotted after Harken, beckoning eagerly for Prissie to follow.

"Come on out," Harken called gently. He wasn't talking to her.

And then Prissie noticed them. Some of the shifting lights that dappled the forest drifted in lazy spirals, resolving into sharper focus as they left the shelter of the trees. She squinted and stepped slowly closer. "They look like—fairies!" she gasped.

"Angels," corrected Harken. "These small ones are the lowest order of angels, but one of the most important."

One of the slender figures lit upon his palm, and he turned to Prissie with it. They were small, hardly the size of her hand, and almost too bright to look at. Peering through her lashes, she could just make out a tiny, perfect person with silvery hair tucked behind pointed ears. Its upturned face was dominated by a pair of slanted eyes; their faceted depths had no whites, reminding her of an insect's. The little creature was *adorable*.

"Hello, there," she cooed, wondering if she was supposed to pet it or shake its hand.

"They cannot speak," Koji informed her quietly. "Yahavim are not quite that clever."

The small being fluttered delicate wings and cocked its head, looking inquisitively from Harken to Prissie, and the old man smiled. "They understand enough and can make themselves understood," he explained. "The members of Abner's flock are not unlike domesticated animals; the yahavim are every angels' primary source of nourishment."

Prissie gave him a horrified look and squeaked, "You *eat* them?"

Koji smothered a giggle. "Nooo," he quickly assured her. "They make manna!"

Harken smiled kindly. "Abner could explain it more clearly, but these small ones are able to perform a great service. Just as plants take in carbon dioxide and release oxygen, the yahavim take in light and produce manna." Turning to the fairy-like creature in his hand he politely inquired, "Shall we show her?"

The tiny angel darted upward on wings like a dragonfly's and turned a somersault in the air, capturing the surrounding light in a brilliant burst and condensing it. Prissie had to shield her eyes for a second, but when the creature righted itself, she saw a small flake drift down onto Harken's hand. "Thank you," he said graciously.

"So bright," Prissie said, blinking her watering eyes. "It's hard to look at them directly."

"Their glory is the least of all the angels, and it is still too much for human eyes to behold," Harken declared. "Be glad that the rest of us are able to rein in the radiance; men have been blinded by the presence of angels in their midst."

"I remember stories," she replied, thinking back over old Sunday school lessons. Again, Prissie was struck by the notion that she was only seeing a part of something much larger, and she squirmed inside, caught between awe and actual fear.

Meanwhile, Koji had three more of the little manna-makers turning somersaults for him. When he was satisfied with their work, he quietly thanked each of them, then hurried to Prissie's side. He held out cupped hands and beamed at her. "Manna is the food of angels. Will you share some with me?"

The delicate wafers were so thin, they were translucent;

irregularly shaped and slightly curved, they looked like golden scales, or perhaps itty-bitty, transparent potato chips. "What's it like?" she asked.

"More desirable than gold, and sweeter than honey," quoted Harken.

"Like the words of God — right and good," added Koji.

Prissie knew they were quoting verses from the Bible, but she didn't understand. How could food taste like words in a book? "That's not a flavor."

Koji lifted his hands again. "Please, Prissie?"

"It's okay for me?"

"The children of Israel wandering in the wilderness ate nothing but manna and were satisfied — for a while," Harken reminded.

"But that was in Bible times," she countered.

"Child, *all* times are in God's hands, and *this* is yours," the older angel pronounced with infinite patience. "Accept an invitation when it is given, for who can tell if it will ever be extended again?"

Prissie thought there might be a rebuke in his tone, but she found nothing but kindness in Harken's deep brown eyes. Her heart clenched with a sudden sense of urgency, and she looked down at the proffered food. Was this her once-in-a-lifetime chance to taste manna for herself?

Koji tilted his head to catch her gaze, his eyes sparkling with hope and friendliness. "It tastes *good*," he promised. "Trust *me*."

Smiling a little uncertainly, she chose a gleaming flake and popped it into her mouth. As an indescribable sweetness spread across her tongue. Prissie's eyes brightened, and Koji grinned.

12

THE SECRET RECIPE

"Thank you for sheltering her."

"Of course," Harken replied as he finished binding the warrior's wound.

Letting the shining raiment fall back into place, the warrior said, "It has been years since the last time the battle raged so close to the center of town. What did they hope to gain from a midday assault?"

"It was dramatic," the old shopkeeper remarked. "Showy, even."

"You think so, too?"

Harken snapped shut the lid of a medical kit and took a seat beside his teammate. "It was pointless, but that may have been the point all along."

The warrior rubbed the side of his face as he thought, but

eventually, he voiced their shared concern. "While all our attention was fixed upon Main Street, was something important happening elsewhere?"

Wordlessly, both angels looked to the east.

"I'm detecting a theme here," Grandma remarked as she placed a plate of sliced starfruit on the table between Koji and Prissie. "Are you fond of stars, young man?"

"Indeed," he replied seriously.

Grandma Nell picked up the box of star-shaped pasta her granddaughter had brought home. "I haven't used these since Beau decided he wanted to be an astronaut when he grew up. Do you remember that, Prissie?"

"Of course," she replied, pushing the plate of fruit closer to Koji.

"We'll have a nice soup with lunch tomorrow," Grandma announced, turning to check the contents of her vegetable crisper. "Naomi and I will raid the garden this evening."

As Grandma Nell bustled out onto the back porch where she kept her big stock pot, Koji picked up a piece of fruit and held it up to the light. "I did not realize I was reaching for stars," he remarked thoughtfully.

"Does it matter?" Prissie returned, nibbling experimentally at the point of her first slice.

"Shimron says that the things we are closest to are the things we usually overlook," Koji replied. "I must ask him if I should begin observing *myself* as well as those around me." He touched his tongue to the starfruit's greenish-yellow flesh, then popped the whole slice into his mouth, closing his eyes as he savored the new flavor.

Prissie took a larger bite, but decided that she preferred the familiarity of apples to newfangled fruits from faraway lands.

Her grandmother returned hugging a speckled pot with one arm and toting a frozen chicken under the other; she *clank*ed the former onto the counter then *clunk*ed the latter into the sink. Wiping her hands on a dishtowel, she crossed to the shelf in the corner, which bulged with cookbooks, and picked up the one waiting on top. "I found it, Prissie—your great-grandmother's recipe book."

"Really?" she exclaimed, setting aside her half-eaten fruit as Grandma Nell offered a worn book with a pink calico cover.

"It took me long enough to find it, but you still have a little time. Give it a look this afternoon, and you can do a practice pie here while I make Koji's soup over in your momma's kitchen. Sound good?"

"Yes!"

Half an hour later found Prissie and Koji on the porch swing. Grandpa Pete's mother's recipes were written in pencil, which had faded in spots and smudged in others, so she turned the pages with great care. "Her name was Mae," Prissie said. "That's my middle name."

Koji nodded wisely, but didn't speak. He was too busy enjoying his cream soda-flavored sucker.

Prissie found the page detailing the secrets to her great-grandmother's pink applesauce, and her brows drew together. "This takes six different kinds of apples, and the measurements are by the half-bushel!" she exclaimed, twisting the end of her braid around her finger before giving it a toss over her shoulder. "How am I supposed to pare this down into one pie?"

"Math?"

"Obviously," she sighed.

It took twenty minutes of figuring and scratching, but finally, Prissie dusted away the eraser crumbs and stared with grim satisfaction at her recipe. "This is as close as I can get," she declared with authority. "But it'll only work if we can find ripe apples on Great-grandma's trees."

Koji bounced to his feet. "I will help!"

Armed with a basket and accompanied by Tansy, Prissie, and Koji set off down the dusty trail that would lead them right to the spot where they first met. As they walked, she thought about all the other angels who'd revealed themselves to her in the last two weeks — Milo, Harken, Adin, Baird, and Kester. According to Momma and Pastor Ruggles, she didn't have anything to fear from them, but some of the things Koji had told her were unsettling. She didn't want to think about an unseen war, or about what had happened to Koji's predecessor, or what kinds of things might happen to her friends if they were captured by their invisible enemies.

She had a nagging suspicion that there must be a *reason* all of this was happening to her, but since she had no idea what that might be, she decided to concentrate on pleasant things, like baking an award-winning pie in time for the county fair.

"Which trees?" Koji asked, interrupting her train of thought.

"These big ones," she replied, pointing to the venerable trees her middle-namesake had loved so well. They were two stories tall, and the uppermost branches were filled with creamy yellow apples, some beginning to show a pink blush.

"They ripen early, but even so, they might be too green," Prissie said worriedly.

Koji studied the trees closely, then chose the one that looked most climbable. He nimbly managed the lower limbs but became momentarily stuck midway up. Then, to Prissie's amazement, he seemed to find a toehold in midair and continued his ascent. "How did you *do* that?" she called.

He turned to look down at her. "With help!"

"Whose?"

For several seconds, he gazed closely at her—observing. Finally, he replied, "I am not allowed to introduce you to anyone you cannot see."

"Someone's here?" Prissie whispered nervously.

"Of course," he replied matter-of-factly.

"Why?"

Cocking his head to one side, he answered, "Because *you* are here."

A few furiously thumping heartbeats later, it dawned on her. "My guardian angel?"

"Indeed," Koji smiled, resuming his climb.

Prissie searched the apple tree for some sign of another angel—a flicker of movement, a shimmer of light, *anything*! "Are they nice?" she finally ventured.

"I am not sure," Koji replied, scrutinizing a cluster of apples that hung right in front of his nose. "I wish Abner was here; he would know which ones are ready."

She hadn't meant the apples, but since they *were* her pressing need, she decided to let it go. For now.

Koji watched Prissie's progress with frank curiosity. He was in full Observer mode, and having his intent gaze fixed on her every movement wasn't doing her temper any favors. Botching a pie was bad enough; doing it in front of a witness made her cranky.

"Can I help?" he offered ... for the third time.

"I'll do it myself," she grouched, pushing a stray tendril of hair out of her face with the back of a floury hand. Grandma had ceded control of her kitchen to them, so Prissie was officially in charge. Koji's role was somewhere between "moral support" and "guinea pig." She carefully sliced a sliver out of one of the apples they'd picked earlier and extended it to the angel. "Do you think it's too tart?"

Koji inspected the wedge, which had pearly white flesh that blushed to a beautiful shade of rose at its center. He crunched into it and puckered, exclaiming, "Sour!"

Prissie's lips formed a grim line as she moved onto the next apple and cut another sample. "If they're still green, I guess I can try adding more sugar," she mused aloud.

"These apples are the secret to your recipe?" Koji asked.

"Well, they're the secret to pink applesauce," Prissie corrected. "Grandma Nell hasn't made it in a while, but it's a Pomeroy tradition that goes back to Great-grandma Mae. The story is that pink was her favorite color, and so her husband ordered those trees especially for her. Grandpa Pete remembers when they were planted."

Koji listened patiently, biting his lip as if trying to contain some comment, but when she paused for breath, he blurted, "Is the oven supposed to do that?"

Prissie glanced away from the cutting board and gasped. Smoke was trickling out from around the oven door and drifting toward the ceiling. "Oh, no! My pie crust cookies!" she wailed.

Grabbing the oven mitts, she yanked the oven open, releasing a cloud of acrid smoke into the room. Neat rows of pastry strips that had been sprinkled with cinnamon and sugar were charred beyond recognition, and once she noticed that some of them were actually smoldering, she hurried the baking sheet to the kitchen sink and dumped the whole lot in. When she flipped on the water, it hissed against the hot pan, sending up a billow of steam.

"No," she muttered grumpily. "That *isn't* supposed to happen. Why didn't you say something sooner?"

Koji blinked. "You did not want my help."

Prissie threw down her oven mitts onto the counter and slapped off the faucet, then stomped to the kitchen table and sat, blinking back angry tears. "This isn't *fair*!" she seethed. "Everyone *else* can do this!" Well, maybe not everyone, but that's the way it felt. Grandma Nell's fabulous pies consistently won ribbons, Auntie Lou's entry was sure to impress the judges, and even her father could probably knock their socks off if he wanted to. Prissie wanted to show everyone that she could do just as well!

"I can see that you wish to do your best," Koji cautiously offered. "But it is not good to compare yourself to others."

"What would you know about it?" she returned waspishly.

Koji didn't react to her tone; he merely answered her question. "I also have a mentor whose reputation precedes him. My placement with Shimron is a distinct honor, and I wish very much to excel."

Interest lurked behind Prissie's sulky expression. "What's he like?"

"Old. Wise. Patient." Koji's eyes shone with admiration for the angel he'd been assigned to work with. "Shimron is one of the First."

"First?"

Koji nodded. "He remembers the creation of this world and has looked upon all of time!" Sobering somewhat, he added, "He also remembers the Rebellion."

Prissie wasn't sure exactly what he was talking about, but it was a relief that Koji could sympathize with her plight. "Does he make everything look easy?"

The young angel considered her question, but he didn't answer it directly. "My task was to watch, to remember, and to testify, but in the midst of my responsibilities, I was seen."

"By me," she supplied, her mood shifting. "Did you get into trouble?"

Koji shook his head. "Shimron was pleased that I was given this chance. He was also able to meet a human and speaks fondly about his experience. They also became friends."

"Someone else who could see angels?" Prissie asked, intrigued.

"Yes. It is not unheard of ... just rare."

"Who did Shimron meet?"

The young angel's eyes took on a mischievous shine. "Elijah."

Prissie gawked at him. "*The* Elijah?"

"Indeed."

13

THE PARTY GIRL

Koji edged closer to Abner, wriggling his toes in the soft grass of their garden sanctuary while he waited to be noticed. The silver-haired angel stood in a veritable cloud of yahavim; the little angels dipped and spiraled around the Caretaker, vying for his attention. Once each bright member of his flock had been counted and coddled, Abner turned his attention to the young loiterer. "What is it, Koji?"

"May I ask a favor?"

Abner clasped his hands behind his back. "You may ask."

Koji nodded solemnly. This was the way of Caretakers, whose powers were awe-inspiring. "I have a friend ..." he began nervously.

"Do you now?" Abner gently prompted.

"Prissie," Koji replied breathlessly.

Abner chose a seat at the base of a tree and beckoned for the boy to join him. "Why don't you start by telling me more about your friend?" he invited.

With a grateful smile, Koji did just that.

Early on the morning of Margery's birthday party, a soft tap sounded at Prissie's bedroom door. "Who is it?" she called quietly.

"Koji. May I come in?"

"I guess," she replied, sitting up in bed and pulling her blankets close.

He slipped into the room and carefully closed the door before whispering, "I have something for you!" Plunking down in the center of her rug, he proudly displayed a small apple basket mounded with distinctively blushing apples.

"Are those from Great-grandma Mae's trees?"

Koji was positively beaming. "Last night, I asked Abner for help. Since he is a Caretaker, the trees yielded their best fruit to him!"

"An angel who talks to trees?" she asked skeptically.

He blinked and replied, "No, but he understands them. Abner promises that these apples are at their peak. They will make good pies!"

So far, Prissie's trial pies had turned out so tart, everyone had needed extra ice cream to get their slices down. Grandpa had suggested some varieties of sweeter early apples to add to the mix, but so far, she wasn't satisfied with the combination. Since the county fair opened tomorrow, and there were just four days left before she and Grandma Nell would be turning in their entries, Prissie was nearly out of time.

"You brought me ripe apples?" she mumbled, finally realizing what Koji's gift meant. "I can try again, and it'll be right?"

"Yes!"

Feeling as if it were *her* birthday instead of her best friend's, Prissie swung her legs out of bed. "I don't have to be at Margery's until noon, so there's time for one more practice pie. I'll let you peel apples if you'd like."

Koji stood and said, "I will start!"

Prissie frowned as she pushed around the bottles of spices in the cupboard. "Cloves, nutmeg, ginger, allspice, where's the cinnamon?" Spotting a jar of coriander, she uncapped it and gave an experimental sniff, curious if it really was manna-flavored.

"What is wrong?" Koji asked from his station at the cutting board. A neat pile of apple peelings had been pushed aside for the chickens, and he'd moved on to quartering and paring.

With a huff, Prissie stalked to the refrigerator, where a magnetized grocery list hung. Sure enough, right at the bottom her father had written *cinnamon* in neat block print. "We're out of cinnamon!"

"Is it necessary?" he inquired.

"You can't make apple pie without cinnamon," she declared moodily.

"Can we get some from your grandmother?" Koji suggested.

"I guess," Prissie sighed. But then the candy jar on the mantle caught her eye, and she had a flash of inspiration.

Maybe since this was just a practice pie, it would be okay to improvise a little. "Wait! I have an idea."

Poking through the contents of the footed carnival glass dish, she extracted the cinnamon candies she'd purchased the other day. "Five left."

"What?" Koji asked, coming over to see what she was doing.

She showed him the red-wrapped sweets. "If I mix these in ...?"

He unwrapped one and his eyes sparkled. "They are the right color."

"And the right flavor," she said with decisive finality. "Let's find a way to smash them into smaller pieces."

After some scrounging around, Prissie dropped the unwrapped candies into a plastic freezer bag, which they took out onto the back porch so they wouldn't wake the rest of the household once they applied the force of a meat-tenderizing mallet.

By the time Prissie's older brothers dragged themselves into the kitchen, her improvised pie was in the oven and beginning to smell good. Neil took a deep breath of spice-scented air and exulted, "I *love* fair time!"

"That's because you're a glutton," Prissie accused the sixteen-year-old, who still wore plaid pajama pants and a wrinkled T-shirt.

"I'm a growing boy!" he protested, yawning hugely as he poured himself a glass of milk.

Tad ambled through the kitchen door already dressed for the outdoors. "Mornin', Priss, Koji," he said as he relieved his brother of the milk jug.

Neil crouched down to look through the oven window. "How long before this one's ready? I'll taste-test!"

"Don't be ridiculous," she retorted. "We're not cutting into my pie until tonight."

The blond teen shrugged and addressed the baking pie through the glass. "Then I guess I'll be seeing *you* later!"

All decked out in the red and white sundress that reminded her pleasantly of Adin and his matching summer suit, Prissie turned in at the Burke residence. Margery lived in one of the big, stone homes in West Edinton's historical district, just four blocks from the bakery. It was an impressive house that felt important, and Prissie was pleased to have been invited there so often over the years — pajama parties, tea parties, birthday parties.

She and Margery had been cohorts since their first day of preschool, when people had said they made such a cute pair. They were both blonde, and they'd both been wearing pink hair ribbons. In the realm of four-year-olds, it had been enough to forge the bonds of friendship.

Prissie hugged a small, wrapped package to her chest as she climbed the steps to the front door, whose beveled glass windows offered fleeting glimpses of rainbows. Pressing the doorbell, she heard a faint chime sound inside.

"Prissie, darling!" exclaimed Mrs. Burke as she opened the door wide. "It's been too long! How are you?"

"Very well, thank you," she replied politely.

Margery's mother beckoned for her to enter, then smoothly plucked the wrapped gift from her hands and placed it next to the others on the hall table. "Luncheon will be served in ten minutes. The other girls are upstairs in Margery's room. You remember the way?"

"Yes, Mrs. Burke," Prissie said with a smile, then began to climb the elegantly curved staircase that dominated their front hall.

She trailed her hand on the banister as she daydreamed about living in the lap of luxury. Margery only had one sibling, a four-year-old brother named Gavin, so even though the Burkes' house was bigger than the Pomeroy's, there was barely enough family to occupy it. Wide open rooms were filled with tasteful decorations and so much quiet; Prissie thought *this* was what heaven must be like.

From Margery's bedroom came the sound of squeals and giggles, and she peeked through the open doorway. "Prissie!" called her best friend, who was sitting on the floor, leaning against her bed. "You made it!"

"Happy birthday," she replied brightly.

She and Margery may have been a matched set back in preschool, but as they'd grown up, differences made themselves apparent. All the Pomeroys were tall, but Margery took after her petite mother. While Prissie preferred to keep the same style, her friend was always trying new looks. At the moment, Margery's blonde hair was teased into a tumble of chin-length curls, and her light green eyes sparkled with excitement. "We were just talking about the class lists! This is the first year Elise will be with us!"

Prissie blinked in surprise. Somehow, in all the excitement, she'd forgotten to check the roll. "We're together again?" she asked, pleased even if she was the last to know.

"Like always!" piped Jennifer, whose deeply tanned skin suggested that much of her annual summer trip to visit relatives on the coast had been spent on the beach. "They wouldn't *dare* split us up!"

"I hate how you have to spend the whole summer not knowing for sure, though," April interjected. She was the resident expert on all things *now* — television, movies, and especially Facebook and YouTube. Her sleek, mouse-brown hair was bobbed, and her baby bangs formed a straight line over the rectangular frames of her glasses. Very little escaped the notice of her sharp gray eyes. "The risk of separation *looms* for weeks on end!"

"I think it's *indecent,* the way they keep vital information a secret until the end of summer," haughtily interjected the one girl in the room Prissie didn't know. Her coloring was dramatic — porcelain pale skin and stark black hair. Hazel eyes were rimmed with a deep purple liner that matched her lace-trimmed leggings, and Prissie's first impression was one of envy.

Margery made the introductions. "This is Elise Hanson. Her family moved in next door during the middle of summer! Elise, this is Prissie Pomeroy."

Elise was flopped on the four-poster bed, reading over Margery's shoulder as she flipped through a magazine. She quirked a light brown eyebrow, and Prissie realized with a jolt that she must color her hair. Elise returned Prissie's assessing look — top to toe and back again — before giving her a mocking little smile. "Hey."

Bristling defensively, Prissie coolly replied, "It's nice to meet you."

"Her family runs the bakery on Main Street," Margery supplied.

Narrowing her eyes, Elise said, "Now I remember! I've

seen you around. Your family adopted that Asian kid, am I right?"

"Koji is an international exchange student," Prissie primly corrected, not liking Elise's tone.

"Whatever," the girl replied dismissively, turning her attention back to the magazine.

"So what have you been doing all summer?" interjected April, and the conversation swerved into familiar territory. Prissie joined Jennifer on the padded bench. Since kindergarten, the four of them *always* caught up during Margery's birthday festivities, trading secrets and making plans for the upcoming school year. However, the addition of Elise felt a bit awkward.

At first, Prissie thought Margery was just going out of her way to make sure that Elise was included, but before long she realized that the flow of conversation centered around the new girl.

April and Jennifer were obviously comfortable with Elise. In fact, Prissie was beginning to feel completely out of the loop. April made a saucy remark about pizza delivery boys that sent everyone else into gales of laughter. When Jennifer noticed Prissie's look of confusion, she giggled and said, "Sorry, guess you had to be there."

As Margery laughed herself silly, a coldness settled in the pit of Prissie's stomach. While she'd been stuck at home, working in the garden and helping Grandma with the canning, an outsider had swooped in and stolen her best friend.

When Mrs. Burke called them downstairs for the luncheon, everyone *ooh*ed and *aah*ed over the decorations. Margery's mother was what Momma called a *crafty* person, and she always put a lot of effort into her daughter's parties. Cold chicken salad and fussy fruit tartlets were served with fizzy lemonade, and Prissie thought everything was perfect, until they were interrupted by the slap of bare feet on wood floors. Margery's little brother Gavin tore around the table, roaring like a lion and making faces at his sister's guests.

Mrs. Burke hurriedly chased him out, lightly saying, "Boys will be boys!"

"Ugh! I *hate* brothers!" exclaimed Margery indignantly.

"Tell me about it! They are *such* freaks," growled Elise.

April smiled mischievously. "Poor Prissie, she has *five*!"

"Five!" Elise snickered. "That's almost indecent!"

Prissie wasn't sure if the girl was talking about the number of boys or the number of kids in their family. "Hang on a sec," Elise demanded, looking at Prissie with new interest. "*Pomeroy*? Is Neil your brother?"

Prissie's unease doubled. She'd had to deal with plenty of girls who wanted to get close to her in order to find out more about her brothers. She offered a sharp, "Yes," and snapped her mouth shut, her eyes sparking warnings.

Thankfully, Mrs. Burke chose that moment to sweep back into the room. "Ready for cake, girls?"

Once they'd been served, Prissie spoke into the lull. "The fair starts tomorrow. What day do you want to meet up?"

"No thanks! County fairs are so lame," scoffed Elise.

Jennifer and April exchanged an uncertain glance, and Jennifer said, "Ours is pretty good."

"Yeah, if you like cows and kiddie rides and pickles and stuff," Elise said, sounding supremely bored.

Margery had the grace to look embarrassed; she knew just

how involved the Pomeroy family was in the fair every year. Prissie stared fixedly at her plate, too stunned by the girl's rudeness to find words for her indignation. How *dare* she?

"The music is worth it," April cautiously interjected. "Free concerts from local bands all day long."

"And there's a midway with rides ... and fireworks," Jennifer added. "*Everybody* goes at least once."

Prissie was grateful her friends were defending their fair, but she wished it didn't sound as if they were apologizing for liking it. She glanced toward Margery, but her best friend was suddenly fascinated with the floral pattern edging her plate.

Elise seemed to decide it was wisest to adjust her stance. With the air of a person making allowances for people who didn't know better, she offhandedly said, "What the heck. Might as well give it a try since I'm stuck out here."

When the time came to open presents, Prissie nervously clasped her hands in her lap. For Margery's gift, she'd settled on something she'd found hanging in the window at Harken's. The angelic shopkeeper had called it a suncatcher, and it certainly caught Prissie's eye, for the blue glass diamond looked as if it had been plucked from her bedroom window at home. It was set in a kind of frame studded with clear glass marbles in shades ranging from blue to green — her best friend's favorites. Since Margery knew about Prissie's fascination with stained glass from the many sleepovers that had been hosted at the Pomeroys, Prissie thought her friend would understand.

Margery lifted the lid on the box, and when she folded back the tissue paper, her eyebrows arched. Seeking Prissie's gaze, she teasingly asked, "*Not* an angel?"

It was a friendly jibe, and a smile flickered across Prissie's lips. She just shrugged and watched with bated breath as Margery lifted her present for the rest to see.

"Oooh! So pretty!" enthused Jennifer.

"Let me see!" exclaimed April, and Margery held the suncatcher up to the light. She smiled at it as it spun, and Prissie's relief buoyed her mood ... right up until Margery opened her last gift.

The elaborate package coordinated with the decorations, making it obvious that the box was from her parents. Margery's eyes sparkled with an eager expectation that made Prissie wonder if she'd been promised something specific for her fifteenth birthday. The wrappings fell away, and her squeal of delight was soon taken up by April, then Elise and Jennifer. "What is it?" Prissie asked, craning her neck to see.

"A cell phone!" Margery exclaimed, clasping the wee bit of technology to her heart, then holding it at arm's length to give it an adoring look. "Finally! Thanks, Mom!"

"Who will you call?" quizzed Elise.

Jennifer bounced and said, "Me first!"

"Only if I get her first text," bargained April, a true haggler.

"Okay," Margery giggled. "Let me get your numbers entered."

Everyone dipped into pockets and purses and produced cells of their own. Margery's new number was exchanged, photos were taken, and the conversation zipped along, leaving her in the proverbial dust. She idly poked at the icing roses left on her plate and tried to imagine her mother's reaction if she said she wanted a cell phone. Laughter was pretty high on the list of possibilities, just under flat-out refusal.

With a soft sigh, Prissie quietly announced, "Be right back."

Jennifer was too busy comparing features with Margery to notice, and April was focused on quizzing Mrs. Burke about texting or tweeting or something. Only Elise glanced up from her cell phone. *Did she smirk?* Prissie wasn't sure, but she just kept walking.

Bypassing the powder room, Prissie snuck toward one of her favorite places in the house. Mrs. Burke called it the solarium, which Momma said was just a fancy name for a sunroom. It was airy and bright with a high ceiling, yellow walls, and plant stands in front of every one of the tall windows — like window boxes on the inside of the house.

Duchess, a regal, long-haired feline with a flat nose and orange eyes, flicked her plumed tail as Prissie tiptoed closer and offered her fingertips to be sniffed. "You're very different from Tansy," she murmured softly. "She's just an ordinary barn cat." Duchess stood, stretched, leaped from her perch, then stalked out of the room, leaving Prissie alone. The snub stung more than it should have, and she had to take deep breaths to keep from dissolving into angry tears.

It looked as though her best friend *wasn't* anymore. Sitting on the floor, Prissie hugged her knees tight to her chest and tried to ignore the stifling sense of dejection. She didn't *like* feeling like an outsider in a place she had always belonged. Groaning softly, she hid her face and wished she could get away. They'd probably never notice she was gone.

For now, all she could do was get through whatever was left of the afternoon with her dignity intact. But how? Prissie was concentrating so hard that she nearly jumped out of her skin when the doorbell rang. Turning her head, she listened curiously as Mrs. Burke exchanged a few words with someone on the front porch. A moment later, the woman's voice carried through the house. "Prissie, your escort's here!"

Mystified, Prissie slipped out of the solarium and hurried toward the front hall just as Margery and the other girls poked their heads out of the dining room.

There on the front step, with his hands clasped before him, stood Koji. He leaned forward just enough to peep past Mrs. Burke, avidly studying the ornate chandelier that hung above the curving staircase. As soon as Prissie came into view, he straightened and beamed at her. "I came to get you."

They'd made no such arrangement, but she was glad for the out. Flashing an apologetic smile, she said, "I need to go. I'll see you guys soon." She nodded to Mrs. Burke and said, "Everything was beautiful. Thank you for having me." Not stopping to introduce Koji to her friends, she escaped out the front door, which closed on the sound of curious whispers.

Prissie marched down the cobblestone walk, back rigid. Once they reached the street, she asked, "Is anything wrong?" Koji solemnly searched her face as if unsure how to answer, so she tried again. "Why did you come? Is something wrong at home?"

"No," he quickly assured. "All is well. Why are *you* distressed, Prissie?"

She was so hurt and angry, she didn't need any more urging to unburden her heart. As they walked slowly toward the bakery, Prissie told him about all the little slights she'd endured and her fears where Margery was concerned. "I'm her best friend!" she ranted. "How could she *do* this?"

"If she *is* truly your friend, she will not abandon you," Koji offered.

"I think she already has," Prissie replied sourly.

Koji gazed at her raptly, and Prissie turned her face from his curiosity. There were times when a person didn't *want* to be analyzed. However, when he spoke, it wasn't to pry. "There are many who have known great distress and loneliness because of the faithlessness of one they called friend."

"I guess," she murmured. She couldn't argue with that, but it didn't really make her feel any better. She kicked at a pebble on the sidewalk and wondered why life was so unfair.

"Prissie?" Koji asked tentatively. When she looked his way, he stopped and so did she. "I cannot promise that I will not fail, or that I can be here for always, but while I am here, I will be your friend."

"*While* you're here?" she asked curiously. "Where else would you be?"

"Wherever I am sent." He smiled tentatively and asked, "Is that not enough?"

For right now, it *was*, and Prissie nodded gratefully. "It's almost like you knew I needed to get out of there," she remarked with a weak laugh.

"Yes," he replied solemnly.

Prissie looked at him keenly. "Why *are* you here?"

"I was sent."

"Who sent you?"

"Can you not guess?" he asked cryptically, and began walking again.

She looked over her shoulder uncomfortably and asked, "My guardian angel?"

He shook his head. "There was no need to relay messages from one angel to another. He who dwells in you said you needed me, so I am here."

Prissie was amazed that Koji could say it as simply as that, as if it were the most natural thing in the world. "God told you to pick me up early?" she asked incredulously.

"Yes."

"That was nice of him," she mumbled.

"Indeed."

Dinner that night almost made up for the afternoon's drama.

"Oh, man! This is actually *good*!" Neil moaned, an expression of ecstasy on his face.

"You sound surprised," Tad remarked blandly.

"You aren't?" he challenged, shaking his fork at his brother before digging in again.

"Nope."

Zeke squinted at his serving of pie. "Isn't this one of Grandma's pies?"

"No, buddy. This is your sister's handiwork," corrected Jayce.

"But it's just as good as your grandma's," declared Grandpa Pete, giving Prissie a wink.

"Yeah, it's actually edible," commented Beau around a mouthful. Prissie wrinkled her nose at him, and he blinked innocently. "What? It *is*!"

Naomi Pomeroy smiled approvingly. "It's *delicious*, sweetheart! Is this your recipe for the contest?"

"I was thinking ... maybe?" she replied, a little flustered by all the compliments.

"Oh, *definitely*," retorted Grandma Nell in no-nonsense tones. "The flavor is outstanding!"

"Its a winner," mumbled Neil. "Something's different about it."

Jayce held up his plate to inspect his wedge of pie, whose filling had a definite cast of pink. "Good color, good flavor," he mused aloud. Catching his daughter's eye, he added, "I hope you can replicate this!"

Prissie flushed with pleasure over her father's compliment. "Yes, I'm sure I can."

Neil leaned over to steal a forkful off of Tad's plate, but his older brother fended him off with a swift elbow to the ribs. Instead, Neil turned to Jude and attempted to wheedle an extra taste off of the six-year-old's plate. "C'mon, Judicious, please?"

The youngest Pomeroy smiled sweetly but answered, "No way!"

Prissie couldn't recall a single time when something she'd made had been such a big hit. Her brows slowly lifted as her brothers fought over her cooking, and she began to smile, a little giddy over her first real success in the kitchen. Wanting to share her happiness with *someone*, she glanced at Koji, whose plate was already licked clean. The young angel, who'd been picking up human gestures from her little brothers, cheerfully gave her a thumbs up.

14

THE CRAZY DRIVER

"Were you listening, sir?"

Abner turned from the yahavim who flitted around him, sparing his apprentice a wry glance. "Why do you assume I wasn't?"

"It's usually the case, sir."

The silver-haired angel frowned thoughtfully and murmured, "So it is."

"Things are stirring, and the girl seems to be at the center of it all."

"You cannot see the center if you cannot see the whole," the Caretaker absently chided. "And it would seem that we have a more pressing problem."

"Do we?"

"Mmm," Abner hummed in concern. "One of my flock is missing."

The Milton County Fair was a long-standing Pomeroy family tradition. According to Grandpa, the fairgrounds were spitting distance from the farthest edge of their property, between them and the sprawling acreage of Sunderland State Park, north and east of town. Prissie had always wondered if you could catch any of the sights and sounds of the fair from their house, but she doubted she'd ever find out. From sunup on the first day until the last fireworks finale, her family practically *lived* there.

Every summer during the festivities, Jayce Pomeroy closed up Loafing Around, making the ten-day event a kind of family vacation. Not that they didn't work. Far from it! Grandpa had staked out a prime location back in the day, so Pomeroy Orchards maintained a presence on one of the fairgrounds' busiest corners, right in the middle of everything. They were famous for kettle corn and caramel apples, and ever since Jayce had entered the bakery business, they'd added apple turnovers.

Early on the first day of the fair, Neil helped Grandma Nell manhandle the huge coffee pot into place. Once it was perking, it would lure in the rest of the crews who were still setting up. The weather promised to be gorgeous—bright and clear, with just enough of a breeze to carry the scent of pancakes and sausages from the restaurant run by the Lion's Club. The only thing that detracted from Prissie's excitement was the offending presence of her father's trainee.

She didn't appreciate Ransom butting in. The very

thought made her angry enough to use a little more force than necessary when putting the big kettle corn scoops into their place at the end of the cooling tray. Ransom glanced over from where he was loading trays of baked goods into a glass display case, but didn't comment. If nothing else, it gave her the chance to turn up her nose at him.

"Okay there, Priss?" Tad asked.

"Grandpa will have a fit if you dent his baby," Neil remarked warily.

"I know," she mumbled irritably. Really, it was all Ransom's fault.

Koji had gently pointed out that the teen was putting in a lot of hours helping Jayce and Auntie Lou stay a step ahead of each day's turnover quota. Prissie grudgingly admitted this was true, but a part of her had hoped that her father would ask *her* to lend a hand.

Last night, Dad hadn't come home until late, and when Momma had gotten them up at the crack of dawn, Prissie had wished she was more like Koji, who didn't need to sleep. Tad plodded along as usual, but then her oldest brother really only had one speed. Still, she could tell he was sleepy, and Neil's contagious yawns weren't helping.

Beau and Koji trudged past, sharing the handle of an old red wagon loaded with boxes of popcorn that were to be stacked against the far wall of their booth. They'd already made several trips, bringing the oil, salt, and the special powdered glaze they needed for whenever Grandpa took it into his head to do a batch of caramel corn. The young angel's gaze darted around, trying to take in everything at once. Catching Prissie's eye, he smiled brightly. "This is exciting!"

"Can you believe he's never been to a fair before?" Beau announced to the rest of the group.

"No kidding?" Neil remarked in surprise.

"Make sure you show him around," Grandma Nell urged, including each of her grandchildren in a sweeping gaze.

"Thank you very much!" Koji exclaimed, then followed Beau back toward the van to get another load of supplies.

"Weird kid," remarked Neil.

Prissie gave him a scolding look. "That's *not* nice."

"He obviously grew up with different traditions," Grandma Nell said in a quelling tone.

Neil ruffled his blond hair with a chagrined expression. "I didn't mean anything by it. He's just a little ... I dunno."

"Yeah, I know what you mean," interjected Ransom, whose gaze followed the young angel. "So where's he from, anyhow?" Prissie froze and glanced nervously at the teen. He noticed and quirked one brow at her. "You don't *know*?"

"I *do,*" she retorted.

Nell Pomeroy calmly answered, "His paperwork said he's from the Northern Marianas."

"Where's *that*?" Prissie asked in surprise.

"They're islands in the Pacific Ocean," her grandmother explained. "It's halfway around the world, but they speak English ... which is why we haven't had to deal with a language barrier."

"Oh," she managed, realizing that Koji would *have* to have a cover story. Random kids didn't just show up on people's doorsteps. As Prissie puzzled this out, she happened to look in Ransom's direction. He looked the same as usual in jeans and a T-shirt, though he also wore a plain white apron like the kind her dad used when he was at work. The addition struck her as odd, until her dad showed up, hauling a cooler. Ransom snapped to attention so fast, he practically saluted. "Can I help you with that, sir?" he inquired.

"No need," Jayce replied amiably. "Did you finish loading that case already?"

"Yeah, pretty much."

Prissie was annoyed. In class, Ransom always acted so carelessly, far more interested in making people laugh than in anything the teachers had to say. Yet here he was, falling all over himself to impress *her* dad. Someone who was supposedly up until midnight icing turnovers had no right to be so energetic, and a non-family member shouldn't be so enthusiastic about their booth. She watched him closely, and when the opportunity presented itself, she confronted him. "Aren't you tired?" she blurted.

Ransom shrugged and said, "I'm okay. What do you care?"

"I don't!" she protested. "I was just wondering."

"Uh-huh. Well, for your information, I'm a morning person."

She narrowed her eyes suspiciously. "Since *when*?"

If any of her brothers had been on the receiving end of this look and tone, they knew enough to back down, but Ransom was either very brave or very stupid. He did that funny little eyebrow quirk again. "Since always. I've been up early for a paper route since I was twelve, and I run in the mornings."

"You run?"

"Yep."

"You're not on our track team," Prissie argued.

"Nope. That was at my old school, before. . . ." He hesitated, then crossed his arms over his chest and finished, "Before I moved here. Satisfied?"

Prissie wasn't satisfied, but she was ready to be done. "If I were you, I'd go home," she snapped.

He snorted quietly. "I knew you were bossy, Miss Priss, but I didn't know you were lazy."

As Ransom sauntered off, Neil snickered into his sleeve, and she rounded on him instead. The fact that her older brother dove for cover only partially soothed her ruffled feathers. Her archnemesis had forced his way into her world, and she was certain it would ruin everything she loved about the fair.

Momma was the one who insisted that the day Prissie turned in her pie at the judging booth should also be her first free day, and she was grateful for her mother's foresight. She was suffering from a bad case of nerves, knowing that the judges would soon be tasting her entry. It made her jumpy just thinking about it.

Prissie doubted she could have remained in the confines of the booth without exploding like so much popcorn. So instead, Momma turned her loose on the fairgrounds, but not alone. She was secretly thankful that she had a ready-made distraction in the form of her youngest brother, Jude. Taking Jude's small, sturdy hand in hers, Prissie asked, "What first?"

"Can we check on Maddie?" he asked hopefully.

They crossed to the far end of the fairgrounds where the barns were arranged in neat rows. Beyond these was an open field backed by a steep, forested ridge that was fenced off—the boundary of Sunderland State Park.

Inside the poultry barn, she and Jude made their way

along the wide aisles lined with wire cages. There were all kinds of chickens clucking and crowing in concert. Further along, the ducks, geese, and a handful of turkeys added to the cacophony. Grandpa had obviously been around earlier, for their ducks and chickens — including Maddie — had already been cared for, and their eggs had been collected.

Jude gave his hen some last minute advice regarding her upcoming judging, then promised to stop back later that afternoon. "We'll bring popcorn," he whispered, and Maddie ruffled her feathers and offered a crooning *buuuck-buck*.

Satisfied that he'd done right by his pet, Jude announced, "Ready!"

For Prissie, today would be a free day from Koji. The young angel had wanted very much to experience all the wild rides, but Prissie couldn't stand them. She preferred to keep her feet firmly on the ground, thank you very much. After some discussion, they'd decided on a three-way split. Prissie would watch over Jude, Beau would show Koji around, and Momma would take on Zeke. The family joke was that five Pomeroys took up the fingers on one hand, but Zeke was a handful all by himself.

Dad had given them enough money for all-day midway passes, so Prissie led Jude to a ticket booth where they were fitted with bracelets. These were great because her brother loved to do one ride over and over again until he was satisfied with it. It took a long time for Jude to tire of anything, but it was kind of fun to watch him thoroughly enjoy each part. She waited patiently while he trotted up the stairs to the giant slide again and again, then joined him on the merry-go-round for half a dozen turns. That ride was pretty much the limit of her daring. They rode side by side, she on a white stallion with pink roses braided into its forelock, and he on a coiling dragon with fierce red eyes.

By midday, things were picking up, and they had to wait in line for each of the rides. Much to Prissie's chagrin, they ran into Ransom and his friends in front of the bumper cars. "Aren't you supposed to be working?" she asked loftily.

"I have the afternoon off," he replied with a careless shrug. He turned back to talk to the other members of his gang before Prissie could properly snub him, so she settled for glaring at the back of his head.

Ever since Ransom had transferred into their school, he'd been hanging out with the same group of guys. Brock was a husky teen with curly black hair and a surly tough-guy attitude, and Joey was skinny and shy, with straight dishwater blond hair falling over his eyes. Both of them played on the football team with Neil, but she didn't know either very well because they were in the grade above hers.

Ransom's other friend was Marcus, a guy Jennifer had been wondering over ever since he'd joined their class the year before. While her friends could go on and on about his dusky complexion, big brown eyes, and cleft chin, Prissie couldn't get past his hair, which probably would have been uniformly brown if it weren't for a wide section at the top that was dyed platinum. When you added to the equation his ever-present brown leather jacket and rumors that he'd been shuffled around from one foster home to another, it equaled trouble.

As they neared their turn, she couldn't resist another jab. "Aren't you a little *old* for a ride like this?" she asked snidely.

"Nope. Nobody's too old for fun," Ransom replied amiably. "Besides, you're here."

"I'm with him," she countered, nodding toward Jude.

He smirked at the six-year-old. "Hey, squirt! You taking your big sister for a spin?"

"Yep!" he replied cheerfully.

The teen leaned forward and conspiratorially added, "Bet she's a backseat driver!" Jude giggled, and Ransom offered, "You stick with me, and we'll wreak a little havoc out there."

Before Prissie could protest, her brother exclaimed, "Cool!"

When the ticket-taker let them through the gate, Prissie moved resolutely toward a red car, but her younger brother hurried past her and hopped into a green one. He beamed at her and said, "Since we're on the same team, we should have the same color!"

For a moment, Prissie had no idea what he meant, but then she followed Jude's pointing finger toward Ransom, who was strapping into another green car. "Oh, honestly," she grumbled, but she let her brother have his way. Stepping in, she smoothed her skirt over her knees before making sure he was securely buckled, then folded her arms over her chest.

As the crackle and snap of electricity signaled the start, Ransom whizzed past and circled to come alongside them. "Not gonna drive, Miss Priss?"

"I'm just along for the ride," she replied with a disapproving frown.

"Guess that makes *you* her chauffeur," he said to Jude. Gesturing urgently, he pointed to someone in the opposite corner. "See that guy in the orange car ... the one with crazy hair? That's my good friend Marcus, and he's our target. Come on, squirt!" With a whoop, Ransom led the charge against their unsuspecting prey.

Prissie pursed her lips as the chase sent them careening all around the floor. If there were rules to this game, they made absolutely no sense. She couldn't tell who was "it" because they kept switching midstream. As far as she could tell, the game was just an excuse to ram into each other as often as possible.

Ransom cruised by and cheerfully asked, "Why so grumpy?" She just scowled, and he grinned more broadly. She wasn't quite sure what irked her about Ransom, but he just seemed to push all her buttons.

Circling around, Ransom pulled up alongside them. "Maybe we should put you in your own car next time. You're building up a lot of road rage! I'll bet you could even give Brock a run for his money out here!"

Jude gasped and eagerly begged, "Can we go again, Prissie? *Please*?"

"*May* we," she corrected, shooting a sulky look at Ransom. There was no missing the challenge in his quirked brow, and she smoothly answered, "Whatever *you* want, Jude."

They queued up at the end of the line along with Ransom and his buddies. Once their turn came around again, Prissie asked, "Are you sure you'll be okay on your own?"

Jude fixed her with a reproving look. "I *know* how to drive, Priss. Haven't you been watching?"

"Fine," she sighed, but when they stepped through the gate, she made sure her little brother was securely buckled into his green car before choosing a red one for herself.

As soon as the sparks skittered across the ceiling grid, the cars lurched into motion, and "the game" entered its second round. Jude zoomed over to Ransom, who didn't seem to mind adding a six-year-old to his gang of hoodlums, and they put their heads together for a quick conference. Prissie took a moment to locate Brock, Marcus, and Joey, but they were off along the far edge of the ring doing their best imitation of whirling dervishes.

Knowing she was outnumbered, she decided that her best bet was to go on the offensive and exact a little vengeance on Ransom's bumper. As soon as she saw her way clear, she punched the accelerator and aimed for the two green cars.

"Scatter!" Ransom yelled, and he and Jude split up.

Prissie might prefer to behave like a lady, but that didn't mean she didn't know how to give as good as she got. She *did* have five brothers, after all, and she'd been driving tractors since she was eight.

Jude wasn't at all surprised by his sister's single-minded intensity behind the wheel and squealed in delight every time she rammed him, but Ransom opted to steer clear.

He played hard to get, swerving back and forth, wending his way through the other drivers as he offered offhand apologies for the madwoman in his wake. Ransom laughed every time he looked over his shoulder at her. "Last hit earns the win," he taunted.

After several near misses, the teen made a series of hand signals that alerted Prissie to the danger of an ambush, though she couldn't tell who he was communicating with. He circled around and let go of the steering wheel, casually clasping his hands behind his neck and smirking at her. He was wide open, and that was good enough for her. Prissie had to admit she was having fun, and it looked like she would get the last hit. Putting on a burst of speed, she raced into a head-on collision, but before she could exult over her final triumph, Jude broadsided her just as the power was cut, and their turn ended. "Gotcha!" the boy shouted gleefully.

His gray eyes shone with happiness, and before she had

time to get irritated again, Prissie's face softened at the sight. It was impossible not to smile when Jude was happy. "Yes, Judicious, you got me," she graciously conceded. Unbuckling, she stepped out of her vehicle and gave her skirt a brisk flap before flipping her braid over her shoulder. Ransom was still buckled in, his arms draped over the small steering wheel as he gazed bemusedly up at her. "What?" she asked sharply.

"So you *do* know how to have fun," he remarked blandly. "I never woulda guessed!"

"I have more fun depending on the company, " she said.

"I had fun, too!" Jude exclaimed as he tucked his hand into Prissie's. "Thanks, Ransom," he said politely.

"Sure, kid," he replied, unbuckling and unfolding his lanky frame from the bumper car. With a careless wave, he backed toward his friends. "See you later, Miss Priss."

"I don't think so," she returned haughtily.

"Can't avoid it. We're both working the evening shift at your folks' booth," he rejoined, then slouched off with his friends, bound for the roller coasters.

"He's nice!" Jude announced.

"He's *annoying*," she corrected, tugging him off in the opposite direction.

By mid-afternoon, Jude was sticky, sleepy, and satisfied to be led back to the family's booth to rest. They followed their noses toward a rich, sweet aroma that could only mean one thing. "Grandpa's making caramel corn!" Jude exclaimed. Forgetting his weariness, the boy pulled at his sister's hand, practically dragging her the rest of the way back.

Beneath the canopy behind their stand, Prissie could hear

the hiss of the burner under the kettle, and when she rounded the corner, there was her grandfather, using the long wooden paddle to keep the popcorn moving over the heat. The air was thick with the smells of sizzling oil, popping corn, and burnt sugar — perfect for bringing in customers.

Grandpa Pete tipped the batch out onto the cooling tray and broke apart some of the larger clusters. Beau and Koji spread the pile across the cooling trays with their scoops, giving the batch a little time to set up before bagging it for sale. Waving at everyone, Prissie circled around to the very back, where a picnic blanket and a few seats were arranged in the shade. Jude ignored the mismatched collection of lawn chairs and flopped down onto the blanket with a handful of caramel corn. Within minutes, he was asleep.

Grandpa ambled over and chuckled at the site. "Looks like you did a good job of wearing him out," he said. He tapped the cooler with the end of his paddle. "Get something to drink and rest a bit. Your mother and grandmother should be back soon, and you can all go to the exhibition hall together."

Prissie's heart skipped a beat then raced ahead. She'd nearly forgotten the upcoming judgment, possibly because she'd spent most of the day trying not to think about it. The results of the pie baking contest would be announced at four o'clock.

A little while later, Grandma Nell and Auntie Lou came into view. They had their heads together and were talking a mile a minute. Just behind them came Pearl, pushing Amberly in a stroller. Her husband Derrick manfully toted the oversized boxes they used to transfer the caramel apples from the bakery. Uncle Lou brought up the rear, hands in the pockets of striped shorts that left his knobby knees exposed.

His straw hat, dark sunglasses, and camera made him look like a tourist in his own town.

For several confusing minutes, everyone was talking at once, but eventually, a small group split from the rest, moving purposefully toward the exhibition hall — Grandma Nell, Momma, Pearl, Prissie, and both Lou's.

With a wistful expression, Koji asked, "Should we go along to offer our support?"

"Nothing doing!" Neil replied. "That's girl stuff."

Koji considered this for a moment, then pointed out, "Both your father and Ransom bake."

"Well sure," the teen replied with a shrug. "But that's business. *This* is competition!"

As Prissie and the other ladies disappeared around a corner, Koji tried one last angle. "You like pie, though."

"You bet, but I like pie on my plate. Looking at pies I'm not allowed to taste is just asking for trouble."

The young angel studied Neil closely for several moments before declaring, "Turning away from temptation is very wise."

Prissie's older brother grinned and said, "You're not the first person to notice I'm a wise guy."

"Nor the last," Grandpa Pete snorted. Dropping a hand onto Koji's shoulder the old man said, "In my experience, this is best. Let Prissie share her news in her own way when she gets back. I'm prepared for any eventuality."

Koji gazed at him expectantly.

Crossing to the stack of boxes that held all their supplies, Prissie's grandfather fished out a box of glaze and showed it to the boy. "If she wins, we celebrate with pink popcorn. If she doesn't, we cheer her up with pink popcorn."

"This, too, seems wise!" Koji said in delight.

Grandpa gruffly replied, "Like they say, the apple doesn't fall far from the tree."

The fairgrounds boasted two large halls. One was given over to merchants who sold everything from knives to woodburning stoves, however, the second hall was home to all of the arts and crafts competitions, including the cooking contests. It was a great place to get out of the August heat and look at all kinds of interesting things — jars of jams and jellies, knitted afghans, colorful quilts, paintings, lace doilies, pottery, woodcarving, and photography.

Grandma Nell was of the opinion that hovering around the judges while they did their tasting soured the flavors of the pies they were sampling. It was her custom to deliver her entries, then leave well enough alone. Because of this, Prissie hadn't seen any of the other entries yet. Together, they walked up and down the rows of long tables, sizing up the competition. Grandma Nell and Auntie Lou were old pros, so they recognized the names of their usual rivals and exclaimed over the most promising newcomers to the contest circuit.

"Where's *your* entry?" Aunt Pearl asked in a low voice.

"The junior class entries are over on the far table," Prissie replied, pointing.

"Let's go check it out!"

Taking a deep breath, Prissie slowly followed Pearl along the lineup. There were more than she'd expected. Lemon cheesecake pie, blueberry crumble pie, raspberry mousse pie, crème brulee pie — each sounded more sophisticated than the last. "These are pretty fancy," she remarked, feeling foolish. Next to all these other adventurous recipes, her apple pie must have looked awfully plain. When they finally made it to her entry, she was actually surprised there were pieces missing. "At least the judges tried it."

"Let's get a picture of you with your pie." Uncle Lou's voice just behind her shoulder made her jump. He held his camera at the ready, waving her to get closer. "What did you end up calling it?"

"Candy Apple Pie," Prissie murmured, offering a wan smile before the flash popped.

"The name suits the color," he commented. "Kinda pretty, unusual for apples."

"Do Nell or Naomi ever make those candied apples? Not the caramel ones, but the ones dipped in sugar syrup?" Aunt Pearl asked. "That's what this makes me think of!"

"Crust looks good," offered Lou, still eyeing Prissie's entry critically.

"It *won't* win," Prissie stated flatly.

Uncle Lou straightened and peered at her from under his bushy brows. "How do you figure?"

"It's too plain."

"Louise has been entering these competitions at the county level and the state level for forty years, so I'm something of an expert when it comes to pie," he declared, patting his stomach for emphasis. Waving toward the long line of entries, Uncle Lou said, "People always try to dazzle folks with their presentation, but all that gussying up won't fool any judge worth their salt."

"Really?" Prissie asked.

"Taste is what counts," he asserted. "Now, as much as I'd like the chance, I can't very well taste these entries, but I've got a nose. The smell will tell you if the taste is there!" With that, Uncle Lou leaned down and took a good whiff of her pie. "This here's a *good* pie," he announced with authority.

His compliment helped bolster Prissie as the minutes crept along, and promptly at four, a group of five people wearing official-looking badges filed toward a podium standing in the corner of the room. "Good afternoon, ladies and gentlemen! The time has come to announce the winners of this year's competition. However, before we do that, I'd like to take a moment to thank the contest organizers and introduce our judges."

As the woman at the microphone droned through the credentials of the men and women who'd tasted all their pies, Grandma Nell, Auntie Lou, and Naomi Pomeroy found their way over, and they formed a little huddle of hopefulness in front of Prissie's entry. Aunt Pearl crossed her fingers and whispered, "Isn't this exciting?"

Prissie could only shake her head. It wasn't exciting; it was *excruciating*, and she thought she might be happier never knowing the judge's verdict. Glancing around desperately for an escape route, she spotted someone who *wasn't* supposed to be there. Ransom stood just inside the doors, his hands shoved casually into his jeans pockets. "What's *he* doing here?" she protested.

Aunt Pearl followed her gaze, then smiled warmly. "Why wouldn't he be? That boy's bound and determined to be a fancy pastry chef. He's probably getting ideas."

She glared, but Ransom's attention was where hers probably should have been, because she didn't realize that they'd announced her name until Auntie Lou whooped and Grandma Nell pulled her into a hug. "Congratulations, sweetie!"

"Not bad at all for your first time out!" declared Uncle Lou.

Then she was in her mother's arms. "I'm so proud of you, Priscilla!"

Finally, they released her so she could walk up to the front and receive her ribbon. It wasn't until she had thanked the judges and turned back toward her family that she saw the words printed in the center of the rosette — *Second Place.*

15

THE DASHING ESCORTS

"Which is their goal?" inquired the warrior, gazing in frustration between the two Protectors.

"Does it matter?" his captain replied. "Either way, there is cause for concern."

He nodded curtly and said, "I should get back. She is with her family right now, but..."

"The others have been alerted to the potential dangers, so there are many who are willing to lend you their aid. Unless she is somehow lured away from the rest, she is safe."

"I wish we were not so close to the Deep." Gazing unhappily toward the east, he added, "It cannot be a coincidence."

"No, it cannot."

When Margery and company turned up at the Pomeroy's booth a few days later, Prissie had no idea they'd be spending the day at the fair. The sting of being left out of the planning was somewhat soothed by the fact that the first thing her friends had done was come to find her. She was scheduled to work all day, but her family pulled together so she could go with the other girls.

"I'll work doubly hard!" Koji pledged gravely.

"Is it all right?" Prissie whispered to her mother, who was taking a turn at the register.

Momma smiled. "Go ahead, sweetheart."

Without further urging, Prissie anxiously smoothed her hands over her skirt. She wasn't wearing anything fancy today — a faded pink gingham sundress and sneakers. But April and Jennifer both wore shorts, while Margery and Elise sported mini-skirts, so she didn't think she'd stick out *too* much. Before she stepped out from behind their stall, her grandfather slipped her a little spending money. "Tomorrow's the last day of the fair," he said gruffly. "Treat yourself to some favorites."

"Thanks, Grandpa!" she said softly, carefully tucking the funds into the small backpack that doubled as her purse. Adding a couple of bottles of water from the cooler, she met Koji's gaze. "You'll be okay?"

He curved his thumb and forefinger into the accompanying hand sign and echoed, "Okay."

While she was settling up with her family, Elise scooted around the side of their stall and smiled at her brother. "Hey, Neil! Remember me?"

The sixteen-year-old looked up from where he was cleaning out the kettle in preparation for the next popping. "Uhh, sure. You're one of the girls who hangs out at the field during practice."

She pouted, then prompted, "I'm Elise, one of your sister's friends."

"Nice to meet you."

Prissie knew her brother was only giving her run-of-the-mill courtesy, but as Elise practically batted her lashes at him, her annoyance flared. "I'm ready to go," she announced crisply, gesturing for Elise to precede her to the front of the booth. With a last wave to her family, Prissie followed her friends through the crowds.

One of the first things she noticed was that all four girls had an assortment of beads and bangles dangling from their pockets. When she asked April about the odd accessories, her friend extracted her cell phone from her pocket and passed it to Prissie. "Oh, wow," she murmured, slowing her steps as she looked over all the doo-dads attached to the phone's strap.

April pointed to a tiny stuffed rabbit. "This is from my sister because my birthday was on Easter this year, and I won this one at the arcade next to the pizza place." There was a tiny pair of fuzzy dice, an ornate letter *A* and even a flash drive hanging amidst the odd collection.

Prissie thought it looked like an oversized charm bracelet. "This is *so* cute!" she said enviously.

"You should totally start your own set." April unhooked a strand of sparkling crystal beads in shades of silver and gray that reminded Prissie of April's eyes. "Here," she offered. "You can have this one."

"But I don't have a cell phone."

"Well, until you get one ..." April replied, her eyes roving. "Ha! This will work!" Prissie stopped walking and peered over her shoulder as her friend deftly attached the decoration to her backpack's zipper, where it sparkled in the sunshine.

Prissie was touched by the gesture. "Thanks, April," she said sincerely.

"Sure!"

For the next couple of hours, they roamed through the fairgrounds, tallying up how many things could be sold on a stick and sampling most of them. Going with the flow, they ended up on the edge of the crowd that had gathered to watch a square dancing demonstration. A little farther along, they ran up against a watermelon seed spitting contest. They played a ring-toss game for about twenty minutes. Eventually, Margery insisted on showing Elise the bazaar set up in half of one of the exhibition halls, where local artisans sold everything from handmade jewelry to tie-dyed scarves. Prissie was glad to be with her friends again, but it bothered her that, for the first time *ever,* she wasn't suggesting what to do next. She didn't even feel like part of the decision.

Margery had always willingly fallen in line with Prissie's plans, so much so that Grandpa teasingly dubbed his granddaughter the queen bee of her set. But now, her closest friends kept laughing over inside jokes and making references to phone calls, text messages, and past conversations she knew nothing about.

Normally, she would have told them all about her ribbon from the baking contest, but Prissie suspected that Elise would put her down. She'd rather keep her happiness to herself than see it trampled on.

The summertime separation had always been difficult, but up until now, everything went back to normal once classes started up again in the fall. This year, Prissie doubted that school would automatically fix things. She strongly suspected that the only reason she'd been included at all was because Elise wanted to get closer to Neil.

"Should we do some rides?" Jennifer suggested.

"Not until after dark; it's *way* better with lights," said April.

"Hey, look!" Elise said, pointing, sounding surprisingly excited. A large, square tent stood between a gyro stand and a cart selling cones of red, white, and blue shaved ice. It was set back from the main thoroughfare, and tapestry rugs were strewn on the ground leading to the entrance. Off to one side stood a fancy sign on an easel — Lady Ophelia, Seer of Fortunes. The heavy purple fabric of the tent was stitched with moons, stars, pretty little spirals, and zodiac figures. A curtain of multicolored beads swayed across the opening. "Let's see what she has to say about our futures!"

With excited agreement, the girls moved to follow, but Prissie stayed put. Margery glanced over her shoulder and noticed. "Come on," she invited.

Prissie shook her head. "I can't."

"What?" Jennifer asked in concern. "Why not?"

"Don't you have enough money?" guessed Elise.

"I'll lend you some," offered Margery.

"No, that's not it," Prissie hedged. "I just don't like fortune-tellers."

"Have you ever been to one?" quizzed April. When she shook her head, her friend reasoned, "Then how would you know?"

She couldn't explain exactly *why* it was wrong, but she knew that fortune-telling was one of the adamant *thou shalt nots*. If she told her friends that she couldn't go in because she believed it was wrong, they'd probably laugh at her. So, Prissie stood there, wanting nothing more than to have the ground swallow her, but keeping her chin up. "I should check in with my family," she lied, cheeks flushed with embarrassment. "I'm supposed to be working today ... and I really need to get back."

"Oh ... well, maybe we'll see you later?" Margery said awkwardly.

Prissie smiled weakly, knowing they wouldn't. "Okay."

Elise shrugged and turned to Jennifer. "I had my cards read once at this place near my old house, and you wouldn't *believe* ..." With a swoosh of heavy fabric and the clatter of beads, four giggling girls disappeared into the fortune-teller's tent, and Prissie could have cried over the unfairness of it all.

For a moment, she was tempted to follow them, but her conscience pricked. "I can't," she muttered unhappily. It would have been nice to have Koji with her right then, because he would have assured her she was doing the right thing. As it was, she just felt left out.

"Miss Priscilla!" hailed a familiar voice.

"Prissie!" came another enthusiastic call.

She turned to see Milo and Baird weaving their way toward her through the crowd, Kester close on their heels. Up until now, the only time she'd talked to Baird, he'd been up on stage, so she hadn't realized how short he was until he strolled up to her. They were eye-to-eye. "Hi," she managed weakly.

The Worshiper's wild hair was pulled away from his face with a series of little clips that made it stand out like a red mane, and his sleeveless gray shirt was printed with a huge *D.V.* in grungy blue letters. Baird grinned unabashedly and gave her shoulder a gentle poke. "Good girl!" he proclaimed. "Difficult choices are difficult!"

"Would you like to join us instead?" invited Milo.

"It'll be fun!" coaxed Baird.

"Really?" she asked, glancing toward Kester, who brought up the rear at his own pace. "Would that be okay?"

"Most assuredly," the tall angel replied kindly.

With a tremulous smile, she whispered, "Thank you."

"Do you come to the fair often?" Prissie asked.

"Every year! Practically every day, too," Baird answered. "Yesterday, I helped chaperone a DeeVee event, and my band is on rotation for music at the bandstand. But today, I'm here with friends!"

"Speaking of which, I hear you're making sure Koji has a good time," Milo interjected.

"Of course."

"I'm *also* showing a newbie around," Baird announced, gesturing broadly to his apprentice, who held a paper sack of mini-doughnuts. The tall musician's charcoal gray slacks and white button-down shirt looked far too formal in the middle of the shorts and tank top crowd, but Prissie suspected that this counted as relaxed attire for Kester.

Baird opened his arms wide to encompass the entirety of the fair. "There's nothing like looking at something familiar through the eyes of someone who's seeing it for the first time!" Giving his partner a sidelong glance, he added, "Though I suspect Koji was *much* more enthusiastic."

"Undoubtedly," agreed Kester calmly.

"Don't they have fairs in . . . wherever you came from?" Prissie asked.

Kester smiled faintly. "I have been to bazaars and street festivals all over the world, but they were nothing like this. Each land has its own flair and flavor, and this one's is uniquely, uh, deep fried."

"At least *try* the doughnuts," said Baird.

His apprentice opened the small bag and poked through the contents with one long finger. "I think it may be wisest to eat when we return home."

"Spoil sport," Baird sighed. "Food is a part of the whole fair experience!"

Milo chuckled. "It's not exactly healthy, but it's not forbidden fruit, either."

Prissie hesitantly offered, "The apple turnovers my dad makes are baked, and they're really good. Would you like to try them?"

Kester smiled and graciously accepted her invitation. "I would like to sample your family's wares. Thank you, Prissie."

When they reached the Pomeroy's booth, Prissie wrinkled her nose at Ransom, who only rolled his eyes before nodding to Milo. "Hey, Mr. Mailman," he greeted.

"Hello, Ransom," he returned amiably. "Four apple turnovers, please. And you can call me Milo."

"Sure, okay," the teen replied, efficiently bagging the pastries.

"Did you have a hand in these delectables?" Milo asked conversationally.

"Yeah," Ransom admitted.

"They look delicious!"

"They're *good*," the teen asserted, looking a little defensive, but mostly pleased.

Koji waved to Prissie and asked, "What happened to your friends?"

She grimaced. "Long story."

Neil glanced her way and jokingly asked, "Did they ditch you?"

"She ditched *them*," Baird corrected, propping his arms on the edge of the stall. "Nice operation you guys have here. Working hard?"

"Yo, Baird," Neil grinned.

Beau raised a hand in greeting, and Koji followed suit, adding, "Hello, Kester!"

"Good day," he replied, meeting each person's gaze in turn. "It is a pleasure to see you again."

Prissie glanced around to see what had become of Milo and spotted him talking to her father, who was minding the kettle in Grandpa's place for the afternoon. With a wave, the mailman called Baird over and introduced him; Kester followed, and the three angels talked with Jayce for several minutes. Prissie fiddled with the end of her braid as they chatted, wondering if they were talking about her. When her dad finally looked her way, it was with a smile. "Come back in time for dinner, my girl," he urged.

With a jolt, Prissie realized that Milo had wrangled permission for her to stay with them for the rest of the afternoon. She didn't have to be told twice. When Baird led the way back onto the fairgrounds, she walked beside Kester with her head held high.

"Thanks again!" Milo called to Jayce, and Prissie peeped over her shoulder. To her complete and utter delight, Ransom was watching them go. If only Elise could see her now, being escorted by three handsome men — well, *angels.* The possibility buoyed her spirits even further. Maybe her luck had taken a turn for the better!

16

THE SWEETEST SONG

"Well?"

The single word echoed off barren walls in the bleak cavern as Murque hauled himself the rest of the way out of the pit and leered cruelly. "He's weakening, my lord. I can make him whimper."

"Has he told you where it is?"

"Not yet."

Dinge crouched at the edge of the gaping hole and asked, "What makes you think he knows anything?"

"The Faithful do not lie, so silence is his last refuge," replied their leader with a delicate sneer. "He *has* the information I seek."

Murque drew a twisted dagger. "Want me to dig deeper to find his voice."

"You'll get your chance, but first, I'd like a word with our caged bird." With an explosion that sounded like shattering glass, the Fallen leapt, sending up sparks and a metallic squeal as he plummeted into the makeshift prison cell.

The two demons exchanged dumbfounded glances, and Dinge muttered, "I've *never* seen him willingly go into the presence of a Faithful."

Murque picked at his teeth with the point of his blade. "What's the hurry? It ain't as if anyone wants this Observer back. He's already been replaced."

Suddenly, a thin wail pierced the darkness, rising in desperation. For a moment, light blazed through the darkness, sending the pair scrabbling away from the edge. With a final shout, it flickered, then failed, and by the time it dimmed to nothing, their leader had returned.

"What did you *do,* my lord?" Dinge murmured in awe.

"Robbed him of his purpose."

He tossed something at the cowering figures, and two pale orbs wobbled to a stop at their knees. Murque grunted in surprise, but only muttered. "Can't *observe* much without those."

"From now on, fill his pointed ears with doubts. Perhaps in his despair, he will find the courage to fall. Now, come."

Once the captors were well out of earshot, their prisoner broke his long-held silence with hoarse sobs.

"And I hear that congratulations are in order?" Milo inquired knowingly.

Prissie blushed and smiled. "Thank you."

"Will we get to sample this award-winning pie of yours sometime?" asked the mailman, a hopeful light in his eyes.

"You could all come over for dinner, maybe," she shyly offered.

"Dinner?" Baird asked, perking up.

"Harken and I are regularly favored by the Pomeroys' hospitality," Milo boasted.

"Don't I know it," the redhead drawled. "Harken goes on and on about Nell Pomeroy's home cooking. So!" Baird exclaimed, clapping his hands. "What would it take to get us through the door? I could sing for my supper."

Prissie giggled. "I'll talk to Momma. I'm sure we can plan something soon. Maybe before harvesttime." Glancing up into Kester's face, she asked, "Would that be all right?"

"I would not be opposed to spending more time with your family," he replied. "Your father would certainly be a congenial host."

"What kind of word is that—*congenial*?" Baird asked, giving his apprentice a sidelong look.

Milo snickered. "It just means friendly."

"Then why not *say* friendly?" groused the redhead.

Their banter continued as they wandered onto the midway. Rumbles and raucous music clamored around them, and Prissie glanced around, hoping for a glimpse of Margery and the others. She smiled to herself when they passed the bumper cars, but it didn't occur to her that her companions were planning to go on any of the rides until Baird stopped at a ticket booth and purchased a sizable roll. "This should keep us busy for a while!" he declared with a wink.

Prissie's steps lagged when she realized where her companions were headed, but her reluctance went unremarked.

Baird was rambling on about a bird's-eye view when all three angels halted in their tracks as if they'd hit a brick wall. The worship leader lifted his hands defensively. "Whoa now! No need to go ballistic! Put the sword away!"

She had no idea who the redhead was talking to, but in the next moment, it ceased to matter. All three angels turned to face her, each with a measure of guilt written on their faces.

"It has come to our attention that this ride may not be to your liking," Kester announced neutrally.

Milo looked stricken, but Baird took their gaff in stride. "You're afraid of heights?" he asked curiously.

"A little," she replied carefully.

"O-kay," he replied thoughtfully. Then he snapped his fingers and pointed to the three of them. "Are we enough to lend you the confidence to face this fear?"

Prissie glanced nervously at the towering Ferris wheel, indecision robbing her of words. She'd stood her ground against Elise and the rest when it came to visiting the fortune-teller. As miserable as it had made her, that had been a place she *didn't* want to go. But now, there was somewhere she *did* want to go, but she was afraid to accept, which made her even more miserable than before.

Milo lifted his brows expectantly, and Baird winked, but it was Kester who tipped the scales. Without downplaying the reality of her anxiety, he stepped to her side and offered his arm. "Lend me a little of your trust, Prissie?"

Pleased to be treated like a lady instead of the frightened child she felt like, she slipped her arm through his, accepting the angel's invitation.

When their turn came to enter one of the large, pink-roofed gondolas, Kester courteously saw her to a seat, then took his place on the hard bench across from her, folding his hands in his lap and gazing thoughtfully toward the sky. Baird dropped down next to him and leaned back casually, an arm draped across the back of the seat, and one ankle propped on his knee. He drummed his fingers against a jeans-clad thigh and hummed a little tune under his breath. The two Worshipers were each calm in their own way, which eased some of Prissie's tension.

Then Milo took the seat next to Prissie. He was far too subdued, which put her back on edge. "I have a message," he murmured, his blue eyes solemn. The other two angels looked surprised, and Milo smiled sheepishly. "It's an unofficial one."

"From who?" she asked tightly.

Baird snorted. "From an overprotective she-bear who's bending the rules."

"There isn't a *rule*," countered Milo.

"It's hardly the norm," Baird pointed out.

"This entire situation is exceptional," Kester calmly interjected.

Before their little discussion could go any further off topic, a lever was thrown and the wheel lifted them off the ground. Prissie squeaked as the gondola swayed back and forth, and her hands locked onto the bench. Frantically, she wondered why there weren't any seat belts.

"Prissie?" Kester called softly. "You are quite safe."

Distantly, she heard Baird sharply order, "Go *on*, Goldilocks! You're closest!"

"Miss Priscilla," Milo spoke, and the note of urgency in his tone made her look up. "If it would help," he offered, awkwardly patting the seat beside him.

She lunged, and he wrapped an arm around her shoulders. Later, she knew she'd be mortified, but right now Prissie just wanted to feel safe, and if anyone was safe, it was Milo.

"There's nothing to fear," he offered reassuringly. "We're with you."

"*Breathe*, Prissie," Baird urged.

Kester quickly crossed to sit on her other side, wedging her between two solid bodies. "Your Guardian," he stated, answering her earlier question. "Milo's message is from your Guardian, an angel whose sole purpose in this moment is to watch over you."

They were still rising, and Prissie hunched her shoulders; however, she listened intently to Kester's voice, needing the distraction his words offered. Their gondola seemed to rush toward the pinnacle, and the winds changed as Prissie was carried up over the top. In a moment, she knew, she would be falling, and she choked on a scream.

"Tell her, Messenger," Kester prompted as the ride swung them downwards.

Milo held her hand as he relayed the Guardian's pledge. "He gives you his word, 'I will catch you if you fall.'"

"But you won't fall," Baird cheerfully interjected. "Not this time."

After another revolution, the Ferris wheel stopped to take on passengers, leaving them suspended somewhere three-quarters of the way up. "Take a look around," suggested Milo.

Prissie slowly opened her eyes and took stock of her surroundings. Baird was still humming lightly, and the tune sounded familiar; after searching her memory, she realized it was the lullaby his apprentice had played for her on the day they'd met. Kester had one of her hands in his and was idly chafing her cold fingers as he took in the view.

Then, he began to hum in unison with his mentor, and after a few moments, Baird broke off, taking a higher set of notes. As his descant rose above Kester's melody, Milo added his voice to the others', dueting in close harmony with the other apprentice. The humming transitioned into a series of soft nonsense syllables, *doo*-ing and *la*-ing. Their trio was simple, even playful, yet their song reached out to her, soothing her until something eased at her core. The calm that settled over her was soul-deep.

The ride resumed, and this time, the revolutions weren't quite as frightening, even when the next stop left them teetering at the very top of the wheel. "I can see your folks' place from here," Milo remarked, pointing.

For some reason, Prissie assumed that he meant the kettle corn stand, but the blond angel ignored the sprawl of tents below, pointing into the hazy distance beyond the fairgrounds. It took a moment to realize what she was seeing — neat rows of trees on a distant slope. "Our orchard?" she asked.

"Yes," Milo confirmed. "Your farm is the closest residence to, well, to *here*."

Baird was looking toward the ridge that marked the border of neighboring park lands, a slight frown marring his face. "Which may have something to do with this ..."

" ... exceptional situation?" Kester offered, finishing his mentor's sentence.

The redhead tapped his fingers against his thigh. "Mm-hmm."

"Pardon me," Kester murmured, drawing back in order to return to his own seat.

In the process, Prissie noticed something peeping out from under the partially rolled cuffs of his shirt. Startled, she blurted, "Kester, do you have a tattoo as well?"

"Ah, you have noticed?" He obligingly pulled back his shirtsleeve, revealing the twining ends of a pattern that lay dark against his olive skin. Where Baird's tattoos were a vibrant shade of red, Kester's gleamed black. "Does it surprise you?"

"A little," she admitted, and his deep brown eyes crinkled in amusement.

"Let me guess," drawled Baird, whose markings were often on display. "You assumed I was the rebellious type?" Prissie refused to answer, but the blush rising in her cheeks confirmed enough. "Take a gander at Milo's," he directed, and the mailman unbuttoned his own sleeve and rolled it back. His fair skin was decorated with tracings of blue as bright as the sky.

"The pattern is different," she noted in fascination.

"As unique as snowflakes," replied Baird, looking pleased.

"What are they for?"

"Should we tell her?" Milo asked, looking to Baird, who had seniority.

"A demonstration would be more fun!" suggested the redhead.

"Here?" gasped the mailman.

"I think *not*," Kester interjected.

They were an angel thing, obviously, but one that made no sense. "I'm not sure my parents approve of tattoos," she announced nervously.

"They're *not* tattoos," Baird announced. "It would be more accurate to say that tattoos imitate these."

"Many people groups seek to emulate the supernatural, reaching for the divine," Kester offered.

At her blank expression, Baird helpfully rephrased, "They copy us."

The gondola jerked and the wheel began to turn again, but Prissie hardly noticed. That's not to say she was *enjoying* the ride, but it was easier to endure when the angels were distracting her.

Baird snapped his fingers. "My band doesn't have any more sets, but the organizers asked Kester here to come back, so he's doing one later. Perhaps we could show her then?" With a sly glance at the dark-haired Worshiper, the redhead continued, "Kester pulled in so many people with his performance this morning that they want him to play again this evening."

Prissie glanced curiously at him. "What did you do?"

Baird leaned forward and said, "Why don't you come and see for yourself?"

She thought fast. "I'll have to ask Momma how late we're staying. If my older brothers want to stick around for fireworks and everything, then I probably can, too."

"Excellent!" the redhead exclaimed. "Tonight's concert will be perfect for a demonstration of what these are good for."

"In front of all those people?" she asked.

"Sure," he confirmed. "Kester is just the one for the job. He's got all kinds of subtlety and whatnot. If *I* tried, I'd probably end up blinding everyone in the first several rows."

"You're kidding," Prissie gasped.

"Nope," Baird grinned. "I'm an all or nothing kind of guy."

"Quite," remarked Kester.

Baird shook a finger at him and warned, "Just a peek, though. Can you manage that, oh apprentice of mine?"

"Of course," the tall angel replied seriously. "It would be my pleasure."

The sun had long since set when Baird led Prissie through the backstage area behind the bandstand to help him give Kester a "pep talk" before his performance. Groups from all over the county took their turn in the limelight, and at the moment, the local chapter of the Sweet Adelines was on the stage, singing an upbeat medley of tunes from *The Music Man*.

A marker board to the right of the stage announced upcoming acts in larger letters, so she could see that they'd just missed the Tiny Tots Tap-dancing Troupe from Fancy Footwork in West Edinton. In the next scheduled slot was written, Kester Peverell, Deo Volente, Harper.

They found Baird's apprentice standing in one of the pools of light that were spaced intermittently along the passage, a black instrument case at his feet. The redhead sidled up and elbowed the taller angel. "Patiently waiting in the wings?" he asked mischievously.

"It shall be just as you say," Kester replied with gravity.

The redhead shook his head. "You *really* need to lighten up!"

"Hmm ... it *is* possible," Kester allowed. "However, I do not believe it is essential."

Prissie couldn't help it. She giggled. Baird's eyebrows shot up, but his surprise melted into satisfaction. Giving Kester's shoulder a friendly cuff, he said, "You might be right."

"I'm looking forward to your performance," Prissie offered.

"May God grant you ears to hear and eyes to see," he replied.

"This is gonna be *so cool*!" Baird assured.

The contrast between their manners had Prissie biting her lip. Baird and Kester might not be good friends yet, but she was sure they would be. Or maybe they already were, in their own way.

The redhead waved casually to his apprentice, then led the way through the narrow passage behind the stage, where the chorus was nearing the climax of a dramatic ballad.

Prissie suddenly wondered what Baird's last apprentice was like, and since he was so easy to approach, she decided to ask. Hurrying her steps, she tapped his shoulder and raised her voice to be heard. "You used to have another apprentice?"

"That's right," Baird replied.

"What happened to him?" Prissie asked curiously. "Was he captured, too?"

The Worshiper turned to look searchingly at her. "Did Koji tell you about Ephron?"

"A little," she admitted, wondering if maybe the young angel had told her something he shouldn't.

Baird simply nodded and said, "My last apprentice simply transferred out in much the way that Kester and Koji transferred in. We go where we are Sent, so personnel changes are natural, especially for teams that include Grafts."

"Grafts?" she echoed, testing the term. Having been raised on an orchard, Prissie knew exactly what a graft was. It was possible to make a place for the branch of one tree to be on the trunk of another. The new limb that was grafted in would take hold and flourish, bearing its own, unique fruit. In fact, Grandpa had a special tree planted in full view of his front porch that he called his Family Tree. With the birth of each of his grandchildren, he'd carefully grafted in a new branch until now, the tree bore six varieties of apples.

"Angels like Harken, Milo, Kester, and me ... and Koji, too. We're grafted into human society and live as a part of it for a time," Baird explained.

"Are there a lot of Grafts?"

"Not really," he replied, waving at someone in the crowd. "I guess it might seem like it, but our team's a little different. Jedrick is responsible for all of the Grafts in the vicinity of, well, around here. Oh, look! They saved us seats!"

"Who's Jedrick?" she asked in as low a voice as the crowd noise would allow.

"Our group's captain," he replied with a wink.

They turned out to be Prissie's parents, Beau, Koji, and Milo. Once greetings were traded and seating shuffled, she ended up between Baird and Koji. "Did you enjoy your afternoon?" Koji asked, studying her face with all the intensity of his kind. "You seem happy."

Prissie thought about the roller coaster her day had taken and answered, "Parts were bad, but other parts were good."

"It's about to get better," predicted Milo, who sat on Koji's other side.

The hubbub of the crowd didn't change when Kester strode onto the stage and quietly placed a stool at its center, but Prissie sat up a little straighter. He carried the harp he'd shown her the week before, and as he took a seat, she whispered to Baird, "He doesn't need a microphone?"

The worship leader waved toward the band shell. “This isn’t exactly symphony hall, but the acoustics are good. Just wait. In a little bit, he’ll be the only thing you hear.”

Prissie glanced around skeptically. The crowds always picked up in the evenings on weeknights, what with people coming after work. Since tomorrow was the final day of the fair, people were anxious to pack in their last bit of fun. Even though the bandstand was on the opposite end of the main thoroughfare from the midway, she could hear tinny music carrying through the night, and from every quarter, the noises multiplied — hawkers and barkers, bells and buzzers, laughter and shouts. She doubted anyone would notice the sound of a harp in the midst of the din.

Kester braced a foot upon one of the stool rungs and leaned his instrument against his shoulder. Without fanfare, he placed his hands against the strings, then plucked a rippling chord. As the sweet, lyrical notes filtered over the crowd, the noise dropped off, and Kester looked toward Prissie, a little half-smile on his face. Somehow, she knew that this song was for her, and that something amazing was about to happen.

Leaving off his tuning, the Worshiper launched into a song, and a hush swept the area as people took notice. Again, she recognized the tune from before, but this time, there were words. Prissie didn’t recognize the language, but that didn’t detract from the piercing beauty of the song. Kester’s mellow voice rang clearly in the open air, accompanied by the sweetly rising notes he plucked from the harp’s strings. She’d thought it would take a miracle to get everyone to pay attention, but perhaps the presence of an angel was a miracle in itself. The noises of the fair didn't stop, but they faded into the background.

As a second verse began, it occurred to Prissie that in spite of his reserved nature, Kester found just as much joy in music as Baird, with all his overt enthusiasm. The redhead leaned closer and whispered in her ear, "Watch closely."

At first, there was nothing different, but then she realized that she could see Kester's tattoo-like markings glowing. The curving patterns decorating his back and arms lifted away, passing right through his clothes, spreading as they stretched over his shoulders, unfolding like a graceful set of…

"Wings," she breathed.

"And she gets it in one!" praised Baird in an undertone.

Prissie couldn't tear her eyes away. As Kester extended his wings, shifting shards of color appeared, suspended above him like fragments of a rainbow strung upon threads of lightening.

Each piece was tapered, almost like a feather, but when Kester shook them out, it wasn't anything like the flapping of birds' wings. As they brushed together, Prissie heard the distant notes of wind chimes, a symphony of sounds that added an artless complexity to the harpist's song. Without a doubt, the first people to put stained glass windows in cathedrals had seen the wings of an angel like Kester.

As he began another refrain, Prissie realized that each tiny glass-like pane seemed to be lit from behind, as if the windows offered a glimpse of heaven itself. From deep within, her soul responded with a wordless longing, a homesickness for a place she'd never been. Prissie didn't realize there were tears on her cheeks until Milo leaned across and pressed his handkerchief against her limp fingers. As he pulled back, she grabbed his hand, and he met her gaze steadily, searchingly.

It was silly, really. They'd been telling her as much since the beginning, but for the first time, Prissie found she could believe it completely. "You're *angels*," she whispered in awe.

Milo relaxed imperceptibly at her declaration. With a gentle smile, he said, "Yes, Miss Priscilla, we are."

17

THE GUARDIAN'S VOICE

In the circular chamber with a ring of stones set into the floor, Harken waited restlessly for Abner's arrival. A burst of silvery light resolved itself into the familiar form of the Caretaker, who regarded the Messenger with icy gray eyes. "Why the hasty summons?"

The tall, dark angel stopped his pacing and replied, "Two things. First, Baird says that the breaking point is near, and I wanted to make certain that those things which are concealed remain hidden."

"Without a doubt," Abner replied confidently. "That which is lost may be found, but that which is hidden by God cannot be discovered."

"It is as you say," Harken affirmed. "I suppose recent events have unsettled me."

The Caretaker absently pushed at glasses he wasn't wearing at the moment. "Too many things have been lost."

"Which brings me to the second reason for calling you here. I have good tidings," the Messenger announced. "It's time to renew our search."

Mid-morning on the last day of the fair found Prissie and Jude in the poultry barn, collecting Maddie. Because of the purple ribbon tied to the front of her cage, Jude had been invited to keep her in the barns as a part of their showcase. It was only an Honorary Mention, but Jude consoled himself that the judges had obviously seen just how pretty and smart his chicken was. Since the results had been announced, Tad had taken to referring to the judges as "Judicious and the Right Honorable Madder," which pleased the boy immensely.

"Let me help," Prissie begged, barely holding on to her patience as she watched her littlest brother manhandle the wire cage.

"I can do it," he insisted. "Me and Maddie will be fine."

"Maddie and *I,* and be *careful,*" she said, as she followed him into the broad alley between the barns.

"I will!"

They turned toward the lot where Grandpa's pickup truck was parked. However, they'd only gone a few steps when Jude tripped over his own feet and went sprawling on the straw-scattered pavement. Maddie's cage door flipped open, and the hen tumbled out with a squawk of protest.

"Oh, *no*! Look what you've done!" Prissie said.

Jude's gray eyes widened in dismay. "I'm sorry, Maddie! Are you okay?"

The hen fluffed her feathers and eyed the ground with interest. As soon as she began scratching, Prissie rolled her eyes. "She's obviously fine, but we need to get her back in her cage."

"Help me catch her!"

Maddie had other ideas. As far as she was concerned, a free-range chicken was meant to be free, and she'd had enough of confinement. Prissie made a grab for her, but the hen darted forward, staying just out of reach. Jude chased her along the alley, but she used her wings for an extra burst of speed and circled back toward Prissie. "Maddie, come back!" the little boy urged anxiously. "It's time to go home!"

For the next several minutes, they ran in useless circles. Prissie knew she must look absolutely ridiculous chasing a chicken and was extremely grateful that no one was around to see her. Of course, that was the very moment that Ransom and Marcus rambled past the end of the alley. Clutching at the stitch in her side, Prissie prayed that they'd keep walking, but the boy with two-toned hair punched his companion's shoulder and jerked his head in their direction.

Ransom slowed to a stop, then called, "Need help, Miss Priss?"

"Not from you, I don't," she grumbled under her breath.

Jude wasn't as fussy about where his help came from. "Ransom! Maddie got out!" he shouted urgently.

"Yeah, I can see that," the teen replied, keeping an eye on the loose chicken as he ambled toward them. "She's the one you were bragging on earlier, right? Nice looking bird."

Jude nodded, still frantically following Maddie, but then his lip began to tremble. "It's my fault she got out. Will you help us?"

"No problem," Ransom replied casually. "But I don't know much about catching chickens. Do you have to throw something over her?"

"Go for the legs," Prissie directed.

"If you say so," he shrugged, then angled toward Maddie. "Will it bite?"

"Maddie's a good chicken!" Jude assured.

Prissie propped her hands on her hips and challenged, "Don't tell me you're *afraid* of chickens."

"Gimme a break. I'm not a farmer," Ransom replied. "I just want to know what to expect." He glanced back toward Marcus, who lounged by the end of the building, and asked, "Can you block that end? I'd rather not chase her through the midway."

His friend pushed off the wall. "Yeah, she won't get by me."

Prissie frowned at Marcus and warned, "Don't hurt her!"

Indignation flashed through his eyes, but he held his tongue and stood his ground.

"Lay off Marcus," Ransom said sternly. "If you hadn't noticed, he's *helping*."

"I didn't ask for your help," Prissie snarled.

"No, but your brother did."

He was right, and for Jude's sake, she'd put up with just about anything. "Fine," she snapped. "Let's try chasing her back into the barn. It'll be easier to corner her there."

"Right," he replied.

A wild goose chase might have been easier. The hen managed to stay just out of range, clucking and scolding as she ran in ever-widening circles. "Maddie, c'mere!" Jude coaxed, desperation edging his tone.

Ransom got close enough to swipe at her feet, but with a series of sharp clucks, she launched herself over his head, taking a short flight in her bid to escape. "I didn't know chickens could fly!" he exclaimed, coming out of his duck-and-cover crouch. Meanwhile, Maddie made a beeline toward Marcus. "Heads up!" Ransom called.

"Don't let her through!" Prissie exclaimed.

"Yeah, yeah," called Marcus. He held his arms wide and scowled at the oncoming hen, then barked, "No!"

To Prissie's astonishment, the chicken obeyed. Maddie back-winged, then wheeled to run in the opposite direction. Unfortunately, Maddie didn't give her or Ransom the same courtesy. "Stop!" she shouted.

"Whoa, chicken!" Ransom tried.

"Maddie, not that way!" Jude wailed as his pet raced past them, straight out into the bare field beyond the barns.

"Oh, this is bad," Prissie said worriedly.

Jude stood stock-still in the midst of the passage, clasped his hands together and squeezed his eyes tightly shut. "Please, God, save Maddie," he prayed aloud. "She's just a chicken, so she doesn't know any better."

Ransom quirked a brow at the boy, then asked Prissie, "Now what? Follow?"

Her heart clenched for Jude's sake; her little brother's face was tragic, and she needed to do something. "I'll go after her," she decided aloud. Fixing Ransom with a fierce look, she said, "Take Jude back to my family's stand, and tell Koji that I need him."

"What good will it do if *he's* here?" Ransom asked.

"Just do it!" she yelled over her shoulder, taking off across the field.

He paused uncertainly, then beckoned for Jude to follow him. "Let's go, kid. We could use the extra help." As an afterthought, he called, "Hey, Marcus, go after her!"

His buddy shoved his hands into his jacket pockets and glared toward the forest. "I'll do what I can," he replied, waving Ransom toward the fairgrounds. "Get Jude outta here."

"Thanks, man!"

Prissie jogged across the rough-cut field, trying her best to keep up with Maddie, but the chicken no longer scurried in endless circles; she ran flat-out, her neck low to the ground, as if she was after a grasshopper. The uneven terrain forced Prissie to keep half an eye on her footing as Maddie swerved toward the shelter offered by the pine-covered ridge that loomed nearer with every step. Jude's chicken was acting odd, as if the hounds of hell were at her heels.

"Not in there!" Prissie yelled as the hen reached the boundary, but Maddie quickly disappeared into the forest beyond. She stopped to read one of the bright yellow signs posted at intervals along a barbed wire fence — State Protected Land, No Hunting. The countryside was filled with raccoons, foxes, and coyotes, and even skunks that could be a danger to a lone hen. Prissie needed to protect Maddie from herself because the foolish chicken didn't realize she was headed for trouble.

Prissie glanced back across the empty field toward the fairgrounds, then gathered her courage. She was on her own. This was up to her. Consoling herself that since the signs didn't forbid trespassing, she wasn't *really* doing anything wrong, Prissie pushed apart the wires and stepped through the fence.

Not far ahead, she could hear Maddie's nervous clucking. "Wait, you silly goose!" she called. "Do you know what kinds of things live in here? It's dangerous for chickens!"

Ferns and bracken covered a hillside so steep, Prissie needed to use the surrounding trees to pull herself up the slope. Small branches caught at her hair and skirt and slapped across her bare legs as she followed Maddie's agitated clucking. She didn't see the chicken until she hit upon what seemed to be a deer path hugging the side of the ridge; instead of trying to charge straight up and over, the narrow trail zigzagged steadily higher.

"Maddie, wait up!" Prissie panted as she clambered after the bird. "You'll make Jude sad."

After another switchback, the ground leveled, and she caught up to the black and white hen. Her nervous clucking tapered off, as if she'd reached safety. "Thank goodness," Prissie sighed, then looked around for the first time. They'd climbed much higher than she realized; the wide shelf rose high above the place where she'd entered the forest. *Too* high. Prissie scrambled backward to hug the rocks that lay farthest from the precipitous edge.

Maddie certainly didn't mind the height. The hen was suddenly calm, carelessly skirting the drop-off as she eyed the ground and began to scratch and peck. "At least I'm on solid ground," Prissie muttered, more frightened than she wanted to admit. For Jude's sake, she made an effort, calling out to Maddie in a coaxing voice, "Come back with me; I know the way home!"

The hen clucked indulgently and let her get closer, but before Prissie could snatch at her feet, the chicken threaded her way through a stand of fern and disappeared from view.

When she moved to follow, a deep voice halted her. "Priscilla Pomeroy, *stop!* Please."

She froze in surprise and peeked over her shoulder, then turned around fully to face the stranger who knew her name. Without a doubt, he was the most fearsome person she'd ever seen, and she quickly took a step backward into the ferns.

Prissie's family was tall, but the man who'd followed her up onto the ridge would have towered over her father. The powerfully built, broad-shouldered stranger gazed intently at her with eyes that seemed to be a murky shade of ... *purple*! A leather band across his brow held back the black hair that stood up all around his head, and his clothing was just as outlandish — a warrior's attire, from the soles of his heavy boots to the jewel glittering darkly from the pommel of the sword that peeped at an angle from behind his shoulder.

He shifted his weight from one foot to the other, and Prissie tensed, sure he was going to attack. Instead, the man grimaced and slowly extended one hand as if trying to call her back. "Fear not," he begged gruffly.

Prissie stopped her backward shuffle and cautiously asked, "Who are you?"

"I am Taweel."

She stared hard at him and noticed for the first time that under his breastplate, he wore a tunic similar to the one Koji had worn when she first met him. The raiment shimmered slightly, even in the shade. "You're an angel?" she guessed.

He nodded once and offered, "I am a Guardian in Jedrick's Flight."

Prissie sagged in relief. Baird had mentioned Jedrick, so Taweel was another member of their team. Help had arrived. "I don't suppose you happen to guard chickens?" she asked, pointing in the direction Maddie had run. Taking a large step backward, she continued, "Because I'm trying t—!"

"Wait!" Taweel exclaimed, but it was already too late.

The ground crumbled beneath her feet, and she was falling.

As soon as the world was right-side up again and Prissie caught her breath, she mumbled, "Wh-what happened?"

"You fell," replied Taweel, his deep voice rumbling against her ear.

She wriggled a little and opened her eyes. Just as she suspected, the big Guardian held her in his arms. "You caught me?" she asked blankly, trying to piece together fleeting impressions. "But how is that possible?"

A soft grunt was his only answer, and she gazed up into his craggy face. Thick black eyebrows gave him a brooding look, and faint scars showed here and there against his dusky skin.

"Are you my guardian angel?" she inquired tentatively.

"No."

Prissie was beginning to think that her own Guardian was some kind of deadbeat. Pouting a little, she asked, "Then why are you here?"

"I was Sent."

It was straight and to the point, but it didn't answer enough of the questions swarming through her mind. "*Why* were you sent?" she asked, hoping for more specifics.

"You were in danger."

"From whom?"

Taweel's jaw clenched, and he replied, "The enemy."

That didn't sound good, and suddenly Prissie wasn't sure she *wanted* more answers. Just then, a glimmer of light shone over Taweel's shoulder, and a tiny face appeared, blinking at her with dark eyes. "Hello, little manna-maker," she greeted, quite forgetting the proper term for this sort of angel.

"His name is Omri," Taweel announced.

"Hello, Omri," she said politely, squinting as the tiny figure crawled closer toward the Guardian's ear, then stood, latching onto the silver chain that dangled there, connecting a cuff to the ring that pierced Taweel's lobe. Omri's gossamer hair looked like spun gold and was pulled up into a ponytail that fluttered in the brisk wind.

Prissie stiffened when that particular detail registered. Tilting her head back, she peered past Taweel's bristling hair at the overlapping patterns of smoky purple light that stretched above them. "We're flying," she whispered.

"Yes."

In an instant, Prissie was curled into a ball, her face hidden in her hands. "I don't like high places," she confessed in a trembling voice.

Taweel's arms tightened around her, offering silent reassurance. A moment later, Prissie felt something warm pat against her hands, and when she peeped between her fingers, Omri was waiting there, a quizzical expression of concern on his face.

"You wouldn't understand," Prissie muttered glumly. "You've got wings!"

She felt Taweel turn in the sky and glanced up at his outspread wings. They didn't flap; instead, they shifted as if to catch invisible air currents. He wheeled slowly, gliding far above the trees. Finally, he spoke. "When the others have driven back the enemy, I will return to the earth. Until then, you *are* safe."

Prissie stared up at him, and he met her eyes reluctantly. "I know," she said softly. "But if it's all the same to you, I'm not looking down."

His gaze shifted self-consciously, and he replied with another vague grunt.

Glad for a distraction, Prissie coaxed Omri into her hands and cradled the pixie-like creature to her chest. He grabbed a hold of her thumb, hugging it fiercely and rubbing his cheek against its pad. She smiled at his antics, and he beamed up at her — quite literally.

"They get brighter when they are happy," Taweel remarked.

"He's humming, too," she replied. "Does that mean something?"

"Omri takes great delight in fulfilling his purpose."

Prissie frowned in confusion. "Isn't his job to make manna?"

Taweel peered down at the little yahavim. "If you were hungry, he would feed you. Omri is responding to a more urgent need."

"What?" she asked wonderingly.

The tiny angel looked expectantly into Taweel's face, and the Guardian replied, "He knew you needed something to hold onto."

By the time Taweel began his slow descent, Prissie had decided that yahavim were even better than kittens and wondered if Abner could be coaxed into loaning her one of his flock. The thought of pets suddenly reminded her of the reason why she was here in the first place. "Maddie!" she gasped, looking fearfully into Taweel's face. "I forgot all about Maddie! Jude will be heartbroken if I don't bring her home!"

"Milo is the swiftest in our Flight," the Guardian replied calmly. "He was Sent for her."

He angled his wings, and they dipped lower, skimming over the tops of trees. Prissie squeezed her eyes tightly shut and didn't open them again until Taweel traded his smooth gliding for a measured stride upon solid ground.

When Prissie opened her eyes, the first person she spied was Milo, whose jeans bore an impressive grass stain. Maddie was tucked securely under his arm, and he hurried toward them across the meadow. "Miss Priscilla!" he exclaimed. "I see you've met Taweel."

She nodded numbly as Taweel set her on her feet.

At that moment, two more angels strode out of the trees to join them on the edge of the field, and she gasped. Like Taweel, the newcomers were unusually tall, and this time, there was no mistaking them for anything other than angels. Both had their wings unfurled, though not extended for flight. Shifting mantles of light trailed behind them like capes.

Prissie edged a little closer to Milo just as Omri wriggled free of her grasp and darted forward to intercept the oncoming figures. The little yahavim flew in dizzy loops that seemed to be a greeting. "Who are they?" she whispered.

"You can see them?" he asked in surprise.

"Obviously," she muttered.

"Jedrick and Tamaes," Milo answered simply.

They approached with swords in hand, alert gazes sweeping the landscape, which seemed peaceful enough to Prissie. The taller one's well-muscled arms were bared and probably would have been tattooed if his vibrant green wings hadn't been on display. Light brown hair streaked with gold was cropped short except for a single lock, which hung in a braid over his left shoulder. When they reached her and Milo, this stern-faced warrior gazed down at her with piercing eyes — green flecked with gold. "Are you well, Priscilla Pomeroy?" he demanded in a surprisingly gentle voice.

"I'm fine … thanks to Taweel," she replied a little nervously. These new angels were really very intimidating.

"Miss Priscilla, this is Jedrick, our captain," Milo introduced.

"You have been causing quite a stir," the leader remarked.

She looked around in confusion. The sky was blue, the grass was green, the sun was high, and the shadows were few. "I don't see anything dangerous," she ventured.

Jedrick sheathed his sword and said, "Be grateful you cannot see. The Fallen are fearsome, twisted creatures."

"They've been driven back for the time being," Milo explained quietly.

"Is everything okay?" Prissie timidly asked the mailman when the three warrior-like angels drew aside to compare notes.

The Messenger's usual smile was tainted by sadness. "No, but you're safe, and for that I'm grateful."

She tugged at his sleeve and immediately felt childish, but Milo and Maddie were the only familiar things in the midst of strange people and stranger ideas. Clinging to the safety he represented, Prissie whispered, "Have these guys been around the whole time, and I just couldn't see them before?"

"Something like that," Milo admitted. "They're members of our Flight."

"Is that like a team?"

"Yes. Each team is comprised of a Flight of angels," Milo confirmed.

"These guys don't look anything like you and Harken, or Baird and Kester."

"No, they wouldn't. They don't need to fit in. They need to fight."

"Taweel said he's a Guardian, but he's not mine," Prissie shared.

Milo nodded patiently. "That's right."

"Whose is he?"

"That's not my story to tell," the Messenger replied gently.

"Oh, so, what about him?" she asked, nodding toward Jedrick. "Is he a Guardian, too?"

"Jedrick is a Protector — a warrior who battles against the Fallen," Milo explained.

"What's the difference?"

The Messenger considered, then replied, "Focus, I suppose. A Guardian concentrates on his charge, but a Protector's eyes are always searching for the enemy."

"Enemy? Do you mean the Fallen?"

"Yes."

"So, you're saying that there were demons here?" she demanded, her voice rising.

"Yes, Miss Priscilla, there were."

"Why?"

Jedrick approached and answered for the Messenger. "That is not entirely clear."

"But you're in charge, so shouldn't you *know*?" she argued.

"I am neither all-seeing nor all-knowing."

"But aren't you guys well-connected with someone who is?"

The captain met Prissie's defensive gaze with a serious expression, and Prissie wondered if she had pushed too far. However, he calmly answered, "We were given as much as we needed to know in order to do that which we were Sent to do."

"And what was that?" she asked more meekly.

"Protect you," Jedrick replied.

"And catch Maddie," added Milo.

"Oh." Prissie peeped toward the other warrior-like angel. His auburn hair was sleek and straight, falling well past his shoulders and arranged so that it partially obscured the long, jagged scar that ran down the left side of his face. His armor was similar to that worn by his companions — fitted leather studded with metallic disks that gleamed dully in the sunlight. His wings fell from his shoulders in mingling shades of bittersweet and amber.

Milo guided Prissie over and announced, "And this is Tamaes."

He stepped forward, and after a moment of quiet consideration, Tamaes silently extended his hand.

Prissie offered her own, and as he gently grasped it, a soft smile played at the corners of his mouth. His reddish brown eyes gazed down at her with such warmth, she needed to look away, so she stared instead at the large, sun-browned hand enfolding hers. With a small squeeze, he said, "Do not be afraid."

She glanced up, then realized that everyone was watching the exchange with keen interest. "I'm not," Prissie protested, looking to Milo for support. He nodded reassuringly, and she fully faced the angel holding her hand. "Were you hurt?"

Tamaes brushed his fingers across his marred cheek. "A long time ago."

The scar looked terrible, and Prissie hesitated to ask her next question. "How were you hurt?"

"I was defending someone precious."

Milo helpfully explained, "Though his teammates are always close by, a Guardian is sometimes called upon to battle a Fallen to protect his charge."

"You're a Guardian, too?" she asked glancing toward the gruff angel who'd caught her.

"Yes," Tamaes said. "Taweel is my mentor." He dropped his gaze. Releasing her hand, he stepped back and rejoined the other two warriors.

For the next few minutes, Prissie couldn't shake the feeling that the auburn-haired angel was looking at her, but eventually, she decided that he was studiously *not* looking at her. None of the others were paying her half as much attention, and they had no trouble meeting her gaze. It was strange. Either Tamaes was incredibly rude or incredibly shy, and she suspected the latter. Also, there was something vaguely familiar about him, though she couldn't quite put her finger on what. Finally, Prissie nudged Milo and whispered, "What's *with* him?"

The Messenger looked at her in surprise, then realized what she meant. With a chuckle, he confided, "Guardians are notoriously bashful. I suppose it's too much to expect him to speak up on his own. Come on."

Adjusting his grip on Maddie, he led her back to Tamaes, who apparently knew what was coming. He murmured, "Thank you, Milo."

"My pleasure," he replied, placing his hand on the Guardian's shoulder before turning to Prissie. "I wish I had the words to convey to you just how momentous this is.

Meetings between people and Messengers are rare enough, but this is such a precious thing."

"Milo, you *already* introduced us," Prissie muttered, feeling awkward.

"Yes, but I left out the important part!"

A tiny suspicion stirred in her soul, and she looked up into the Guardian's eyes, searching for confirmation. Milo didn't even need to say it before she *knew*.

"Miss Priscilla, Tamaes is *your* guardian angel."

Milo escorted Prissie back to the edge of the fairgrounds, where Grandpa and Jude anxiously waited. Her youngest brother whooped for joy as soon as he caught sight of Maddie. Grinning toward the sky, he called, "Thank you, God!" and came running to meet them.

"You should thank Milo," Prissie chided.

The mailman chuckled and said, "It's all the same to me."

Still, Jude gave Milo's leg a fierce hug, then squeezed his sister for good measure. Prissie glanced around. "Where's Ransom?"

"Him and Marcus had to go," the little boy replied.

"He and Marcus," Prissie automatically corrected. It didn't surprise her at all that she'd been abandoned in her time of need. Marcus was practically a stranger. At least Ransom had gotten her message through.

Grandpa beckoned the mailman over so they could get Maddie back into her cage for the ride home. Jude followed Milo, not wanting to stray far from his beloved chicken, and while they were busy, Koji stepped forward. It occurred to Prissie that he was being unusually quiet, and she wondered how much he already knew about what had happened on the ridge. At a loss for what to say, she settled on an awkward, "Hi."

"Prissie?" he began, gazing at her with his hopeful expression. "May I express my relief as well?"

"I ... guess." If she'd known what he meant, she probably would have refused, but an instant later, it was too late. Koji's arms wrapped around her, and he hugged her even more tightly than Jude had.

"I was afraid," he confessed, his face hidden against her shoulder.

Could angels be afraid? Apparently so, for the young angel was trembling. She tried to reassure him, awkwardly patting his back. "It wasn't that bad."

"If you had seen what I saw ..." he protested, shaking his head. "Shimron told me that friendship would bring both joy and sorrow, but I did not understand until now. It has never been so difficult to watch and wait!"

Prissie gave in and hugged Koji back a little. "I'm obviously safe. Nothing bad could have happened. Not really."

Just then, Milo placed his hand on Koji's head and ruffled his hair. "We'll be along, Pete," he called.

Prissie looked helplessly toward her grandfather, who was ready to head to the truck. Grandpa Pete harrumphed as he always did over open displays of affection before leading Jude away.

Koji reluctantly released Prissie and urgently met her baffled gaze. "You saw some of our warriors, didn't you? Do you think they carry weapons for no reason? The threat is as real as we are!"

"I think I'm ready to go home, now," she announced.

Looking from one to the other, she repeated. “I want to go home.”

Koji closed his mouth and lowered his eyes, and Milo quietly replied, “I understand.”

Prissie nodded briskly and turned her back on the whole frightening morning.

18

THE FICKLE FRIEND

Jedrick gazed down at Tamaes, who sat upon the sloping roof just beyond the bright pattern of colors created by the light shining from Prissie's bedroom window. "You seem rattled," the Protector remarked.

The Guardian stared at his hands, which were loosely laced before him. Eventually, he dipped his head. "A little."

"This is the second time you were able to meet Prissie." With a faint smile, Jedrick remarked, "I remember how dismayed you were the last time."

Tamaes huffed in amusement. "She cried."

"And this time?"

The Guardian ducked his head and softly said, "She smiled."

Choosing a seat beside the other angel, Jedrick frankly

broached, "There is said to be a danger amongst Guardians. When they place too much importance on their charge, they lose sight of God."

Leaning back to gaze into the spread of stars overhead, Tamaes lightly traced the scar that cut down his right cheek. "I am well aware of this, Captain."

"I know," Jedrick acknowledged. "However, I would be a poor leader if I did not address the matter."

"I shall remain Faithful."

With a nod, the Protector moved on. "Several in our Flight have already befriended Prissie, and I see no reason why you cannot do the same."

Silence lingered long, but Tamaes finally broke it, wryly admitting, "That may be why I am rattled."

Usually after the fair closed, summer's excitement fizzled away, but Prissie's mind still whirled with new faces, half-formed fears, and an unsettling suspicion that even if she wished it, none of the strange things she'd seen were going to fade away. Maybe it would be better if they did, like waking from a bad dream.

But was it *all* bad?

"No," she sighed, staring hard at her bedroom ceiling. Still, Prissie would have been happier if she could pick and choose the parts that involved her — the friendly, smiling, happy parts. Determined to put the previous days' events behind her, she thrust all thoughts of angels from her mind.

Prissie wandered downstairs in the vague hopes that Momma would be able to suggest something to do. A little excitement might be nice, just not the kind that involved death-defying tumbles, ominous warnings, and keen-edged swords.

She found Momma and Grandma Nell on the back porch, sipping iced tea on the slowly swaying swing. Her grandmother was casually flipping through the pages of Beau's new book about Sunderland State Park, but she glanced up over her reading glasses and blandly remarked, "Here comes another one."

One look at her daughter, and Momma smiled knowingly. "You look restless."

"I'm bored," grumbled Prissie.

Grandma Nell chuckled. "I can't believe you young ones! Anyone with sense would thank heaven for a quiet place to collapse after all the flimflam and folderol of the fair, but here you come, begging for more!"

"But there's nothing to do!"

"Oh, there's always something that needs doing," her grandmother retorted, a teasing sparkle in her eyes. "Are you looking for extra chores?"

"Something *fun*," she hastily amended.

"Why don't you call Margery?" Momma suggested. "You two are usually full of plans about how to spend your last free days before school starts."

Prissie gave her a pained look. "She's probably busy."

Momma chased a droplet of condensation down the side of her glass with one finger, then casually asked, "Did something happen with Margery the other day? You left with one set of friends and came back with another." Studying her daughter's face, she added, "Neil seemed to think you had a falling out."

"Since when does Neil know anything about anything?" Prissie snapped, upset that he'd tattled.

"He was only passing along something that nice young man Baird said," Naomi explained, her voice soft.

Momma always did get quieter when she scolded, and Prissie knew she was pushing it. Still, her tone sharpened defensively. "He has no right to stick his nose into other people's problems!"

"So there *is* a problem." Momma shook her head and prompted, "What happened, sweetheart?"

Prissie only hesitated a little. It felt good to finally tell someone. Momma and Grandma listened patiently as she explained how awful Margery's birthday party had been. Being looked down on, left out, and laughed at — maybe they were small things, but they hurt in a big way. "It's like they've forgotten all about me!" she exclaimed bitterly.

"Then maybe it's time to remind them," Momma suggested. "Do something to show them you still want to be friends."

"Like what?"

Grandma Nell interjected, "It's not like you to sit back and wait for your friends. Don't you usually keep them organized."

Prissie nodded slowly as she thought back. "I did have lots of fun things planned, but right around the middle of summer, everyone was suddenly too busy." It had been frustrating to hear nothing but *no* and *not this time* from Margery and the others, so she'd stopped asking. "Maybe I gave up."

"Try, try again," Momma cheerfully rejoined. "Why don't you invite the girls to the mall?"

"When?"

"The longer you put off reconnecting, the harder it will be," Grandma Nell warned.

Prissie's mother brightly agreed. "There's no time like the present!"

"Today?"

"It's short notice, but why not?" Momma replied encouragingly. "Go see if they're free, and we'll take it from there."

"I thought you were tired," Prissie said, dragging her feet just a little.

"Completely exhausted," her mother acknowledged, waving her toward the door. "Which is why I'll bribe Tad into playing chauffeur if you can get a group together."

Grandma Nell closed the oversized book she'd been perusing and extended it. "Put this in the office for me on your way to the phone?"

Prissie was grateful for the advice, but it didn't really make it any easier for her to make the first move. She shouldn't have to remind Margery, April, and Jennifer that they were friends — should she? But a trip to the mall would be the perfect distraction.

In the end, Prissie couldn't quite summon up the nerve to call. Instead, she fired up the family computer in the little office area off the kitchen and copied them all on an email instead. Down in West Edinton, three cell phones were undoubtedly alerting their owners to new messages.

While she waited for a response, Prissie idly turned the pages of the big book Grandma had passed along. It was the one Harken had given Beau. Apparently, the nearby state park's property had once belonged to A. J. Sunderland, one of West Edinton's founders. She'd always liked the hiking trails that meandered through the nearby woodlands, and she could remember camping there a few times when she was little. Near the center of the book, Prissie found a fold-out map of part of Sunderland's impressive cave system and traced her finger along the maze of tunnels that apparently stretched for miles.

Just then, the computer chimed, and she felt a zing of excitement. April had responded! Clicking the message, Prissie smiled triumphantly. Jennifer was over at April's house, and they were both bored to tears. They could meet up. The sooner, the better!

Margery's reply came through a few minutes later, also agreeing to the plan. Margery used to use a lot more exclamation points, maybe because shopping was involved. Still, a yes was a yes.

She was just logging out when Koji tapped on the door frame. "Are you going somewhere, Prissie?"

Not quite meeting his gaze, she said, "Yes. I'm going to the mall with my friends."

"May I accompany you?"

Prissie appreciated everything Koji had done for her, but she replied, "Not this time. Girls only."

Momma leaned into the office niche and announced, "Your brother is ready and willing, but you'll need to leave on the early side so he can put gas in the van."

"Thanks," Prissie replied with a weak smile.

Koji's steady gaze was discomfiting. "Tad is not a girl."

"He doesn't count!" she exclaimed defensively. "He's our driver."

Nodding, the young angel solemnly said, "I understand. Please, be careful."

As soon as he excused himself, Prissie wished she'd been more honest with Koji. She felt guilty, especially since she knew what it was like being left out, and she was kicking herself for using the very words she'd come to hate — *not this time*. In trying to prove she still fit in with her old friends, she'd pushed away her new one.

The mall was packed with teenagers also making the most of their last week of summer vacation. To Prissie's delight, Jennifer wore a long, crinkly skirt with little seashells stitched along its hem. "I bought it at the *cutest* little shop close to the beach!" she enthused, twirling to show off her summery souvenir.

Prissie exclaimed over the perfect little seashell earrings that matched. "It's perfect! You look beautiful!"

Her friend's big, brown eyes took on a happy shine, and she linked arms with Prissie, pledging, "We're gonna have so much fun today! I'm *so* glad you called! There was absolutely nothing else to do!"

April gave the girl a poke and demanded, "Coming over to my house was nothing?"

"Your house doesn't have a coffee shop, summer clearances, or cute guys!" Jennifer argued.

Prissie glanced after their driver, who'd manfully escaped in the direction of the food court. "Are you talking about my brother?"

"Not Tad," she giggled. "I was talking about hypothetical boys. You never know who we might see at the mall!"

"Hypothetical, huh?" April countered with a smirk. "Are you sure you're not thinking of someone in particular?"

Margery glanced up from her cell phone and remarked, "I think it's pretty obvious who she's hoping to see. Jennifer has a one-track mind."

"Right up until she changes it!" April teased.

Jennifer giggled all the more, and Prissie smiled. It was almost like old times. Almost. Despite being exactly where she wanted to be, and with the people she wanted to be close to, something felt a little odd. Without meaning to, she found herself scanning the crowds and wondering if everyone's guardian angels were camped out on the roof. The middle of the mall was spacious enough for flight. Even now, it could be a battlefield.

"Oooh, he's gorgeous!" Jennifer swooned, her gaze fixed upward as they rode an escalator down.

"Interesting fashion sense," April remarked, tapping Prissie's shoulder to get her attention. "You two match."

By the time she figured out where to look, the young man had turned away, so she only caught a glimpse of sleek, dark hair and a shirt in the same rich shade of violet as hers. Prissie's heart gave a little leap, for she was almost positive it had been Adin.

"I saw him earlier, outside the dressing rooms," Margery interjected.

"Maybe he's following us!" giggled Jennifer.

April snorted. "Even if he's pretty to look at, that would be creepy."

Prissie hadn't wanted anything supernatural to follow her to the mall, but Adin fit neatly into the category of pleasant angelic encounters. "I hope we see him again," she murmured.

They wandered through shops for a couple of hours, then agreed it was high time for a treat. Migrating toward a popular establishment on the first floor, they ordered iced coffees and crowded around one of the tiny tables out front to watch passersby. Prissie was still on the lookout for men in violet shirts.

"Omigosh! Did you see him?" Jennifer squealed.

"Can you be more specific?" April asked, glancing around quizzically. "There are a lot of guys to choose from."

"The gorgeous stalker again?" Margery guessed.

"Marcus!" the girl hissed, her eyes wide. "I can't believe he's actually here! And he was looking right at me! Omigosh!"

"Marcus from our class Marcus?" Prissie checked, trying to keep the incredulity from her tone.

"More like *the* Marcus," April replied. "And I don't see him. Are you sure you're not hallucinating, Jennifer? It's a dangerous business, mixing caffeine and crushes."

"He was right up there a second ago!" Pointing to the mall's second level, she muttered, "And of course I'm sure!"

"He's hard to miss with that hair," Prissie reasoned, scanning the upper walkway.

"I know!" crooned Jennifer, a dreamy expression on her face. "I wonder why he's here."

"Destiny," April deadpanned. "Or there's the remote possibility that he has shopping to do. How about we ask him?"

Shaking her head, Jennifer mournfully said, "He's gone."

"He can't have gotten far," April challenged.

"You wouldn't!"

"Wouldn't I?"

"Dare you to," Margery interjected, egging them on.

"Done!" April had never been shy about approaching people, and she was on her feet in a moment. Slinging her bag over her shoulder, she loudly announced, "I'll just go say hello!"

When she sauntered off without a backward glance, Jennifer wailed in dismay and snatched up her various bags before chasing after her. Shaking her head, Prissie remarked, "I can't believe she's being so silly over someone like Marcus."

Margery's green eyes were oddly flat. "You're one to talk. When we were kids, you were in love with the mailman."

Whether intended or not, the barb cut deeply, and it took a while for Prissie to work around the sudden tightness in her throat. "You're right," she managed. "I shouldn't criticize."

Her friend shrugged and carelessly said, "At least Marcus is good looking."

Prissie wanted to defend Milo somehow, but to do so would mean confessing too much. Valiantly changing the subject, she asked, "Do you have any shopping you need to do?"

"Not really," Margery replied, sounding bored. "I was here yesterday."

"Oh." Her mind was a blank, so she sipped her iced coffee in awkward silence. When her friend's phone gave a perky *ching-a-ring*, Prissie honestly thought she'd been saved by the bell. Margery whipped it out and smiled at the display. "Message?" Prissie politely inquired.

"Yep."

"Is it April?"

"Nope," Margery replied, slinging her purse strap over her shoulder and standing. "Come on."

"But what if they come back, and we're gone?"

Rolling her eyes, she held up her phone. "All they have to do is call, and we'll tell them where we are!"

Feeling stupid, Prissie mumbled, "Obviously." Margery headed straight for the main entrance, and she had to lengthen her strides to keep up. "Where are we going?" she finally asked.

Her friend didn't answer. She was too busy waving to someone leaning against the wall just inside the bank of sliding doors. "Elise! You made it!"

"I pulled it off," she said.

Margery turned to Prissie and smiled sweetly. "It turns out Elise could come, too."

"It's not like you guys were excluding me on purpose," Elise said.

At a loss for what else to say, Prissie lamely said, "Hello. It's nice to see you again."

Hooking her arm through the other girl's, Margery demanded, "Where were you all morning?"

"Out."

"Doing what?"

"Stuff," Elise replied with a haughty glance that suggested she wasn't going to say anything while Prissie was in earshot.

Although she'd thought Margery was being unusually quiet, Prissie felt sick when her best friend suddenly transformed into her old, chatterbox self, gushing with news as she led Elise toward the glass elevators. Her steps lagged as the other two girls boarded. Elise quirked a brow. "Are you coming, or what?"

Prissie shot a pleading look at Margery, who knew about her fear of heights. The message carried across, and Margery exclaimed, "Oh! That's right!" However, instead of getting off, she nodded toward the high-end department store at the far end of the mall and said, "We'll be up in the makeup department. Catch up to us there."

"Or not!" Elise added with a smirk. And the doors slid shut.

Too stunned to move, Prissie watched the elevator soar upward without her.

"That wasn't very nice." Prissie turned in surprise to find

Adin standing nearby, also watching the elevator's ascent. His gaze slanted her way, and he mildly inquired, "Friends of yours?"

"Not so much," she murmured, grateful that God had again seen fit to send reinforcements. With a wan smile, she asked, "Are you here to keep me company?"

Glancing around, he remarked, "Since you're suddenly on your own, how can I do otherwise? It'll give us the chance to catch up!"

"I'd like that," she admitted, grateful that Adin had showed up right when she'd needed him most. Only Koji would have been more welcome right now. Unlike Margery, he was a friend she could count on.

As if he could read her mind, Adin remarked, "I hear you're keeping an Observer around the house these days."

"Koji," she replied warmly.

"I see he's endeared himself to you," he said with a soft laugh.

Smiling readily, she explained, "We're friends."

"I'm surprised he isn't with you."

Prissie looked away sheepishly. "Oh, he would have been, but it's just girls today."

Adin leaned down in order to get her to meet his gaze. "Are you regretting that choice?"

"Just a little."

His brows lifted, and she blushed.

"Okay, maybe a lot."

They strolled along companionably. "The two of you must be close."

"I guess." Was it possible to be closer to Koji, someone she'd only known for a few weeks, than to Margery, someone she'd known for years? That's certainly how she felt. Prissie suddenly realized why Adin's assessment rang true. "I trust him."

"Naturally," Adin rejoined. "The Faithful are faithful, after all!"

"Oh, right," she murmured, embarrassed to have taken so long to come to such an obvious conclusion.

"I'm sure he trusts you, as well."

"I suppose." Prissie wasn't so sure Koji could count on her, not when she was so frightened by what friendship with him might lead to. The Faithful were one thing, but the Fallen were another. Getting mixed up in an invisible war sounded like a very bad idea.

"Prissie?" She nearly bumped into Adin, who'd swung around to face her. "You're not listening to me," he scolded in sing-song tones.

"Sorry. What?"

"I was only saying that good friends often trade secrets."

Color rose in her cheeks as Prissie recalled some of the secrets she'd entrusted to Margery. Would the girl keep them even if their friendship ended, or would they be betrayed to the likes of Elise?

Adin's brows lifted inquiringly. "Is that a yes?"

"Naturally," she murmured, unconsciously borrowing his word. "The longer you know someone, the more secrets you share."

Suddenly, something bright zipped between them, and they both stepped back in surprise. More dazzling lights arrowed past, like so many shooting stars. Prissie gasped in delight and backed up even further to watch a cluster of yahavim spiral toward the ceiling far overhead. "Did you see? I wonder what they're doing here!"

Her companion laughed lightly and said, "It seems a new escort has arrived."

More tiny angels darted in from every direction, as if drawn by the others. Several tapped her, as if to say, *I found you!* She smiled at their antics, and her heart melted every time one smiled back. The only problem was, the more of them there were, the brighter it became.

"Since these little ones seem to think you need them, I'll leave you to their tender mercies!"

"Thank you, Adin." With a slightly harried smile, she earnestly said, "You always seem to cheer me up."

"Don't mention it," he demurred. "And don't be afraid to get closer to your Observer friend. Something tells me his secrets will be well worth finding out!"

More little manna-makers rushed around her, and Prissie was nearly blinded by their combined glory. Trying to act naturally in case anyone was looking, she slipped into a long, empty hall with lockers, pay phones, and an exit sign flickering at the far end. Blinking away the spots that danced before her eyes, she quietly demanded, "What's gotten into you guys?"

When Prissie held out her hands, two of the tiny angels settled on her palms. She didn't really recognize them, but that didn't stop her from enjoying their company. She seemed to have attracted an entire flock, and their soft humming and affectionate gestures banished many of her fears. Even at the mall, God was watching over her.

All at once, the yahavim scattered, just as someone swung around the corner, nearly knocking her off her feet. Hands grabbed her shoulders, and a gruff voice muttered, "That was close." Prissie stared blankly into the scowling face of Marcus Truman. "You okay?" he asked.

Badly startled and more than a little afraid, she twisted away from him, demanding, "Get away from me!"

"'Scuse me," he quickly apologized, holding up his hands. "Didn't mean to scare you."

Prissie glanced around, wondering where all the manna-makers had disappeared to. Had Marcus's arrival driven them off? With the beginnings of a very bad feeling in the pit of her stomach, she edged toward the safety in numbers that the mall offered.

Her classmate shoved his hands into the pockets of his leather jacket and bluntly asked, "Do you think maybe you could call off that friend of yours?"

"Jennifer?"

"That's the one," he confirmed.

"Oh." With a glance down the empty hallway, Prissie asked, "Are you hiding from her?"

"Sorta. Are you?"

She shook her head. "We were separated."

"No kidding," he muttered, looking disgusted. "Try the food court."

"Why?" she asked suspiciously.

He grumbled something under his breath, but his answer was civil enough. "Because I last saw her in the food court with April. They were talking to your brother."

With a hasty word of thanks, she fled, wanting nothing more than to reach Tad and convince him it was time to go home. Although she hated to admit it, hiding was exactly what she wanted to do right now.

19

THE SUMMER'S END

Jedrick," the Fallen said, pleased when Ephron twitched at the name. "He's your captain. No ... he *was* your captain. I've been looking into the members of your former Flight."

His prisoner turned his face to the wall.

"Such an unusual group, with a shocking number of Grafts." His voice dripped with sweet poison. "But there's someone even rarer under his watch-care, isn't there, Ephron?"

The Observer sat rigidly against the wall of the pit, his breaths shallow due to pain, or possibly fear.

"*Two* someones!" he revealed, exulting in his discovery.

Ephron sagged a little, resting his forehead against his prison wall.

His captor scowled, for the whelp's reaction felt more like

relief than resignation. Features twisting into an ugly mask, he spat, "You served with two Caretakers, yet you fester in this hole! What more proof do you need that God has turned his back on you?"

This time, the angel turned his bandaged face toward his tormentor. Lifting his pointed chin, he spoke in a light voice left ragged by pain, yet filled with grim resolve. "Even so, I will remain faithful."

One day followed the next, and Prissie kept waiting for something else to happen, but it didn't. Her family went on as if everything was perfectly normal, and after all the excitement, she found the ordinariness of the week reassuring. From sunup to sundown, Grandma Nell kept her running between the garden and kitchen and from the kitchen to the cellar, where long shelves were filling up with jars of summer's bounty. Same old, same old had never been more welcome.

While Prissie's hands were busy, she tried very hard not to think about angels with swords, invisible wars, and the existence of demons. It was *much* nicer to dwell on visions of rainbow-hued wings, the elusive sweetness of manna, and the feel of Omri's tiny arms wrapped around her thumb. As she carried quart jars of tomatoes down the basement stairs, she sighed and muttered, "It's no use. I can't un-know what I know."

There were things out there that were bad enough to make Koji tremble and to rob Milo of his smile. Protectors and Guardians carried weapons and bore the scars of battle because the conflict was real and closer to home than she'd ever imagined. But at the same time, there were good things that she didn't want to give up. While she added to the neat rows of canned fruits and vegetables, she put together a wish list. "I want to hear Kester play every kind of instrument, and ask Harken if I can go through the blue door again, and see if any of the little angels in Abner's flock are as nice as Omri, and hear Baird's songs, and see Milo's wings, and tell Tamaes that I think I remember him a little."

She hadn't seen any sign of her guardian angel since they'd been introduced. To be honest, Prissie was relieved. It had been weird enough to deal with the invasion of her privacy that Koji represented, but what was she supposed to do about an invisible protector who had been with her since she was born? Sure, he existed to protect her, but he was still a *guy*. While she appreciated knowing her guardian angel's identity, the whole situation was awkward.

Still, Milo had called their meeting *precious*. Not a word she would have used, but Prissie had a vague idea that the Messenger had been looking at things from Tamaes' point of view. Suddenly, it occurred to her that her reaction had probably been a big disappointment for the Guardian. For days, she'd been pretending he wasn't there. Had she hurt his feelings in the process?

Prissie peered uncertainly around the cellar. Light from two bare bulbs gleamed off of whitewashed stone in the cool, slightly musty storeroom. She certainly felt alone, but that didn't necessarily mean she was. "Are you here, Tamaes?" she whispered.

No answer came.

A moment later, footsteps sounded on the stairs, and Koji called, "Prissie?"

"Y-yeah?" she replied, feeling a little guilty without knowing why.

Since the events at the fair, Koji had been the one constant reminder of the presence of angels. He sat across from her at meals and helped her in the garden, but he was also holding back. She thought he always looked as if he wanted to say something, but he held his peace, spending more and more time with her brothers. Maybe it was her imagination, but it felt as though the young angel was waiting for her. If only she had a clue what he wanted.

Koji stopped partway down the stairs and sat, wrapping his arms around his knees. "Do you need help?"

"Not really. I just finished."

He considered her solemnly, then announced, "It would be just as silly to pray to an angel as it would be to pray to your cat."

"I wasn't!" she protested. "Not *really*. I was just checking?"

With a nod, Koji said, "I understand, Prissie. I simply wish to make sure that *you* understand."

"How did you know I was down here?"

"I was Sent."

"So you're a Messenger now, too?" she asked lightly.

"Indeed," he replied with a brightening smile. "Speaking of which, the mail will be here in a few minutes. Will you come with me to see Milo?"

"Oh." She'd been avoiding the mailbox — and the mailman — all week, and it was no shock that the Observer had noticed. It wasn't that she was angry with Milo or anything like that. Prissie had just needed some time to get used to the new ideas they'd dumped on her. There it was. With a long-suffering sigh, she tucked her skirt around her legs and sat next to Koji on the stair. They'd been giving her a little time and space, and he wanted to know if it had been enough. "I guess I haven't seen him in a while."

"Does that mean yes?" he asked hopefully.

"Obviously."

"Good."

With slow steps, they followed the narrow lane through the orchard, she in the left-hand track, and he in the right. Nothing much was said, but that was fine. This was one of those times when being together was enough. It was a friendly sort of silence.

When they arrived at the dirt road, they could just hear the rumble of an engine in the direction of the highway, so they hurried toward the twin mailboxes and climbed onto the plank fence behind them.

Milo pulled up and leaned out the car window. "Hey there, Miss Priscilla! Long time, no see!"

"It hasn't been *that* long," she huffed, fiddling with the end of her braid.

The mailman turned off his engine and hopped out of the car. "Guess it just felt that way," he replied with an amiable smile. He handed off his last mail delivery of the day. "How have you been?"

"Busy." It was small talk, and it wasn't what she *really* wanted to say at all. Gathering her courage, she asked, "Do you have time to visit?"

"I have nowhere else to be," he replied casually. Milo climbed up on the fence to sit on Koji's other side. "What's on your mind?" he invited.

The admission wasn't easy, and it came out as a whisper. "I don't know what to do about Tamaes."

"Do?" the Messenger echoed, clearly confused.

"There's a big *guy* following me around everywhere," she whispered urgently. "It's like having an invisible stalker. *Please* tell me he stays out of my room." Prissie's eyes widened in dismay, and she hissed, "and the *bathroom*!"

Mercifully, Milo didn't laugh. "Didn't you share these concerns with Koji?"

"She has been avoiding me as well," the young apprentice announced bluntly.

Prissie wrinkled her nose at him, and Milo sighed. "If I had considered things from your point of view, I would have spoken sooner," he assured. "I'm sorry you've been worrying needlessly over this."

Needlessly sounded promising, and she perked up a bit.

The mailman nodded approvingly and said, "You are *very* special to Tamaes. He's known you since the moment you were conceived, and he will remain by your side throughout this life. He's never far from you, but that doesn't mean he's shadowing your every step. For instance, he's not here at the moment."

"Isn't he supposed to be?"

"Oh, he's here," Milo said, waving in the general direction of the farmhouse. "He's just not *right here* with us. If you think about it, there are ten Pomeroys living here, each with a Guardian of their own. These angels work together, establishing a hedge of protection around your home."

"And when Dad leaves for work?" she asked.

"His Guardian travels with him, and joins the group who watches over the other members of the bakery staff."

"It sounds sort of crowded."

Milo laughed and said, "Very."

Koji swung his legs back and forth and commented, "Milo has a Guardian, too."

"You do?" Prissie asked.

The mailman's blue eyes sparkled. "Unofficially, yes. He really should show himself since Miss Priscilla has already been introduced."

"Oh!" she gasped as Taweel appeared, sitting on the roof of Milo's car, his elbows resting on his knees. He cast a moody glance at his teammates, as if he resented being tattled on. In the next instant, Omri flitted into view, zooming in excited circles around the three fence-sitters before settling in his favorite spot upon the big Guardian's shoulder. Briefly meeting Prissie's astonished gaze, he inclined his head in greeting. "Hello, again," she murmured back.

"Taweel has been watching out for me since, well, since midsummer," Milo explained.

"Don't you have a person to look after?" Prissie asked curiously.

"No," Taweel replied shortly. He stole a glance at her out of the corner of his eye and grudgingly added, "She lived long ago."

Milo hopped off the fence and asked, "Can I call Tamaes over? I think he's missing out."

The Guardian's mentor merely gave a little half-shrug, but the Messenger read it as acceptance. Taking several long strides so that he had a clear view up the driveway, Milo let loose with a piercing whistle, signaling with his hands. Prissie twisted around and tried to see what he was looking at, and Koji helpfully offered, "Tamaes has been on the barn roof since sunrise."

There was an explosion of orange light that almost looked

like flames as the previously invisible figure leaped into the air. Even in the bright afternoon sunlight, her guardian angel's wings shone vividly against the blue sky. "Is that where he usually goes?" she wondered aloud.

"The barn is his second favorite. There is a spot near the gable above your bedroom where the dormer meets the main slope," Koji replied, using his hands to form the angle. "It is a good place to sit."

"How do *you* know that?" Prissie demanded.

"I stayed with Tamaes a few times ... before."

"Oh." Prissie's eyes were drawn skyward as Tamaes sailed overhead, then angled his wings to wheel around, lining up to use the gravel road as a runway. He dropped between the surrounding trees with easy grace, back-winging to a stop a short distance away. As he strode toward them, he scanned the surroundings. It was bizarre, having an armed and armored warrior walking around as if he owned the place. "And there are nine more of him hanging around?" she muttered.

Koji gave her a strange look. "No one but Tamaes is like Tamaes."

"Ten Guardians, each with a mentor," remarked Taweel. "So, twenty?"

Milo grinned and pointed to himself and Koji, saying, "And each Guardian pair has teammates who check in with them from time to time."

"Observers, Protectors, Messengers," Koji happily listed. "They are always coming and going."

Prissie studied the empty front lawn, the various outbuildings, and the clear skies overhead. The only activity she could see in the entire farmyard was the handful of ducks who were waddling past the garden gate and Tansy, whose tail occasionally flicked as she dozed in the sun in front of the barn. It was quiet. Boring, even. But only because she couldn't see the whole picture.

The Guardian slowed to a stop a few paces away, but Milo smoothly drew him forward, saying, "Tamaes! Join us."

With the beginning of a smile tugging at the corners of his mouth, he nodded and said, "Miss Priscilla."

Once again, Prissie found it impossible to hold his gaze. He had the kindest eyes she'd ever seen, but it was difficult to face so much warmth from someone who was basically still a stranger. She fiddled uncomfortably with her skirt, at a loss for words.

Thankfully, Milo was right there, ready to step into the awkward silence. "Miss Priscilla was concerned to discover that you spend so much time on rooftops," he said conversationally. "Perhaps the Guardians should borrow the postal carrier's slogan — neither rain nor snow nor sleet nor hail will keep you from your appointed rounds?"

The orange-winged angel looked at her in surprise. "I do not mind."

"Don't you get cold?" Prissie asked curiously.

"Well, yes," he slowly admitted.

"Or wet?" she demanded.

Tamaes glanced uncertainly at Taweel, who looked to Milo. The Messenger chuckled and continued in his role as spokesperson. "We *do* experience the elements, feeling the same sensations as you, but we don't react the same way. For example, Tamaes can sleep all afternoon on the barn roof without any worries of sunburn, and Koji could run barefoot through snowbanks without ever risking frostbite."

"We understand cold without knowing its bite," her

guardian angel offered. "So there is no need for concern on my behalf."

"That must be nice," Prissie remarked.

"There's one exception," Milo shared. "None of us likes to linger long in the dark."

"You're afraid of the dark?" Prissie asked, surprised.

"You could say ... as children of light, we yearn to walk in the light," he replied with a wink.

"Omri *must* have light," Taweel said, speaking up on behalf of his small companion.

Looking between the angels gathered around her, Prissie shook her head. "What do you all do at nighttime, then?"

"Night and dark are not exactly the same," Koji piped up. "The stars are good company after the sun has set."

"And the moon offers its radiance," Tamaes quietly added.

Milo beckoned playfully to Omri, who took wing and circled the Messenger once before landing on his outstretched hands. "Plus, there are places like the garden beyond the blue door, which offer respite for those of us who have been sent into creation. Abner's flock thrives there because it's always light."

Unsure if the little golden-haired angel would respond to her call, Prissie crooked a finger at Omri. To her delight, he came straightway, alighting on her palm and promptly flopping down onto his stomach and propping his chin in his hands as his feet waved in the air. At Prissie's soft giggle, the brightness that haloed him increased in intensity.

Taweel snorted at Omri's antics, and Milo laughed outright. Glancing up to share her excitement with the others, she found Tamaes's gaze. His brown eyes widened for a moment before his expression relaxed into a gentle smile. The Guardian's reaction reminded her of how startled Koji had been to be seen on the day she found him sitting in the apple tree. Invisible people weren't used to being seen, and it was a little comforting to know that she wasn't the only one adjusting. Prissie had no idea *why* she was meeting all these angels, but deep down, she was really glad to know them.

He came to her in a dream that was so bright, it outshone the sun.

It was Harken, she was certain, yet he wasn't quite the same Harken she knew. He looked much younger; he stood straighter, and there wasn't a trace of gray in his thick black hair, which had been twisted away from his face in a series of long coils like heavy ropes. He wore shining raiment, and from under the edges of his sleeves, she could see the twisting ends of his furled wings, the deep red pattern clearly visible against his dark skin.

"Mr. Mercer?" she asked, just to be sure.

"Yes, Prissie," he answered in a deep voice untouched by age. "Are you surprised?"

"I think I should be," she admitted. "But you look more angelic this way."

He beamed at her with that wide, white smile she'd known since childhood, and she found herself smiling back. "I have a message for you," he revealed.

"Again?" she whispered nervously.

His deep chuckle set her at ease. "It's a simple message this time. One I'm sure you'll understand."

"All right," she replied bravely. "I'm listening."

Holding her gaze, he paused dramatically, then quietly said, "Wake up."

Prissie opened her eyes.

Moonlight streamed through the diamond panes of her window, scattering pastel colors onto the floor beside her bed. A glance at the clock showed that it was still the wee hours of the morning, and though the house was quiet, she sat up, listening. Her dream was already fading, but she felt restless.

A soft thump. A distant whimper. The muffled patter of footsteps. Prissie swung her legs over the side of her bed and tiptoed to her door in her nightgown. There it was again. A soft cry from down the hall. She peeked out just in time to see a light come on in the next room over, illuminating the space under the door. A few seconds later, her younger brother poked his head into the hall, and she quietly asked, "What's the matter?"

Beau beckoned to her urgently. "Sis, come help me. Something's wrong with Koji," he called, trying to keep his voice down.

Hoping that the young angel hadn't gone all pointy-eared and glowy on them, she hurried down the hall. The little boys' room was actually the largest of the upstairs bedrooms, and it was shared by Prissie's three younger brothers. Two sets of bunk beds filled up most of the space, and Koji had been given the bunk under Beau's. "What happened?" she whispered, hoping they wouldn't wake Zeke and Jude.

Beau shrugged. "Not sure. I think it's a bad dream, but I can't wake him up."

To her relief, Koji still looked like the normal kid he was supposed to be, however, he also looked anxious. His face was creased with worry or fear, and he tossed his head from side to side while making indistinct noises of protest in the back of his throat. "A nightmare?" she murmured, but that didn't make any sense. Koji shouldn't have nightmares because he didn't really sleep.

Prissie thought back on what Koji had told her about his nights. There had been something about communicating through dreams, so maybe his mind was elsewhere? Sitting on the edge of the bottom bunk, Prissie grabbed the young angel's shoulders and gave him a firm shake. "Koji ... *Koji,* come back. Are you listening? I need you to listen to *me,* Koji!"

Dark eyes sprang open, wide and unseeing as he struggled to catch his breath. Slowly, Koji focused on Prissie's face. "There you are," she scolded. "You had me and Beau worried for a minute."

"Prissie?" he whispered, his voice hoarse.

"Obviously," she returned tartly. He sat up awkwardly, glancing around the room with a mixture of confusion and dread. And then, the young angel whined softly, threw his arms around Prissie, and began to sob. "Wh-what's all this?" she stammered, looking to Beau for help.

Her brother backed up a step. "Lemme get a glass of water ... and tissues?" he offered.

Prissie was about to protest when Tamaes stepped into the room behind her brother. Trying not to gawk, she nodded to Beau. "That would be good."

The Guardian dropped to one knee at her side and lightly touched her shoulder. "Don't be afraid," he urged earnestly. Placing his large hand upon Koji's back, he said, "You're safe, now. Tell me, where did you go?"

"I ... I am not certain," he replied in a muffled voice. "It was dark. So dark."

"Something in the darkness frightened you," Tamaes prompted. "Did you encounter the enemy?"

Koji shook his head, then turned his face so he could meet the Guardian's eyes. Tears still streamed from his eyes. "I was simply drifting when he found me."

"He?"

"Ephron," Koji answered in a tremulous voice. "Oh, Tamaes, we have to tell the others! Ephron needs our help!"

The story continues in Book 2: The Hidden Deep …

DISCUSSION QUESTIONS

1. Do you believe in angels? What has influenced your perception of them? Why do you think they exist?
2. In Chapter 2, Harken says, "You can learn a lot about a person from what they choose to read." What books have you read recently? Do they say something about you? Have they influenced what books you'll reach for next?
3. Prissie turns to various people for advice and information before getting closer to the angels in Jedrick's Flight. Where do you turn when you have questions? Are search engines enough? Who do you trust to give wise counsel? Is no advice better than bad advice?
4. Baird and Kester are so different from each other that Prissie thinks they wouldn't make a good team. How much common ground do people need to get along? To work together? To be friends?
5. Where's your comfort zone? What happens when you leave it? In Prissie's case, how do you know when broadening your horizons is a good thing (like allowing Milo to introduce her to Baird) and when new experiences cross a line (like dabbling in fortune telling)?
6. Do Prissie's pie-baking aspirations seem too old-fashioned? Compare and contrast her goals with Ransom's. What's the difference?
7. Harken remarks that when people are faced with something that doesn't appeal to them, they often refuse to acknowledge it. If you don't believe in something, does reality change?
8. Prissie asks Koji if being invisible is lonely. What do you think?
9. Can you sympathize with Prissie's problems with her girlfriends? What kind of advice would you give her?
10. In Chapter 10, Kester says, "Do not rely too heavily on appearances. They are not the most important consideration." If not, then what is?

THRESHOLD SERIES

THE HIDDEN DEEP

BOOK TWO

1

THE NAMING DEBACLE

Milo cut through the air, skimming across shifting beams of light with what *looked* like reckless abandon. However, this angel had learned caution. Though there was joy in his flight, he continuously scanned above and below for signs of danger. Just off his flank, a flare of dusky purple revealed the presence of his armor-clad companion. Taweel flew with his sword in hand, ready to defend his teammate.

"Race you back!" Milo challenged, folding outstretched wings and streaking through a sky as blue as his eyes.

With a soft grunt that may have been amusement, the Guardian followed.

Just north of the small town of West Edinton, the Messenger banked into a steep spiral that ended with an expert flick and fold, then he climbed back into the driver's seat of his old green car. Checking his reflection in the rear view mirror, Milo ran his hand over short-cropped blond curls and buckled his seat belt across his mailman's uniform.

As the engine rumbled to life, Taweel leaned down to peer through the open window.

"We'll try again after I finish my route," Milo promised. Then he put the car in gear and took off down the road, kicking up gravel and a small cloud of dust.

Prissie and her next-younger brother Beau climbed onto the white-painted plank fence that stood behind the twin mailboxes at the end of their long driveway. An oval-shaped sign showing an overflowing basket of apples proudly announced, "Pomeroy Orchard," and the block letters on the pair of red and white flags on either side of the gate let people know the apple barn was open for business.

Throughout the summer months, afternoons had found Prissie right here, waiting for the mail, but today was different. Today, she was waiting for the school bus. Settling onto her perch, she crossed her ankles in a ladylike manner and smoothed the skirt of her pink and white sundress. "It shouldn't be much longer," she remarked, gazing off in the direction of the highway.

Beau nodded. He never said much. To be honest, Prissie was a little surprised the thirteen-year-old had volunteered to join her. He usually buried himself in a book or spent time on the computer after school. Their bus had dropped them off nearly an hour ago, but they were waiting on Zeke and Jude, who would be arriving on the elementary bus.

Six-year-old Jude was going to school "for real" this year. According to him, kindergarten was just a warm-up, but he was finally following in the footsteps of his older siblings. At Momma's request, all of the Pomeroy kids were sticking around the house to have milk and cookies with the little guy to celebrate his milestone. Prissie and Beau listened closely for the telltale rumble of an engine, but the only sound was the lazy buzz of the bees that droned in the riot of purple coneflowers that Grandma Nell had planted around the mailboxes.

"You think the bus will beat Milo?" Beau asked.

Prissie favored her brother with a long look, trying to decide if he was teasing her. Milo Leggett was a long-time family friend, and her fondness for him was something of a sore spot. Everyone in town knew the young man, but Prissie always thought of him as *theirs*. He went to their church, taught Zeke's Sunday school class, and regularly dropped in to chat since their farm was the last stop on his route. Milo's visits had been a cause for excitement ever since she was a little girl because he was *special*. Of course, up until this July, she hadn't realized just *how* special.

There was no sly glint in Beau's blue eyes, so Prissie resisted the urge to snip. "It'll probably be close. They might even get here at the same time."

"Jude would like that," he remarked thoughtfully.

Privately hoping Milo's timing was providential today, she replied, "It *would* be nice."

Another minute ticked by before Beau spoke again. "Say, Priss ... about Koji." He was peeking at her out of the corner of his eye.

Prissie began to fiddle with the end of one of her honey-colored braids. Was *this* why Beau was here? In a house as crowded as theirs, it wasn't easy to hold a private conversation, and it was even harder to find a time when Prissie and Koji weren't together. The boy probably would have been with her now except that he'd begged Grandpa Pete to let him help out with the farm animals. Tad was showing Koji the ropes of his new responsibilities.

"Did he do okay at school today?"

"Of course!" she said defensively. "I made sure of it!"

Officially, Koji was an exchange student who was boarding with the Pomeroy family for the year. To everyone else, he seemed like an overly curious boy with exotic features — golden skin, almond-shaped eyes, and glossy, black, shoulder-length hair. Her whole family believed he was from a set of tiny islands in the middle of the Pacific.

Only Prissie knew the truth.

Meeting Koji had been an accident, or at least something that didn't happen very often. For reasons no one yet understood, Prissie had spotted the young angel watching her from a branch in one of her grandfather's apple trees. In the weeks after that first meeting, one thing led to another. Or maybe it was better to say that one angel led to another.

Prissie had discovered that angels were living as regular people in and around West Edinton. It had been hard learning that Milo was one of them. Their mailman was a Messenger, as was his mentor Harken Mercer, who owned a used bookstore on Main Street. After getting over her initial shock, they'd introduced her to Baird and Kester, "Worshipers" who led music at the DeeVee, a church down in Harper.

Since then, she'd met or heard about other varieties of angels. Each angel had a special role. For instance, Koji was an apprentice Observer, and he was thrilled by his chance to live as a human instead of just watching them from afar. For the most part, Prissie didn't mind having him around. Koji's delight was contagious. He had proven himself a good friend, but it was still difficult to reconcile everyday things with the fantastical things she'd witnessed.

Beau stared up into the sky. "Koji is ... strange sometimes."

"How do you mean?" Prissie asked carefully.

"Well, I know he's from another country and everything, but some of the questions he asks are way out there. It's almost like he's from another planet, sometimes."

She rolled her eyes. "He's not an alien."

"I know, I know," Beau muttered. "But sometimes he takes foreign to a whole different level. Have you ever tried to explain sneezing to someone? And he'd never tasted bananas before."

"Maybe they don't have them where he comes from?"

"I checked online. That island where he's from has whole banana plantations."

"I'll tell him not to bug you with such weird questions," Prissie offered.

"I don't mind," Beau quickly assured. "His questions make me think, and it's kind of interesting to try to answer them."

Prissie frowned. Beau didn't speak up unless he had something to say, and it felt as though he was still working up to it. "I think Koji looks at things differently than most people," she suggested.

"Do you know that he'd never used nail clippers before? He watched me trim mine, then asked me to do his, too."

"That was nice of you," she said nervously.

Beau shrugged. "It's kind of like having another little brother, except that he's older than me. *You're* his favorite, though. Does Margery know she's been displaced?"

Prissie's expression clouded, and she crisply answered, "I doubt she minds." She and her best friend Margery had drifted apart over the summer. Since Prissie needed to show Koji around, she'd barely said two words to her in school today. Not that Margery noticed. *She'd* been busy giving the grand tour to Elise Hanson — another newcomer to West Edinton.

Her brother took a deep breath. "You're not going to ditch Koji, are you?"

"*What*?" she exclaimed.

With a determined expression, Beau forged ahead. "I

know you don't mind being his best friend around here, but how are you going to treat him when other people are around? You might get teased because he's different."

With flashing eyes and flaming cheeks, Prissie demanded, "You think I'd be that awful to someone?"

"Hope not," he muttered.

He dropped his gaze, but his back was straight, and that meant he was sticking by his question. She scowled. "There's no way! Koji's *ours* now, and I'm not letting *anyone* make fun of him!"

"Ours, huh?" Beau looked embarrassed and relieved at the same time, as if his almost-accusation had been as hard for him to say as it had been for her to hear. "So you really *are* okay with him and his weirdness?"

"Obviously."

"Good."

Although Beau let the subject drop, Prissie's conscience nagged at her. It was easy to overlook Koji's bizarre qualities because she knew he was an angel. If he'd been a regular boy, would she treat him the same way? Thankfully, she didn't have to answer that question. Just then, the school bus swung into view — right behind an old, green car. "Milo!" she cheered, immediately feeling better.

There were times when Prissie hated how crowded and noisy her house could get, but there were also times when she wouldn't trade the hubbub for the world. Today, she was glad to be part of a big family.

Momma herded everyone into the kitchen, where Grandma Nell lifted fresh cookies onto cooling racks, filling the room with the mouthwatering smell of melting chocolate. Grandpa Pete found an excuse to come in for a cup of coffee, but even with Milo and Koji added to the mix, there was no need to squeeze around the sturdy kitchen table. It had been built to serve a crowd.

Questions and answers flew through the air as notes were compared. Yes, Prissie's oft-rehearsed fears of alphabetical seating arrangements had been realized. No, Zeke's teacher hadn't fainted dead away at the sight of him. She'd taught Neil, after all. She was brave. Yes, the school bus driver still listened to country music while he drove. No, Beau hadn't forgotten his lunchbox in his locker. He was turning over a new leaf now that he was out of elementary school.

Milo was right in the thick of things. He asked Tad if he'd still have time to work on the old truck he was rebuilding now that classes were back in session, and he checked with Neil to see if the football coach had finalized the roster for Friday's game. However, it didn't take long for Zeke and Jude to mob the mailman, eager to share their grade school adventures.

As the conversation took a turn towards pencil sharpeners and dodge ball, Koji claimed a place at Prissie's side. "I *drove*!" he whispered eagerly.

"Tad let you drive the quad?" she asked, amused by his excitement. All the Pomeroys learned to drive as soon as their feet reached the pedals of the various mowers and tractors on the farm. One of the jobs Grandpa had given Koji was to help Tad feed and water the pigs, and since their shed was in the back forty, they used a four-wheeler to drive out there.

Koji nodded. "We brought them apple mash from the cider press, and I tried to use the pump. It was difficult, but Tad is quite able."

"It sounds like you had fun, but it's a lot *less* fun if the weather's bad," Prissie warned.

"I will not neglect the task your grandfather entrusted to me," Koji promised.

When they turned their attention back to the group, her family was a sight to behold. Prissie shook her head at the level of ridiculousness on display, but with five brothers, she'd come to expect it. She knew from experience that it could get much, *much* worse.

"Beat this!" Neil gloated.

"Mine's better!" Zeke argued.

"Milo's dripping," said Jude with a giggle.

Koji gazed around the table in fascination, then leaned close to whisper, "What is the goal of this contest?"

"No point," Prissie said. "Just silliness." Zeke crossed his eyes as he tried to catch a glimpse of his milk moustache, and Jude beamed up at Tad.

"Come on, Prissie," coaxed Neil. "Don't be such a stick in the mud!" Even Milo's smile wasn't enough to tempt her into joining in. "No thank you. I prefer to drink my milk, not wear it. Who started this, anyhow?"

Everyone immediately pointed to Milo, who sheepishly reached for a napkin. Prissie looked at him with raised eyebrows. "Sorry, Miss Priscilla." Once she'd accepted his apology with a smile, he cheerfully changed the subject. "It sounds like everyone made it through their first day intact."

"Not me!" Beau replied with a groan. "Mr. Hawkins started role call before I could tell him not to use my full name!"

"So it's out," Tad said sympathetically.

"Maybe no one noticed?" Prissie ventured, earning a flat look.

"It will take *months* to live this down," the thirteen-year-old grumbled.

Koji looked from one sibling to the next. "What are you talking about?"

"Names," Tad supplied.

"My name isn't *really* Beau," the middle brother explained. "That's my nickname. It's short for ... my full name."

Neil reached for another chocolate chip cookie, then shook it at Koji. "We who bear the name of Pomeroy share a tragic flaw, handed down to us by our parents." Glancing around the table, the sixteen-year-old asked, "Shall we let him in on our darkest secret?"

"Why not?" Tad replied with a friendly smile. "I think he'll keep quiet."

Koji's eyes widened. "Thank you for your trust."

"Okay, then," Neil agreed, picking up his tale. "It may interest you to know that Momma and Dad gave all of us Bible names."

The young angel looked from one sibling to the next, then glanced towards Mrs. Pomeroy, who stood on the other side of the kitchen. Naomi had obviously heard these grievances many times before, and her gray eyes were dancing. "I think they're fine names," Momma said, trading an amused glance with her mother-in-law.

"Very traditional," Grandma Nell agreed.

"And very unfortunate," countered Neil.

Tipping his head to one side, Koji said, "I do not recognize most of your names from Scripture."

"We shortened them," Beau said with a disapproving look in his mother's direction.

Tad took this as his cue, folding his hands on the table and fixing Koji with a serious gaze. "I don't like it to get around, but my full name is Thaddeus," he revealed. "I've been calling myself Tad since the first grade."

"Indeed," Koji replied before looking to the next brother. "Neil is short for...?"

"Cornelius," he replied with a grimace.

"I might have guessed that one," Koji replied. Gazing into Prissie's face he asked, "Are you unhappy with your name?"

She shook her head, but admitted, "I do usually introduce myself as Prissie, though."

"Aquilla and Priscilla were lovely people," Milo interjected.

Prissie blinked in surprise. It sounded like the Messenger had known them. Was it possible for Milo to be *that* old?

Koji's dark eyes sparkled with interest as he looked at eight-year-old Zeke. The boy's unruly mop of blond hair was a testament to his energetic nature. "Zeke must be short for Ezekiel?"

"Nope. Hezekiah," announced the boy.

"Is that worse?" inquired the young angel curiously.

"*Way* worse."

Turning to the humiliated teen, Koji asked, "What is Beau short for?" The thirteen-year-old put his hands over his face and mumbled his reply, but the young angel's ears were sharp. "Your name is Boaz?"

"The kinsman redeemer," Mrs. Pomeroy said with a dreamy sigh. "I just love his and Ruth's story! *So* romantic!"

One blue eye peeped out long enough to roll expressively. "Maybe so, but that doesn't mean you should inflict his name on a poor, unsuspecting baby."

"What is Jude short for?" Koji inquired, looking towards the youngest family member. "Judah?"

Neil leaned forward. "Here's the thing. When Momma was expecting Jude, we ganged up and issued a formal protest. All of us are stuck with impossible handles, but we thought the new little twerp should be spared the indignity."

Tad nodded. "We begged our folks to come up with a name that wasn't embarrassing."

"Of course, Momma didn't want to settle on something *easy* like John or Mark," Neil continued. "She said those were too *boring*."

"Calling him Jude was a compromise," Mrs. Pomeroy said as she nibbled her own cookie. "Short, but different enough to be interesting."

"So we call him Judicious, just to be contrary," Tad concluded.

Koji smiled at the littlest brother, who was obviously proud of both his name and the story behind it.

Once the conversation moved on, the young Observer nudged Prissie with his elbow and shyly confided, "Koji is my nickname, too."

"Really? What's your full name?"

"I cannot tell," he admitted. "It is a name only known to me and the One who gave it."

"Only God knows your real name?" she asked, mystified.

The angel searched her face, then nodded once. "It will be the same for you one day."

Prissie's brows rose. "Don't be ridiculous. Everyone already knows my name."

With a hint of a smile, Koji replied, "You will be given a new one. It is promised."

"Oh," she replied blankly. After some thought, she had to admit she was looking forward to finding out what her new name might be.

Later that evening, Prissie stood beside Grandma Nell at the stove, carefully stirring applesauce so it wouldn't scorch. During harvest time, this was pretty much a daily chore, and the two of them had the routine down pat. The only difference this year was the addition of a new helper. While Grandma Nell ladled hot cinnamon-spiked sauce into gleaming jars, Koji added the lids. When they were done, Prissie's grandmother tallied up the quarts. "Two more batches should do it, so report for duty again tomorrow night."

"Isn't this more than last year?" Prissie ventured as she lugged the big pot over to the sink to wash up.

"We have an extra mouth to feed this year," Grandma Nell countered, smiling Koji's way.

Once the kitchen was restored to order, Prissie's mind turned to homework and the reading she needed to do for the week, but Koji tapped her shoulder. "I am going outside to talk with the others for a while," he said quietly.

Prissie's heart sped up. "May I come along?"

The boy's face brightened. "I would like that."

Since the evenings were growing chilly, she slipped a sweater over her light dress and followed Koji onto the back porch. Stars were already out, and for several moments, the young angel stared up at them. "They will come to us," Koji announced.

Prissie often wondered how he knew where his teammates were, what they were doing, and sometimes even what kind of mood they were in. She guessed it was probably the same as her and Grandma making applesauce. He'd learned their routine and knew what to do. Either that, or he'd received a message. It was strange to think that Koji could *hear* God, and even stranger to think that God would pass along a time and place for a meeting.

Tansy offered a soft meow from the seat she'd claimed on the porch swing, and Prissie soon had a lapful of purring barn cat. Koji sat on the steps, his dark eyes fixed on a point in the distance. "What do you see?" she whispered, hoping she would get to visit with Omri again.

"Jedrick is coming!"

"Is that good or bad?" she asked nervously. Koji didn't have time to answer before there was a silent explosion of green light just beyond the garden. Though she'd only seen the phenomenon a few times before, Prissie vividly remembered the beautiful shifting patterns of light and color that made up an angel's wings.

"He is here," Koji announced unnecessarily.

A towering, armor-clad figure strode up the walk, and as he drew nearer, a second angel slipped out of the shadows just beyond the hydrangeas lining the porch. Prissie tried not to stare and failed miserably. Angelic warriors were huge, fantastical, and actually kind of scary, so it was hard to look away, especially once she realized that even without the porch light on, she could see them quite well. It was as if they brought their own light with them into the darkness. Could this be an angel's halo?

Rich green fell from Jedrick's shoulders, flowing almost like a cloak or cape as he strode forward on booted feet. "Are you well, Priscilla Pomeroy?" inquired the stern-faced warrior. Jedrick was a Protector, and he was the captain of the team of angels that Milo, Koji, and the rest belonged to. His light brown hair was cropped close around his head except for one long braid, which hung over his left shoulder; the jeweled pommel of the sword strapped to his back was visible over his right.

His inquiry was hard to answer. It felt like a trick question. Up until a few moments ago, Prissie had been just fine, but Jedrick's arrival brought back unsettling memories and made her wonder if there were invisible enemies prowling around in the dark. She hugged her cat close and shrugged.

Just behind him stood Tamaes, a Guardian whose long, brown hair only partially covered the jagged scar that marred his otherwise handsome face. He stepped forward. "Do not be afraid, little one," he said gently. "Jedrick is *not* here because of danger nearby."

Jedrick looked sharply at his companion, then his expression altered subtly. Though his face lost none of its fierce quality, the Protector's green eyes softened somewhat. "On the contrary, it is a quiet night."

Prissie glanced at Tamaes. It was irksome that he had known exactly what was on her mind, but she shouldn't have been surprised. Tamaes was her guardian angel. Since the moment her life began, he'd been watching over her. It made sense that he would understand how she felt. He looked as though he wanted to say more, but was too bashful to get it out. Instead, Tamaes gazed at her with undisguised fondness, and she was the one who glanced away.

Koji nudged closer on the porch swing and touched the back of her hand. When she met his earnest gaze, he said, "Prissie, I would not lead you into danger."

"There *are* things to be afraid of, though," she countered in a soft voice.

Jedrick solemnly shook his head and declared, "Fear not, for I am with you."

"Indeed," Koji said.

A war was being waged, and there were enemies so terrible, she'd been told to be grateful they were hidden from her eyes. However, here and now, she was as safe as she could be. If only things could stay this way. "So why *are* you here?" she asked in a quiet voice.

"I am often here," Jedrick replied, looking amused. "My responsibilities keep me close."

"What are those?" she asked.

The captain folded his muscular arms and cocked his head to one side. "I protect those in my Flight, and we each have our role to fill. Some stand guard over that which is ours to keep. Some seek that which has been lost. Some can only watch and wait."

Prissie glanced at Koji, whose pensive face was once more turned towards the sky. "That which has been lost? Do you mean Ephron?" she asked carefully. Ephron was Koji's predecessor, an apprentice Observer who'd been taken by the enemy.

"I do," Jedrick confirmed. "Koji, I need to ask you to tell me more about your dream."

"He was somewhere close. Somewhere dark," the boy replied.

This was nothing new, but his captain nodded encouragingly. "Go on."

"He was hurt. Frightened ..." Koji's voice trembled. "And he said he would keep your trust no matter what else was taken."

Jedrick exchanged a long look with Tamaes before saying, "They *are* questioning him. It is as Abner feared."

Tamaes winced. "It is my fault," he murmured.

"Do not think it," Jedrick said. "None of us can take the blame for those who chose to fall."

"What do they mean?" Prissie whispered to Koji.

He looked at her with sorrowful eyes. "Ephron came to visit Tamaes on the day he was taken. The enemy captured him *here*, in your family's orchard."

ROUGH & TUMBLE

While you're waiting for *The Hidden Deep*, you can read more about angels and the Pomeroy family on Christa's website, ChristaKinde.com. **Rough and Tumble** is an adventurous continuation to the *Threshold Series*, about a young angel named Ethan, who's sent to serve with the other Guardians of the Hedge surrounding the Pomeroy family farm. One mischievous little boy is about to turn Ethan's life upside down!

At just one hundred words, chapters are small enough to read on the fly—with daily updates and new installments.

Become a subscriber at ChristaKinde.com!